SCHIZANDRA

and the

GATES *of* MU

BY LAURA BRUNO

"With more people waking up every day, the need for switched-on fiction grows ever more pressing. ... Laura skillfully weaves a tapestry of an orphan's magical journey, the prophecies of 2012, a mystic grandmother descended from witches, twin maiden reflexologist great aunts and alien-like cacao guzzling frog creatures. ... This unique work of heart is so fast paced it almost reads like a short story, yet it's a full-sized flesh on vegan bone novel. I furiously flicked through the pages wanting to know how our own end will spark our own beginning, in rebirth."

–Shazzie, UK author and health pioneer, www.shazzie.com

"Laura Bruno has created a delightful story that both captivates and enlightens. She offers the reader many hours of pleasure as she shares some of her extensive knowledge of reflexology, astrology, numerology, tarot, stones, crystals, Atlantis and Lemuria."

–Shirley Andrews, *Lemuria and Atlantis:*
Studying the Past to Survive the Future

SCHIZANDRA

and the

GATES *of* MU

LAURA BRUNO

ISBN 978-0-615-30133-4

Text illustrations©Tania Marie (www.taniamarie.com) All rights reserved.
Back cover photo©Stephen Bruno (www.stephenbrunophotography.com)
Cover Artwork ©Wendy Purdy, www.BigStockPhoto.com.
Cover design by Cathi Stevenson

The author gratefully acknowledges written permission to paraphrase a line from 2012: THE RETURN OF QUETZALCOATL, (New York: Jeremy P. Tarcher/Penguin, 2006). Copyright © 2006 by Daniel Pinchbeck. Used by permission of Daniel Pinchbeck.

The author gratefully acknowledges written permission from Aztlan.net to share facts from Hector Carreon's article, "Strange Rumblings at the Center of Our Galaxy" (http://www.aztlan.net/rumblings_center_galaxy.htm), October 18, 2005.

The author gratefully acknowledges written permission from Tim Glenn to share facts from his 2007 astrology, numerology and tarot reading for the character Schizandra. (www.soulpurposereadings.com)

Excerpts from "On a Beach at Night" are out of copyright: Walt Whitman, *Leaves of Grass*. 1900. (First published in 1870.)

Most Kabir excerpts are taken from the 1915 Rabindranath Tagore *Songs of Kabir* translation, which is out of copyright. All others reflect the author's own wording. All rights reserved.

In loving memory of Adam

And in loving honor of my husband,
Stephen Bruno

SCHIZANDRA

and the

GATES *of* MU

LAURA BRUNO

"They are ill discoverers that think there is no land, when they see nothing but sea."

−SIR FRANCIS BACON

CHICAGO NEWS-POST

December 21, 2000

OBITUARIES

CHICAGO. Dr. Philip J. Parker, one of Chicago University's most controversial professors of archeology and anthropology, died at midnight after a two-year battle with cancer. He was 45.

Parker was best known for his discovery of ancient Egyptian artifacts buried in the American Southwest. A series of smaller finds led to his 1986 excavation of the legendary "Gates of Mu." This discovery stunned an academic world that ridiculed most theories regarding the Lost City of Atlantis and its Pacific counterpart, Mu (also known as "Lemuria").

Parker's find and subsequent book (*Myth and Mu: Echoes of the Motherland*, Aesclepian Press, 1987) earned him full tenure and a distinguished post at Chicago University because he proved a common cultural ancestor for Ancient Egypt and America's first inhabitants.

Carbon dated at 26,000 years old, the gates were formed of an unknown metal reputed to be the "orichalcum" mentioned in Hesiod's *Hymn to Aphrodite*. Both Plato and Hesiod claimed the gold-colored substance "sparkled like fire" and came from an ancient island that sank in the Atlantic Ocean. Tibetan texts associate this substance with Mu. To date scientists have found no other explanation for the metal's origins or unknown chemical composition.

Parker's research shocked the world, but his behavior after publication confused colleagues and mystics alike. The young professor refused to comment on his famous discovery and spent the rest of his career attempting to refute his own findings.

Retired Prof. Reginald Bernhardt (PhD Anthropology, Yale, 1947) said, "Phil Parker was profoundly affected by the 1987 death of his young bride. His research and focus shifted when she passed." An anonymous colleague added, "Professor Parker channeled his grief into academic rigor and life as a single dad."

Ginger Parker (nee Vreeland) was just 20 years old when she died giving birth to their only child. The Parkers are survived by their 13-year-old daughter Schizandra Ginger Parker.

Chapter One

FIVE-HUNDRED MILLION YEAR-OLD SANDSTONE LOOMED behind the schoolyard. Under the shadow of this red rock, a pigtailed blonde in braces waved. "Hi, Shazzie!"

Schizandra smiled through grapevine curls and grabbed her books. "Hey, Brielle!" Leaping from the car, she sensed Melissa's periwinkle stare. "I'll tell her," she hissed, then slammed the door.

"What's up, Shazzie?" A brunette named Angie had joined Brielle. "You look upset."

"My grandmother won't let people call me *Shazzie* anymore!"

"That's weird." Angie leaned in and asked, "Why can't people call you what you want 'em to call you?"

"I don't know. She has this thing about names! Like a name's important 'cuz it's your identity. Like it reveals who you are or something. She doesn't even let me call her Grandma. I have to call her Melissa."

"*Wild!*" giggled Angie. "What's Schizandra mean?"

"It's a medicinal berry."

"A *berry*?" exclaimed both girls.

Schizandra winced. "All the women on my mother's side are healers. My grandmother's a midwife; my mother was sort of like an art therapist before she died. I think my twin great-aunts are reflexologists." She scanned her audience, reading their faces before sharing the next part. "Generations ago, all the women in my family were witches."

In Chicago, that last part would have at least raised eyebrows, maybe even altered a friendship or two. Angie and Brielle waited for something more. "*And?*"

"And, that's pretty much it. All of us are named for herbs."

"*Melissa's* an herb?" they challenged.

Schizandra nodded. "Another word for *lemon balm.*"

"What the heck is *lemon balm*?" Brielle asked.

Schizandra shrugged her narrow shoulders. "I don't know. My dad didn't believe in any of that stuff. I just know the meaning."

"What was your mother's name?" asked Angie.

"Ginger."

"Like on *Gilligan's Island*?"

"Yeah, and my dad was the Professor." Schizandra smiled in spite of herself, as a bell ushered them inside.

Cherished only child of the late Dr. Philip J. Parker, Schizandra had begun Sedona's Red Rock Middle School a mere week ago. After her father's funeral, she had moved from Chicago to Sedona to live with a grandmother she had never even met. *Melissa*: the same grandmother who had let Schizandra's mother die; the same grandmother her dad had taught her to despise.

Last week, the principal had placed her in the only seventh grade homeroom with any space—Mr. Pisconte's end-of-the-alphabet Room 407. As she slid into her seat, the Peruvian teacher was already taking attendance:

"Turner, Kaela."

"Present."

"Turzen, Vanessa.

"Here."

"Wilson, Ari."

"Yo."

Raising his eyebrows, Mr. Pisconte continued, "Parker, Sandra."

"Pres—um. It's Schizandra, actually."

"Last week you tell me Sandra. What is this Shazania?"

"Shuh-ZAN-druh." Her cheeks burned crimson as she cursed Melissa, praying for the bell.

"You tell me call you Sandra. Which it is?"

"Schizandra."

"OK, Shandrana. Why you no Sandra? Never mind," he waved his right hand in combined irritation and anticipation, "time to stand and pray the flag."

Everyone except Ari Wilson rose and placed hand over heart. Ari slouched in an olive hemp hoodie and low-riding Levi's.

"Wilson, Ari, up! Time to pray the flag. We no have much time today thanks to Shaziandra. This a beautiful country. Now pray the flag, proud to be American."

Ari smirked, but rose.

"I pledge allegiance, to the flag, of the United Sta—"

In a whirlwind, students grabbed books and backpacks, bursting through the door to the clang of Period One. As Schizandra left homeroom, she could still hear Mr. Pisconte "praying" for the rest of them. " ... One nation, under God, with Liberty and Justice for all. Amen!"

Always small for her age, Schizandra looked and felt like a sixth grader walking to first period biology. At four foot nine, she seemed smaller than anyone she knew. It wasn't just her height. She exuded "tiny" like forget-me-not or baby's breath. What she lacked in size, though, she made up for in brains. She had first learned of her father's cancer after winning the fifth grade Illinois State Spelling Bee. Over a shared bowl of Mexican fried ice cream, Daddy had asked her if she knew what "diagnosis" meant. *Diagnosis. D-I-A-* "No, Zany, do you know what diagnosis *means?*" A year and a half later he was gone. At age thirteen, Schizandra knew firsthand what "orphan" meant.

She squeezed past a couple kissing in the doorway and tiptoed to her seat as the late bell tolled. Something in Room 206 smelled wrong. Searching in her backpack for a pen, she tried to place the odor. Burning plastic? *No.* Mildewed car? *Uh-uh, worse.*

Her father's waxen face. That scent behind the flowers at his funeral. First period biology smelled like death, and she was tired of death. Schizandra longed for a world where death did not exist. She looked at the lab table. A supine frog with splayed legs was slit from throat to anus. Haru, her overzealous lab partner smiled at his dripping scalpel.

"I already opened her up. She's pregnant, Shazzie! Look at those eggs!"

Black and white orbs of mutant caviar; yellow fingers of fat clawing to escape the jade and opal skin.

Her tiny heart.

That mouth—slightly ajar as though hushed mid-croak.

"Hey, Shazzie, you OK?" Haru seemed far away. "You look weird. Are you dizzy?"

Schizandra choked back vomit, and the pungent odor disappeared.

So did all the air. Hot blackness prickled up her spine. Engulfing her skull, the void silenced sound and annihilated light. When it reached her eyes, an entire fluorescent sky whirled through one constricted pupil. Everything turned black and heavy, pulling her down and inward.

Chapter Two

S EDONA PULSED WITH THE SOUND of an approaching helicopter. Mark Adams worked the controls with ease. Helicopters were like women. They could shred the inexperienced, but in the hands of a master, women and choppers purred. This Jetranger 206 III was a dream to fly. The most popular turbine ever built, Bell's Jetranger offered superior reliability with the best safety record in its class.

Sam Frey let out a low whistle as they soared over huge red monoliths. "We're in God's country now."

"Or the devil's," Mark said, "Sedona's got some spooky cross winds."

"Spooky? For an adrenaline junkie, you're awfully superstitious!" Sam led Mark's Emergency Medical Service crew on what the FAA officially termed a "lifeguard," any aircraft carrying sick passengers.

"I just like to avoid certain *types* of risk," Mark answered, "sushi, marriage, freak winds controlled by ancient civilizations … "

Sam shook his head and smiled. "Let me get this straight," he said, "retired Warrant Officer Mark Adams, Desert Storm Apache pilot with two bronze stars, sixty-three jumps and twenty-three hundred flight hours, who's had more chicks than he can possibly remember," Sam paused, "is afraid of dead fish, holy matrimony, and ghost stories."

"Laugh it up, rescue boy, how you think I survived seven years as a Green Beret?"

"I know, I know, you followed your intuition. You infiltrated the hottest spots around the globe."

Mark had the throttle rolled full open as they cruised towards Sedona Regional Medical at 130 miles per hour.

"Mom jokes that if she ever wanted to know where I was, she'd turn on the news. Nine times out of ten we were there: kidnapping leaders, supporting coups, doing all that classified shit."

The 45-year-old bachelor moved the cyclic to adjust pitch. As the

Jetranger dipped right and cut west, Sam whistled at the landscape again. "You know I'm kidding, right? If you weren't such a badass it wouldn't even be funny."

Mark half-smiled, but didn't comment. Instead, he radioed, "Sedona Regional Medical, lifeguard helicopter two zero six lima hotel, eta seven minutes."

"Roger 206. Standing by."

He completed the pre-landing checklists—*no warning lights, gauges in the green*—and then said to Sam, "I ever tell you about that time in Kuwait I dreamed about walking down an alley and triggering a land mine?"

"Must've missed that one," Sam replied with mock concern.

"Next night I find myself and two buddies in that same alley. I tell 'em about my dream, but they laugh: call me *superstitious*." Mark shot a look at Sam before continuing. "I turn the hell around and haul ass. The guys whistle after me like I'm some kinda girl. Just then an unlit car explodes. One of them buddies lost an eye."

"What happened to the other one?"

"Dead!"

"Aw, crap, man, I'm sorry."

Mark returned his attention to the controls. "Let's land this baby. Sedona Regional Medical, lifeguard two zero six lima hotel thirty seconds out."

The chopper hovered and then roared to touchdown. Sam's crew hurried out of the Jetranger. A girl lay unconscious on a stretcher, her dark curls spiraling out of control with the rotors' gusts. She looked young.

Once the crew strapped her in back, Mark rolled up the throttle until the governor took over and pulled pitch. The chopper ascended over West Sedona. Sam and his crew continued to monitor the girl. Sedona's ER had ordered her to Flagstaff for more advanced neurological care. She twitched now, in spite of the 206's notably smooth ride.

"Funny thing," Sam told Mark, "everything else about her seems normal. We just can't wake her up."

A stunning expanse of red rock stretched below. Huge brick and peach colored stones mingled around Sedona's shops and restaurants. The helicopter's shadow stretched across art galleries, resorts and romantic getaways dotting the route out of town. As the scenery turned greener and more mountainous, Mark noticed an odd smell in the cabin. A smell every Bell Jetranger pilot had learned to dread. The odor came from the heating of special grease used to lubricate the short shaft—that part connecting the turbine engine to the rotor system.

You can't mistake that smell. If you detect that smell, land immediately! His words to countless former students haunted him now as he searched for a spot to land. In an attempt to save the engine, Mark acted fast, but not fast enough. He felt a jolt, and the engine RPM spiked. *When a short shaft fails, an engine quickly unloads because it no longer turns the main and tail rotors. Once the RPM spikes, that engine dies and will need to be rebuilt.*

The Jetranger rapidly lost altitude. With nothing powering the blades, Mark began an emergency autorotation to the ground, hoping to use wind and any remaining blade spin to land this chopper safely. Mark had forced his students to simulate engine failure hundreds of times in practice. Even so, autorotation was a skill pilots hoped they'd never need to use.

Mark tried to tune out everything except the emergency at hand, but he knew from Sam that the EMS crew had been managing its own crisis. Upon lift-off, the girl had started shaking. At first, it seemed her tiny body just couldn't handle the chopper's vibration, but the violence of her movements intensified as they left town. Then—still unconscious— she began to wail. Her voice sounded otherworldly—like a harmonic play between two chords. Not exactly unpleasant, but disorienting. *And weird. It was definitely weird.* That smell pervaded the cockpit, and the helicopter shook.

Then *Whack!* from the chopper, at which point, the pilot needed to act fast.

"Mark!" yelled the EMS crew leader. "What the hell's going on?"

Mark said nothing. He aimed the Jetranger into the wind to improve their chances, but the wind blew downhill. What they gained in natural lift, the climbing elevation of the land reclaimed.

"Mark!" Again, no answer. Sam's voice sounded strange in the sudden quiet.

Mark wanted a wide open space with no trees in a 40-foot radius, but they had lost too much altitude to be picky now. They would probably hit some branches on their way down. He felt the blades clip a tree. *Damn!*

Thankfully, the rotors kept turning with inertia, lessening impact from a 25-foot drop into the only clearing in sight. The chopper touched down with a jolt, but no explosion. The sudden stillness felt even more eerie than the silence.

Mark sat for a few moments, riding the adrenaline rush. Nothing like a good autorotation to rejuvenate the heart! Despite regular simulations, a less experienced pilot might have panicked and crashed in the real deal. He looked to Sam, "Everyone okay?"

"A few bruises and one bleeder, but safe enough. The girl's untouched," Sam said with deep respect. "Thanks, man."

The EMS crew offered Mark a standing ovation. "'It's simply the most survivable, supportable, mission capable helicopter for the money,'" he quoted Jetranger's key selling features. "Just doin' my job."

Mark radioed flight control: "This is two zero six lima hotel, we just survived a catastrophic failure of the short shaft over Oak Creek Canyon. Engine's toast and we got no blades. Minor injuries, and one unconscious patient. Requesting airlift to Flagstaff Regional Medical. Over."

"Roger that."

Chapter Three

PUSH, ADELE, PUSH!" MELISSA GAZED into the woman's eyes. "Remember your breathing: one, two. Now let it go. Slowly—through your teeth: three, four, five, six. Again! Breathe into the pain—you can do this!"

"Mother of God, get it out of me!"

"That's right, honey, push!" She turned to Adele's heaving womanhood. "Crowning! Oooo, a shock of black hair! You're almost there, now. Breathe."

Melissa lived for these moments. Every time she attended a birth, the beauty snuck up on her. Nine months of sweet anticipation and then this, this ecstasy! Thirty-two years as a midwife, and she had never tired of watching births. No, not watching. She preferred to call it "loving." Melissa was an extra dose of love, a conduit to that Mother love with a capital M.

Melissa had tried to quit once, when her daughter Ginger died giving birth to Schizandra. Even now, the midwife felt her chest constrict. Death in childbirth was always hard—not that she'd had much experience with it. Just her own child, so full and then gone.

There was nothing she could have done to save her. Not even a fully staffed hospital would have changed the outcome. Melissa knew that, but an autopsy couldn't resurrect her only child. A fiery redhead and true artist, Ginger had revealed the beauty in whatever and whomever she touched. Philip had loved her passionately, unable to deny her anything—even her refusal of a doctor at childbirth. Melissa had managed to save the baby, but not her own daughter.

Inhaling deeply, the 54-year-old midwife reclaimed the present moment. Her pager, set to vibrate mode, started buzzing on Adele's nightstand next to a carved jade frog the midwife always brought to births. The frog symbolized fertility, and jade brought luck, especially for childbirth. Melissa's teacher had given it to her at Ginger's funeral.

Hearing what sounded like a fly, Adele turned. Soaked in sweat, she fixated on the frog, now dancing with the pager. Melissa gently brought her back: "You just concentrate on you, OK, sweetie? Focus on your baby. Focus on your breathing. You're almost there."

Melissa always carried a pager, but she had checked in with her other clients this morning on the way back to Adele's, and all of them were fine. One could never know for certain, but she gave her charge another sixteen minutes of labor, twenty at the most. Whoever was paging her would just have to wait.

Adele's sister and sister-in-law held her hands. On the other nightstand stood an eight-by-ten inch wedding photograph and a four-by-six snapshot of a tan, blue-eyed man in Army fatigues. Ralph Rivers, an oral surgeon in civilian life, had been deployed to Kosovo as a reservist two months ago. In December, his sister Sarah had driven to Sedona from Santa Barbara to offer her support. Adele's sister Marina was in her residency at Flagstaff Regional Medical: Obstetrics and Gynecology. She had driven down last night. Melissa herself had been here since 2 a.m., minus twenty minutes driving Schizandra to school that morning.

Earlier, when Melissa had asked Sarah to drop off Schizandra, Marina had said, "That poor child's suffered enough surprises this month. Go. Take your granddaughter to school. I can hold down the fort for half an hour, right Adele?" Melissa wished Ralph could have been here. A firstborn son only happened once, but she knew war stopped for neither death nor birth. Ginger's father had been killed in Vietnam before ever laying eyes upon his child. She prayed that Ralph would make it home alive.

"I see shoulders!" cried Marina.

"Oh, Adele, sweetie, you're almost there. One more push."

Sarah squeezed her hand, and Adele's warrior cry surpassed even Mother Kali's.

Melissa removed the baby—a wailing boy. Marina cut the umbilicus and cleaned him, while Sarah captured scenes on Camcorder for Ralph. Melissa spritzed the sergeant's wife with rosewater, and helped her don a fresh magenta robe. When Adele seemed ready, the midwife delivered the child to mother's arms.

"Welcome, Charles Kagan Rivers," whispered Adele, instinctively holding the baby to her breast.

Melissa smiled. "You look radiant." She kissed Adele's cheek, glancing at the newborn. "And you, Mr. Charles Kagan. You are a perfect little jewel from heaven."

"Thank you, Melissa," Adele said, with tender eyes.

Melissa's pager buzzed again, vibrating so hard this time, that the jade frog jumped right off the table. Sarah laughed. "I guess somebody really wants your attention. Want to use the phone?"

"I suppose I should." Melissa kissed Adele's forehead and hugged Marina.

"I'll take you to the kitchen," Sarah said, smiling at her suckling nephew. "When you're finished, I'll see if I can get Ralph on the line for her."

"Oh, nonsense," Melissa said, "I'll use my cell. You go celebrate, and tell your brother congratulations! I'll go get my things."

In another eight minutes, Melissa climbed into her silver 1966 Jaguar Mark 2. She keyed the ignition while turning on her cell phone. *Five voice messages?* Elation from this morning's birth tightened into concern. Melissa exhaled slowly.

86. Send.

"Please enter your password."

1967.

"You have five unheard messages. To hear your messages pr—"

One.

"First Message. Mrs. Vreeland, this is Nurse Baker at Red Rock Middle School. I tried calling you at home, but there's no answer. We need to get in touch with you as soon as possible. Schizandra's unconscious. My direct line is 555-0120. End of message. To erase this message, press seven, to save it press—"

Nine. Melissa's fingers trembled.

"Message will be saved for thirty days. Next message. Mrs. Vreeland, Nurse Baker again. We can't seem to reach you, and Sedona Regional Medical's had to MedEvac your granddaughter to Flag. I just found your pager listed in the emergency file. I'll try that. If you get this message, please call 555—"

Melissa screeched the Jag to 89A, where she tried to turn left. After six minutes of non-stop cars, she pulled into the gas station on her right. Her tank was low for driving up the mountain.

"Pump number five?" the cashier said.

Melissa nodded.

"That'll be $16.07."

She took out a ten and six ones. "I've got change." She fumbled in her purse, hoping her overflowing eyes would dry before she found the coins. A large, brown hand placed a nickel and two pennies on the counter. Using a tissue to dab her tears, Melissa turned and faced a six-foot-two Navajo in gray. His shoulder-length black hair framed an eerie visage: ancient gaze, unwrinkled skin.

"The child is cursed," he whispered.

"Excuse me?" she asked, "Which child? Not Charles Kagan?"

The stranger shook his head.

Blood tore through Melissa's brain and crashed against the fear growing in her gut. *Schizandra*. She tried to speak but he silenced her by laying those two huge hands upon her shoulders. Dark, liquid eyes penetrated her own. His lips moved closer to her ear: "Sins of the Father."

Melissa shivered as the native released his hold and left the store. A moment later, she ran after him, but the parking lot was empty. At the Jaguar, goose bumps tickled her neck. She turned and a raven flew so close she felt the whoosh of air beneath its wings. Heart pounding, she climbed into her car and locked the door.

Traffic had thinned, and this time Melissa easily turned left. Driving toward Flagstaff—"Flag" to locals—she felt her energy shift with the changing scenery. Red soil turned to greener trees, and looming rocks became some of the most gorgeous views on earth. As she drove through this canyon that had so inspired Zane Grey, Melissa pondered her encounter. Part of her wanted to dismiss it. Psychics littered Sedona, some of them real finds; others blew through like tumbleweed, scratching and grabbing whatever they could.

But the Navajo had asked for nothing.

Her mind returned to Ginger's death. A freak of nature: something so rare that in thirty-two years, Melissa had never even heard of another case. An amniotic fluid embolism. *A.F.E.* The midwife would never explain it this way, but technically Schizandra had killed her own mother. During labor, bits of the baby's cells and fluid had entered Ginger's bloodstream, causing cardiopulmonary collapse.

Philip's grief had quickly turned to rage. He'd ordered an autopsy secretly—as though Ginger's own mother would try to hide the truth. Despite the results, Philip had never returned to Sedona, claiming the rocks would mock his already unbearable pain. The discoveries during his '86 Sedona summer of love became relics of a past he refused to acknowledge. Chicago University honored him with full tenure, and the Egyptian Institute still displayed his surprising *Egyptian* artifacts, but the professor had sealed those catacombs of a broken heart. Melissa always worried that her granddaughter became Philip's new obsession.

Sins of the Father.

No! She would grant no energy to that. Schizandra was just a child.

The child is cursed.

Melissa gripped the steering wheel until her knuckles throbbed. As she entered Flag, the pressure dropped. White marbles of hail pinged off windshields and cluttered asphalt. Melissa approached the hospital, but her cell phone rang, causing her to miss the entrance. She pulled into another gas station.

"Hello?"

"Mrs. Vreeland?"

Static threatened to disconnect the call. "Yes? Can you speak up please? I can hardly hear you," Melissa shouted.

"Mrs. Vreeland, this is Dr. Swinburne's nurse at … –ona Regional Medical."

Melissa mouthed the words, trying to make sense of them.

"Are you still there?" the nurse asked.

"Y-yes," Melissa stammered. "Who's Dr. Swinburne?"

"He's the neurologist treating Shuh-, uh, your grand—" … *scratch, buzz* … "in Sedona."

"I don't understand. Nurse Baker said Schizandra had been MedEvac'd to Flag over an hour ago. I'm just pulling into the hospital now."

"That's why" … *garble, garble, ping, ping, ping* … "change of plans."

"A change of plans?" Melissa yelled.

" … copter … couldn't leave … -gine failure."

"She hasn't left Sedona?" Each shallow breath drew knives into Melissa's lungs. The hail and static ceased. "Is she still unconscious?"

"Yes, but all her vital signs appear normal now."

"Oh my God, she's brain dead?"

"Not exactly. You'll have to speak with Dr. Swinburne when you arrive."

Chapter Four

SCHIZANDRA WAS SOARING OVER MARS. A wormhole had spun, swallowed and spit her out on the other side of space with a velocity that kept her flying. Or maybe the lack of gravity let her float. She didn't care. She felt wonderful. Stars swirled above and around her, and the full moon shone upon a ruddy landscape far below. She had not expected the moon to look the same from Mars.

Or did Mars have its own moon? She wished she had paid more attention in sixth grade astronomy. No one had ever told her that Mars would look so beautiful. Its quiet majesty embraced her soul. The ground reached high in spots—almost touching her outstretched palms. Cold air rushed through her fingers as she swerved to miss a hill that looked surprisingly like …

Bell Rock.

Schizandra inspected the planet again. She and her spirits sank. There they all were, those stupid, ugly red rocks: Bell, Cathedral, Coffee Pot, a few whose names she had managed to tune out during Melissa's tour. She landed with a thud, choking on a cloud of rusty dirt. Head in her knees, Schizandra wept. "Is there no escape?" she sobbed into the universe.

"Escape. Escape. Escape," echoed across the canyon.

The sentinels stared at her—silent and inscrutable in the night. Stars overhead sparkled brighter than any Chicago sky, and the huge moon watched it all, gliding past Cathedral Rock like a giant pearl.

For twelve thousand years, Native Americans had considered Sedona holy ground but not a place for year-round living. Schizandra certainly agreed with them about the year-round living part. Under this starry canopy, a wandering bark shocked the landscape. Yelping now, followed by frenzied wails.

She jumped to her feet. She had heard coyotes howl behind Melissa's house but had never felt like prey before. She realized now why she had mistaken Sedona for Mars: no lights. *They must be having a blackout.* Otherwise, she would have seen houses, traffic lights.

"Unless Sedona's empty," something said inside her head.

"R-rff-a-eeeeee-oh! Ai-eeeeeeeeeee! Ai-eeeeeeeeeee!" screamed the canyon.

"Unsettled," said the still small voice.

"Ai-eeeee! Eeeeee! Eeeeee!"

So many voices closing in. Her skin prickled, and she shivered in the desert air. Its freshness bit her lungs.

Then suddenly, a different noise, this one not so far away, either: a quiet thud. Sounds of kicking, hooves thrashing the ground—then—silence. A rustling: fifteen yards in front of her, two eyes glowed in the darkness. Something was moving slowly, very slowly out of a shadow and into the moonlight. A cougar dragging its kill across the deer path in front of her. She tried to disappear behind some juniper, but the puma had already smelled its rival.

"Rrrrrow-ow-rrf!"

Schizandra had never heard anything so terrifying as the bark-screech of a hundred-pound cat covered in blood. She screamed—her own blood-curdling human voice bouncing around the canyon. Their eyes met, and then the cougar turned, dragging its prey into the night.

Schizandra wished she hadn't spurned Melissa's introductory tour. She needed to orient herself, and without the town's lights, she had no idea which way to go. One thing was sure: she needed shelter, fast. Between the coyotes and the cougar and God knew what else, she might not make it through the night.

God. Where had *He* gotten her? Bereft at thirteen and lost in a red rock hell on earth. Some Savior. No wonder Daddy hadn't believed in anything. He had researched what he called "archetypal archeology" and had once been the world's leading expert on Atlantis and Lemuria by proving connections among Ancient Egypt and prehistoric cultures in the Americas.

As a child, she listened to his tales about the *Motherland of Mu*, an ancient continent in the Pacific Ocean. He sure knew how to tickle her brain! Once, she begged him to tell her his stories were true, but he said, "No, Zany, nothing's true unless you see it with your eyes or hold it in your hands."

"Nothing?"

He paused. The wind howled past and died away. Finally, he said, "No, not nothing." He closed his eyes before continuing, "Pain is true. Sorrow *clings*, so it must be real."

As Schizandra watched him fight his tears, she suddenly said, "Daddy, what's that fog around your chest?"

"*What?*"

"When you tried not to cry the brown fog pushed against your chest."

"A likely story, Zany."

"No, Daddy, I saw it. The fog wrapped itself around you like—"

"Zany, stop. It wasn't real."

"But Daddy, I saw it, and you said—"

"I know what I said, Zany. You're tired. Sometimes we think we see things when we're tired but that doesn't make them real."

After that conversation, her father stopped telling fairy tales. Six months later, the doctors diagnosed stage three lung cancer, which eventually spread to his brain. He didn't tell her until his hair began falling out from chemotherapy. Then she learned another medical term: "Metastasize. M-E-T... "

Schizandra needed to pay attention to her surroundings now, and memories of Daddy weren't helping. She found herself thinking of Melissa. What would *she* do? Schizandra closed her eyes and took a deep breath. She felt her mind empty like the landscape and exhaled fully.

Inhaling, she smelled sage like Melissa used for smudging. She filled her belly with air, letting it expand across her ribs. The air stretched her chest, and she paused. On the exhale, she reversed, squeezing air from her chest, then her ribs and then pushing it all out with her diaphragm. Alone in the desert, Schizandra breathed the universe as it breathed her.

By the time she opened her eyes, she felt clear. She needed to find a safe place to spend the night. As her retinas adjusted to the darkness, she began walking in the opposite direction of the cougar. She looked at the moon again, grateful for its bright appearance. Melissa would call tonight's full moon "a good sign because it represents a mother's love." Schizandra had never known her mother, but she hoped she could tune into Mother Earth tonight.

Conscious that she sounded like Melissa, she pushed away her father's scorn and asked for help. She wasn't sure whom she asked, but her mind requested another sign: "If the full moon really is a good sign, then please, I need another one."

You must believe said a thought in Melissa's voice.

"I want to believe," said Schizandra, "but how?"

Ask for what you need.

Schizandra closed her eyes, trying to conjure a wish, but her mind clamped shut. "I can't," she cried. "I'm afraid to ask."

Which is scarier, my child? Finding you can trust the unknown, or acting as though you can't?

A coyote howled in the distance. Within seconds, others joined, echoing eerie calls across the canyon. Schizandra shivered—her breathing shallow once again.

Ask for what you need.

"What good will that do when I don't even know who I'm asking?"

Then ask for faith. It's ok to ask for faith.

Schizandra's heart beat faster and a wish took shape. A dark circle moved in front of the moon, casting its shadow over everything. Her heart sank, and she shook her head. Tears spilled down her cheeks again. Honestly, what had she expected? Asking the moon or Mother Earth for help!

A lunar eclipse removed the only comfort she had sensed all night. Wandering in the dark, she tripped on a stone and skidded facedown across the ground. As she caught her breath, she turned her head to the right side. The shadow dissipated. Soon the moon highlighted the low lying entrance to an ancient tunnel.

Melissa followed a nurse into what she assumed would be Dr. Swinburne's office at Sedona Regional Medical. She found instead a dimly lit, antiseptic room. In the center stood a table and a machine recording peaks and valleys of information on an endless sheet of folded computer paper. Upon the table lay Schizandra. Her brown curls haloed the red and blue electrodes pasted to her scalp. The nurse monitoring the machine glanced up as Melissa entered.

"Mrs. Vreeland?"

Melissa nodded. "My God!" she whispered, the color leaving her cheeks.

"I'm Amelia Colman-Smith, Dr. Swinburne's nurse. We spoke earlier on the phone. You can call me Amelia. Why don't you sit down?" she motioned.

Melissa composed herself as she sat in the chair closest to Schizandra. "What's all this—equipment? Are you checking her brainwaves?"

"Yes."

"And what do they tell you?"

"Oh, we don't have all the results yet. Dr. Swinburne ordered an electroencephalogram—an EEG—hoping it would make sense of all the other tests. He'll analyze the results once we finish here."

In the background, Melissa heard and saw the EEG's arm conducting paper in a screeching symphony. When Amelia put a strobe before Schizandra's closed eyes, the tempo changed. The perky nurse told her comatose patient, "Almost done, we're almost done."

The whole performance seemed unreal to Melissa's sleep deprived brain—like a sci-fi musical of *Sleeping Beauty*. As the midwife drifted into dreamland, a Navajo doctor descended from the light fixture and cupped Melissa's hands between his own. He looked into her eyes. In a lively tenor, he began, "Your granddaughter's asleep, my dear. / A curse, a kiss, now don't you fear. / Just find a prince, get on with it. / We'll have her conscious in a bit."

Melissa jerked herself awake as Dr. Swinburne made his less theatrical entrance through the door. The first thing the midwife noticed was his height. His head nearly skimmed the doorframe. Nurse Amelia handed him a stack of neatly folded computer paper. "You were right," she said.

"Mostly deltas and thetas?" asked Dr. Swinburne.

"You'll have to double-check, but it seems that way to me."

Melissa looked confused. "I'm not a doctor, but I do have some medical training. Aren't delta and theta waves what we have when we're asleep?"

"Forgive me, Mrs. Vreeland," he said, "I'm Dr. Michael Swinburne." They shook hands. "I know this must be very traumatic for you, but from a research standpoint, Shuh- is it Schizandra?" he looked at his chart. "Yes, *Schizandra* presents a fascinating case."

"Would one of you please tell me what's happening?" asked Melissa.

"Nothing definite," said Dr. Swinburne. "According to her teacher, your granddaughter lost consciousness in biology class while they were dissecting a pregnant frog. Is she a squeamish child?"

"I don't know." Melissa fought tears of inadequacy. "She's only lived with me for two weeks. Her father just died of brain cancer."

Dr. Swinburne and Amelia traded glances.

"You think she has a brain tumor?" Melissa asked, trying to name the worst as quietly as possible.

"Not likely," said the doctor. "We don't have all the blood work yet, but from what we've seen Schizandra appears in perfect health. She's a little small for her age, but nothing to worry about. No anemia, no evidence of diabetes. MRI and CT scans were normal. No visible tumors. Adequate blood flow to the brain. No sign of hemorrhaging. Normal blood pressure. Heart rate and breathing within normal range."

"So what's the problem?"

"Well," Dr. Swinburne chuckled nervously, "nothing seems to wake her up. Not shaking, loud noises, smelling salts, bright lights: nothing."

"She's in a coma?"

Dr. Swinburne sighed. "Technically, yes, but she presents like no other coma I've seen. It's like she's resting, possibly dreaming. Sometimes she turns away from lights, as though they'll wake her up, but they never actually do."

"She screamed earlier," said Amelia. "It scared the b'Jesus out of me, but when I looked up your granddaughter was fast asleep. I think she's dreaming. Sometimes her eyes and legs twitch, like she's scared, maybe running."

"Poor child!" cried Melissa. "What can we do?"

"Well," Dr. Swinburne said, "under normal circumstances, *normal* being the operative word here, we would keep her in a hospital for observation at least overnight, but as you know, we don't have an inpatient hospital in Sedona." He paused and fumbled with her chart. "The other intriguing factor is that we can't seem to remove your granddaughter from Sedona."

"*What?*"

Dr. Swinburne smiled uncomfortably and continued, "As I said, it's most unusual. The first helicopter flew fine without her, but they tell me a rare equipment malfunction occurred with Schizandra on board. They required an emergency landing and rescue operation. The second helicopter fared no better than the first. As soon as they got her on board and headed toward Flagstaff, a different but also notably rare problem disabled that chopper."

Dr. Swinburne fiddled with Schizandra's chart as he talked. "With both helicopters down, they tried transporting her in an ambulance, but it got two flat tires on its way to Flag. By this time, the pilots and EMS crew were pretty spooked. They convinced the next ambulance to take Schizandra back to Sedona—which they managed to do without incident."

The doctor shrugged his broad shoulders. Melissa thought he looked more like a football player than a physician. Tapping his clipboard on the table, he said, "That's how she wound up in *my* office. We can't keep her here indefinitely, though." Schizandra didn't move.

Melissa's dream sequence seemed more plausible than what Dr. Swinburne had just shared. She wouldn't even try to make sense of it yet: first things first. "So what's the plan?"

"Let me read over her EEG. For now, we've arranged a temporary round-the-clock monitoring situation here. Even with normal brain scans and blood work, in this sort of medical case, there could be a risk of her becoming unstable with seizures, breathing problems, secondary cardiovascular effects, fever, pulmonary embolus.... Results from toxic studies performed to exclude occult drugging and poisoning take time to come back—"

"Poisoning!" Melissa said. "Pulmonary embolus!" Her heart ached as she imagined losing Schizandra like she had lost Ginger.

Dr. Swinburne looked kindly at Melissa and said, "We're trying to rule things out. Your granddaughter will need close observation with constant reassessment of potential causes of the problem, including some prolonged cardiac monitoring. If she doesn't wake up soon, we'll need to provide IV nutrients, catheterization, and monitor her for potential infection. We're working on a more permanent location for her, should that prove necessary."

"Prognosis?"

He shook his head. "I don't know what to tell you. The physician in me says, there's nothing objectively wrong with her, but we need to find an etiology for her prolonged unconscious state. *Maybe* she's just really, really tired. Trauma like a parent's death sometimes causes extreme fatigue until a person feels ready to face the loss."

Dr. Swinburne clicked his pen and shook his head. "The Sedona resident in me wonders if there's not something else going on here, some inter-dimensionality, perhaps. A spiritual experience. Shamans go into trances to 'hone their powers.' I'm not saying I believe all that—or even any of it—but after twenty years here, I guess anything's possible."

Melissa nodded. *The child is cursed.*

Chapter Five

HARU GLANCED AT HIS ALARM clock. 2:32 a.m. In three and a half hours, he would need to wake up but he had yet to fall asleep. Would Shazzie be OK? He had missed her in tenth period algebra, so he figured she must have gone home sick. Somebody said an ambulance had rescued a girl at school. He'd heard a siren, but that could have been anything. Despite his attempts to find out more, no one gave any details. All he knew was that if Shazzie needed an ambulance, then it was something serious.

If only you had waited. I just wanted to show off a little, let her know how smart I am. *Stupid, Stupid! Shazzie's smart but she's still a girl and sometimes girls are scared of frogs. If you were as smart as you think you are, you would have waited for Mr. Feinman to tell you how to cut the frog. Then, if she'd looked squeamish, you could have shown your bravery by offering to slice the frog yourself.* Yeah, like her hero. *Exactly. But no! You couldn't wait to be the big shot. And now Shazzie might be really sick.* I know. *I know. What are you gonna do about it?* What *can* I do? Haru wracked his brain.

And so the hours passed, with nothing but a headache and twisted sheets to show for them. When he finally did fall asleep, Haru dreamt of a colony of giant frogs living deep inside the earth.

On one frog's head sat a yellow crown like kids' books use to designate a king. Haru was hiding under an oriental rug. He could hear the frog king and his advisors croaking loudly. Apparently, the queen had hopped away with the king's black pearls, and he was very mad.

As frog knights tried to quiet him, the king's chest expanded. It kept growing and growing and growing, and when the king had finally reached his limit, he bellowed forth a beep. Haru struggled beneath the rug. Beep, beep, beep. A frog leg grabbed him and dangled his body before the king. Haru slammed off his alarm clock and jumped out of bed. 5:55 a.m.

Wearing flannel pajama bottoms, he stumbled to the bathroom. The tiled floor felt cool and earthy between his toes. He washed his round face in a porcelain sink and combed through matted knots of jet-black hair. With a Japanese mother and Navajo father, Haru had a quiet, unassuming appearance—except for that hair.

His hair was so thick he could balance a sombrero three inches above his scalp. Today, he tugged on those locks, even more unruly from last night's restless sleep. As he yanked the comb through the last big knot, something hit the vanity and bounced across the floor. It settled in a line of sand between the Southwest tiles.

Haru knelt and retrieved a black pearl. "That's odd," he thought, examining the little stone, "I wonder how *that* got in my hair?" Things were always getting stuck in Haru's hair. Once, a raven had landed on his head and sat there for two minutes before peoples' stares had made Haru self-conscious. When he'd finally touched the top of his head, wings had bashed his hands, followed by loud squawking. The raven's foot had caught in a stubborn knot, which Haru had needed to unwind carefully in order to free the bird.

Maybe someone's necklace had broken near his head at school yesterday. He put the pearl in his pajama pocket and forgot about it as he dressed for class.

In first period biology, Mr. Fienman asked, "Has anyone heard any news about Sandra Parker?"

When no one answered, Haru raised his hand and asked, "Do you think Shazzie's really sick?"

"I don't know. I hope not," said Mr. Feinman. "There might be something going around. Maybe she just needs a day or two to recover. I'll let you know if I hear anything. Now, let's get out our frogs. We didn't have much chance to study them yesterday."

Haru retrieved his frog from the refrigerator. As he looked inside, the tiny black and white eggs reminded him of his dream. He extracted a black egg and ran it between thumb and forefinger. It was slippery and shot across the room.

"Haru!" Mr. Feinman tried his best to look stern. "*Please* wait for further instruction before playing with your frog. Remember, this is for educational purposes, not just fun. Now pick up whatever you just threw."

"But, I—"

"Just pick it up, OK?" said Mr. Feinman. He secretly admired Haru's curiosity but could ill afford a cafeteria-style frog fight.

Haru found the egg lying on a crack between linoleum squares. Only then did he recall the round black stone that had fallen from his hair that morning. He returned to his seat and looked at the open frog. Revealing her black pearly cache, Queen Froggy suddenly seemed tragic. Had she died on her way to freedom? *How will the king feel when he finds her slashed?*

Haru lifted his scalpel and awaited further instruction. At the end of class, Mr. Feinman praised the boy's unusual restraint today. Haru just nodded. His former exuberance had fled.

Chapter Six

"SEPHORA, BRING ME MY CACAO."

In the twinkle of resident firefly light, the frog queen smiled. Only this time, she wasn't a frog. She stood tall and slender—unmistakably lovely and human. She was what Native Americans called a "shapeshifter," and she enjoyed appearing in different forms. Smoothing black eyebrows reflected in a watery mirror, the queen fondled a string of black pearls encircling her neck. It was nice to have a neck again. Indeed, she preferred this form. One of the pearls had fallen off as planned.

A yellow hummingbird arrived toting the requested beverage in her tiny feet. The green pail looked like bottle glass, but it was actually fifteen-million-year-old moldavite from a meteor crash at Nördlinger Ries. The queen had commissioned her portable cup from some eighteenth century Bohemians whose ancestors had supposedly carved the Holy Grail.

"Thank you, Sephora. You *are* surprisingly strong."

Sephora hovered at eye level. "Serving you's an honor, m'queen, and as you know, despite m' size, I do *dream* big. But I must tell you the king—he's asking for you."

Frauke downed her cacao and grinned. This was nothing like that watered down hot chocolate they drank on Earth's surface! Frauke's cacao came pure—no milk, no sugar—straight from the tree. The bliss chemical *anandamide* suffused her brain, and she felt her heart expand. "Did you tell him I journeyed?"

"No, m'lady. I ... "

"Well, then, I'll just have to surprise him."

"Queen Frauke! Forgive me for asking, but is it truly wise?"

"Ah, sweet thing, you do amuse me. Another, please!" She handed her servant the now empty pail and awaited her return.

One of the crystals—a heavyset amethyst named Lavandula, flashed to get Frauke's attention. "What is it, darling?" she asked. For millennia, the queen's ancestors had used crystals to store and relay information. People on Earth's surface used quartz in watches and silicon in computers, but those in Frauke's kingdom had mastered this form of communication.

Placing her left hand on the crystal's smooth face, Frauke uploaded a message sent by her great-great grandmother: "Unto us, a child has been delivered. Make straight her path. For this meeting, you remained."

Frauke giggled. The Ancients were *so* melodramatic. Lavandula flashed again and before Frauke could remove her hand, the crystal relayed additional instruction: "We assure you this is no laughing matter, Frauke. The girl has crossed the veil and wanders above. You must find her and lead her underground. We have waited 25,989 journeys around the sun for such an opening. Time is of the essence."

Thank goodness Sephora arrived just then with another cacao, or Lavandula might have ruined Frauke's morning. She sipped the smooth concoction slowly this time, letting the bitter liquid caress her tongue. Already she felt better, but one couldn't possibly feel *too* good. "Have you got any nibs, Sephora?"

"M'lady, I really must advise—"

Frauke's eyes smiled at the little bird. "Sweetness, it is not for you to advise. Only to serve, darling, and if you had held Lavandula, you'd want more, too. Now, please, Sephora, the nibs. I will love you forever for thirteen cacao nibs." Frauke's tiny lips puckered, and the hummingbird flew away on a delightfully blown kiss.

Lavandula flashed again. Frauke turned to face the other cave wall, but a hematite-quartz named Mikhail caught her attention there. Large and rutilated with reddish-brown needlelike crystals inside, Mikhail had long ago established a friendship with his beautiful mistress. The tangerine colored messenger glowed. Despite some initial resistance, Frauke tenderly placed her hands around his translucent face.

"Greetings, vivacious one."

Frauke's sigh ended in a cherubic lift at the corners of her mouth. She relaxed her shoulders. They were letting him translate!

Mikhail continued, "The Ancients honor me again by asking me to relay their message to you in my own words. Let us return the honor by listening well, shall we?" Mikhail intensified his orange hue to match the high vibration of their exchange, and Frauke's heart began to sing. She felt a buzzing in her head akin to the effects of her beloved cacao.

Now that he had captured her full attention, the 188-pound crystal began in earnest. "Your Majesty, you have shown great wisdom this morning by laying both your hands upon my face. The information I carry requires access to both sides of your brain. For clarity, I shall speak as though I am myself the Ancients, but know, delightful one, that I've grown flowers from their words for you."

Frauke noticed a pulsating warmth in the center of her chest and felt waves of peace cascading into the top of her head, down and through her body.

"We begin by assuring you that we support, nay celebrate, your love of cacao. Such information no doubt surprises, but lest you forget, oh, youthful one, it was we who first introduced the Maya to this food of the gods. When you drink *xocoatl*, we feel your joy, and we celebrate because in joy, you scatter your love in wide arcs."

Frauke felt a momentary surge of shame. *The Ancients knew about her cacao habit.* But mortification quickly soared into relief: *they didn't care!* In fact, it almost sounded as though she should consume more. Hopefully, their support wouldn't stifle its effects. Why, part of the—

"Cacao, cacao, cacao. Now that I have your attention again, exquisite jewel of the underworld, I must continue their message." Mikhail pulsated twice to emphasize his point.

A radiant Frauke refocused herself on Mikhail's calming glow and the information she had agreed to receive through him.

"We speak to you with great compassion, dear one, realizing you have not known this planet as we once did. O Frauke, Frauke. Our history's a fairy tale to those who've spent 800-year life spans in caves and tunnels. In mind you are all young; there is no old opinion handed down among you by Ancient tradition, nor any science hoary with age."

Three inches inside the back right half of Frauke's brain, something stirred. She could feel it stretch and yawn as though awakening from deep slumber.

"The world has torn asunder and not everyone mourns the rift. You must find the girl who wanders behind the veil. Her name is Schizandra. The girl's fa—"

Just then Sephora returned with thirteen cacao nibs and an urgent message. "M'queen, m'dear, m'goodness, the king!" She fluttered her wings even faster than usual, hovering and spinning rapidly around Frauke's head.

"Sephora, darling, you're making me dizzy. Slow down! What is it?"

Mikhail flashed three times, but Frauke's heart had already fully engaged the little bird.

"It's the king," said Sephora, "M'goodness, m'lady, I feel—" A quick thinking Frauke caught the messenger in her right hand then gently stroked two fingers over an unconscious Sephora.

"Help!" cried Frauke. Both her voice and silent screams echoed through nearby tunnels. "Someone, please! Help!"

Mikhail flashed again, but Frauke didn't notice as she stood there cupping the bird between both hands. Lavandula stepped in, throwing lavender light across the shadowy niche. Others joined, until the room bounced with flickering colored lights. Frauke's call replayed itself throughout the tunnels, and her stomach churned.

A transparent stone named Heliodor began to emit a steady yellowish-green hue. Frauke walked closer to him in order to balance herself. As her breathing returned to normal, something urged her to hold Sephora within his light. After a few minutes, the little bird recovered enough to open her eyes. She twitched as two of Frauke's tears splashed her golden feathers.

"I thought I'd lost you, sweetness."

Calmer now, Sephora still felt the urgency of her errand, but Frauke insisted she rest awhile: "The king can wait, my little darling. It's you I'm concerned about right now." She stroked the spot between Sephora's eyes and the little bird snuggled into her hands.

A gray, long-eared rabbit named Nestor hopped into the niche, sniffing and looking concerned. Frauke felt a tugging on her aura—the electromagnetic field that surrounds the body of all living things. Through a light pressure on the edge of Awareness, Frauke noticed Nestor's presence.

The rabbit could not speak aloud, but she and the queen knew how to communicate with each other. Frauke and Nestor opened their ears wide, and intensified their senses of smell, touch, taste and vision. The queen and rabbit felt each other as tiny impressions, triggering ancient and unused receptors in the brain. Sensitivity to minute changes in auric fields brought bursts of colored information. With practice one could unfurl these tightly curled messages. A spot near the pituitary gland acted as a prism that focused all those perceptions into a readily understood language experienced as thought.

"You called for help," said the wise old rabbit, taking in the scene before her. Renouncing the reputation of her species, Nestor had taken a vow of celibacy and a masculine name. She looked like a normal bunny yet carried the authority of a high priestess. "The bird mirrors your own unease, my child."

"Nonsense!" Frauke said, "She fainted right before my eyes. The poor darling's utterly fatigued."

"Only through serving you." Because Nestor had sent it telepathically, the queen could not avoid the rabbit's meaning.

Frauke lowered her eyes.

"It is normal to try to distract oneself at times, but you must show courage. You are queen, and the king awaits your visit."

Mikhail! Frauke couldn't possibly encounter the king before she received the rest of the Ancients' message. She turned to him, but her rutilated friend had long ago stopped glowing.

"Do not worry," Nestor said, reading Frauke's concern, "I've already notified the Ancients on his behalf. Through no fault of his own did he fail to relay his charge."

Frauke's stomach sank as she registered a bit of her own responsibility— or lack thereof.

"Enough!" tapped Nestor. "Shame is a distraction. You will receive your calling another time. Now go, the king awaits."

Frauke grabbed the thirteen cacao nibs. "The Ancients recommended it!" she said, triumphantly stuffing four nibs into her mouth and the rest inside her cloak. Dopamine, magnesium and tryptophan calmed, while the anandamide reopened her heart. Bliss returned!

"I know," said Nestor, affectionately amused.

Frauke savored the cacao seeds, chewing them slowly in order to prolong the experience. Funny how something so bitter produced an effect so sweet. As the chemicals infused her body, Frauke felt a renewed sense of clarity. She could face the king. She had followed her heart, and the Law of One would protect her. Gently, she stroked Sephora's feathers, surrounding her in love. With a tiny kiss, she whispered, "Good-bye, sweet friend. Nestor will care for you while I'm away. I'm going now to meet the king."

Sephora released a melodic sigh of relief as Frauke floated away on cacao bliss.

"Well done," sniffed Nestor, after Frauke left.

A lively Sephora warbled, "I tell you Nestie, I couldn't think what else to do."

"What she refuses to embrace for the sake of responsibility, she will for love. You acted well, my friend." Nestor glanced at Sephora and nudged her with a twitching nose: "And now, let us enjoy our time together since the queen herself prescribed it. I have a vial of ambrosia for you tucked into my fur, and I've got fresh rocket in my cheeks."

"Nestie!" laughed Sephora, "you always did know how to party!"

Frauke wandered through the tunnels, moving effortlessly in a labyrinth of interconnected rooms and sudden drop-offs. She had lived here for 461 years, so she knew her way even without the enormous crystal markers. If a visitor ever became disoriented, he or she need only place hands upon the ancient monoliths and upload directions stored within their quartz. Royal blue lapis lazuli and teal chrysocolla slabs sat side by side, waiting to awaken intuition and the connection between heart and mind, should someone forget how to utilize the quartz. Just standing in their presence would calm and heighten one's awareness.

But Frauke needed no such tools today. She knew exactly where she was going, and she wished it were anywhere but there. Despite her resistance, she hurried now, having promised Sephora she would attend the king. Having the renowned healer Nestor care for her little friend brought some comfort, but Frauke also remembered Nestor's reputation for wasting neither words nor time. Her very appearance had frightened Frauke into action. Nestor would not have come if Sephora weren't truly on the verge of death.

In the eerie glow of crystals and shimmering walls, Frauke looked even lovelier than usual. Compassion coupled with concern had increased the circulation to her face, filling her normally fair cheeks with a rosy hue. The flawless skin around her eyes and lips belied the queen's age—perhaps a testament to the Ancients' ways, if she ever gave them credit, which, of course, she did not!

No, Frauke preferred to honor beauty and levity above all things. She not only *looked* young; she *felt* so. This kingdom had run itself for thousands of years. Why should she concern herself with details like responsibility or her reason for being here? Clearly, she lived for fun and loveliness. If she had not discovered a higher purpose in 461 years, then who were the upstart king and the Ancients to suggest otherwise?

Really. Just because the king embraced amphibian form more than anyone since the time of the Ancients! That hardly qualified him to create new laws and expectations. Frauke didn't care that prophecies foretold a leader who would master the *amygdala*, the central brain's tiny fear structure. The king had come to prominence by teaching others to "Embrace Brahma. Erase trauma." Apparently, he had passed for a local at several ashrams in India, but Frauke found *that* hard to believe. In any case, her people came to venerate this visitor as a wise teacher and compassionate guide.

Frauke had managed to ignore the hoopla surrounding his rise to power until one fateful morning when the Ancients spoke to her through Mikhail. What they told her would have been unforgiveable through anyone but Mikhail, and even then, it had created an ongoing rift in their relationship. According to the Ancients (through their rutilated messenger), Frauke was to marry this amygdala-touting, compassion-croaking...*frog* man in order to save the planet.

The playful queen initially fainted from the request, stunned to the point of physical shock that the Ancients would require such a sacrifice. And from her, no less! Why, she'd served well as queen, hadn't she? Did the descendents of Mu ever steal or cheat? If Frauke had not journeyed above she wouldn't even know such concepts!

For a long time after that encounter—despite her love for Mikhail—Frauke felt her heart contract whenever he began to glow. She found herself averting eyes in his presence, looking anywhere but his face. She feared his messages and figured if she did not acknowledge his glow, then she could avoid the communication flowing through him. For two years, they lost their easy dalliance. Every transmission seemed to carry the weight of the world.

Frauke suspected that Mikhail had tried to intercede on her behalf, and she felt a little guilty about that. The Ancients did not appreciate a crystal who expressed his own sentiments. Crystals were communication tools and tools alone—servants of The Law of One. For Mikhail to request different messages and to do so in the name of Love, well, that had *never* happened before in thirty thousand years of crystal subjugation.

The royal marriage occurred suddenly, shortly after Mikhail's transmission of the Ancients' orders. Much fanfare accompanied the union, which Frauke determined would never change her. She fought her battle alone and inside, so no one knew that she and the king had yet to consummate their marriage. *Why, she had never even kissed him!* Whether anyone knew it or not, she had managed to preserve her status as Virgin Queen. She intended to save herself until she found "The One."

Fortunately, she and Mikhail seemed on better terms these days. Until this morning, his messages had remained less intense, and at least the Ancients were allowing him to translate again. She always received instruction more easily when couched in compliments.

Frauke put her hand to her throat, catching a sob of affection for her old friend. As her fingers grazed the black pearls, she gasped. Someone must have been watching out for her. She quickly removed the necklace, shoving it inside her cloak beside the nibs. If the king had seen her wearing that!

Frauke smiled mischievously, fingering the cacao nibs in her pocket. Two more wouldn't hurt! As soon as she chewed them, though, she wanted more. The Cacao Room required only a short detour. The king had waited days. Surely he could wait a bit longer. Besides, cacao always made her happy, and certainly the king would appreciate a happy, open heart.

She might even bring him some beans as a peace offering. He was too novel to remember when cacao pods served as money, but Frauke knew. Didn't the value of a gift come from the giver's perspective? In any case, who would not love to peel away the papery skin and devour a creamy fruit with bitter seeds? If the frog king couldn't handle cacao, then what kind of a king was he? Frauke realized she needed to find out.

And so, she turned right on her travels instead of left, her mouth and heart waiting to ride another wave of cacao bliss. She could hear her workers chanting as they harvested the beans.

To a visitor, the queen's Cacao Room might sound surprising, but it seemed only natural to Frauke. *Theobroma cacao* had always been associated with royalty. Three rulers of the Mayan city Tikal had named themselves Lord Cacao, and Montezuma himself drank fifty cups of cacao before visiting his harem. Cacao butter melted at human body temperature. Frauke loved rubbing it into her legs and elbows. She could smell the tantalizing fragrance through her cloak.

Despite its subterranean locale, the Cacao Room looked and felt very much like a jungle. An underground thermal spring fed the trees and hissed warm mist into the air, simulating tropical climes. A ceiling fashioned entirely of heliodor and rock crystal lenses from Ancient Egypt—variants of the same optical technology used to survey and thereafter build the pyramids—had allowed construction of a room whose upper dome could simulate the sun.

The Ancient Britons, in their astronomical studies had also employed crystal lenses at Stonehenge, which was originally a domed observatory of the moon. Drawing upon additional Peruvian relics, Frauke's scientists had combined wisdom from three cultures to create a subterranean micro-system. By projecting mild sun energy into the Cacao Room, the ceiling offered boundless nourishment to thousands of rainforest plants used by Nestor and others in their healing work.

But by far the most important plants (according to Frauke anyway) were *Theobroma cacao* of the superior *Criollo* variety. Indeed, this species produced the finest flavor, ranging from fruity to spicy, even floral. Nothing artificial mingled with her cacao, including her employees, who descended from family lines charged with building the ancient Khufu pyramid. Contrary to popular belief, those workers had not been slaves, and neither were Frauke's. They served her with love and a reverence for life. And she paid them well.

Upon seeing their queen, the Egyptian descendants bowed and rushed to offer her their beans. Frauke laughed. "One at a time, darlings!" She held open her hands for the first elongated red pod. Passionately, she ran her fingers over its ridges and began to peel the skin with a small knife. She bit into the cacao and felt its cool taste dissolve into water on her tongue. As she reached the brown seeds inside, she moaned, enjoying a moment of chocolate ecstasy. In an instant, she came back to herself, hyperaware of an intruder in their midst.

"Hurry," she said, unnerved beneath her smile. "I'll need seven of the most sacred pods to give the king. And then I must leave."

Frauke's workers stuffed her pockets full of cacao beans and fed her spoonfuls of fruit and nibs. Her heart fluttered as she felt a rush of theobromine. A firm believer that one could never feel *too* good, she nevertheless knew when to stop. A hint more cacao and she'd be on the run for days.

"Really, darlings, I simply must depart. Oh, no, really, I couldn't possibly accept some more." She relished their nurturing and let them swab cacao juice off her pretty face. "A sip of coconut water? Darlings, you are too kind, but yes, I do believe I'll take a sip."

Her cloak felt heavy with all the pods, and she remembered to move the black pearl necklace to a different spot. No sense antagonizing the king! She kissed each worker on the forehead and turned to leave.

Chapter Seven

SCHIZANDRA DREAMT OF HARU. His hair pointed even wilder than usual, forming a spiky halo around his earnest face.

"Shazzie!" he whispered. "Over here!"

Haru's eyes motioned toward a tunnel entrance at the rear of the cave. Schizandra registered the scene but found she could not move her legs. When she tried to ask for help, the words died mute within her throat. She screamed inside but no one heard her cry. Haru kept talking.

"Focus, Shazzie! Remember your breathing."

Schizandra inhaled a blast of cool, dry air.

"Again. Breathe! Breathe in the air!"

Schizandra began a tentative series of inhalations and shaky exhalations, terrified that it required so much work. She wanted to tell Haru her fear, but language failed her. Not even her arms responded when she tried to motion to her throat.

"I know," Haru said.

Thoughts tumbled around Schizandra's brain. *He knows? Knows what? How can he know? Where* am *I, and why can't I talk? How can he hear me when I can't even speak?*

"Yes, Shazzie, I know. You're sending me your thoughts. You're in a coma near an ancient portal. I know you're scared, but you need to listen to me." Haru glanced behind him. "I don't know how much time we have," he mouthed, barely letting his own voice escape. Again, his eyes motioned to the tunnel entrance. "You need to go there."

The frozen girl wanted to cry, but nothing happened. Sobs choked in her chest without so much as a flinch. *How?* She screamed inside.

"You have to use your mind," Haru said. "If you can talk with it, you can do other things, as well." He concentrated for a moment and then whispered sternly, "Shazzie, this is no time for *can't*. You need to move. Now! Here, maybe this will help." He placed the black pearl in her left hand, wrapping limp fingers around the jewel.

Schizandra's right side began to tingle. Her icy limbs suddenly grew soft and warm. She wiggled her right toes. *Wow!* With her newly mobile right hand, she removed whatever Haru had put into her still unresponsive left palm.

Holding it tightly in her right hand, she felt a corresponding heat move through her left side. A slow, honey-like presence seemed to activate her body, moving up and down clear, but unknown channels. Sometimes the honey met with resistance, and when it did, Schizandra felt a buzzing in that area—as though the honey had turned into bees. Their flapping wings and pollen coated legs tickled those tough spots until everything turned honey.

She felt liquid gold flowing though her body, and her mind grew sweet. She closed her eyes to savor the aromatic scent of flowers, beeswax and honey-dew, her mind and body buzzing with the softness of wings and the love of bees. When she opened her eyes, Haru had disappeared.

But the sweetness remained. Slowly, Schizandra looked around her. Through the darkness, she could just make out the edges of what looked like some kind of entrance. And then she remembered Haru: *You need to go there.* As she stood and brushed the dirt off her pants, a small stone scattered across the cave's floor. Something told her to retrieve it, and she spent the next five minutes trying to locate its smooth surface in contrast to the sandstone.

Now! She remembered Haru's urgency just as she found the black pearl, putting it in her pocket and crawling quickly to the interior tunnel's entrance.

Once she stepped into the tunnel, a soft glow grew visible ahead of her. She tiptoed her way there, unsure of her footing on the slippery limestone. The air felt moist after her time in the desert, and she breathed it eagerly. Six feet in front of her stood the largest crystal she had ever seen! Normally, Schizandra subscribed to her father's view that crystals were worthless New Age trinkets. ("Newage," he would say, "rhymes with sewage!"). But three feet high and half as wide, the clear column seemed to beckon her. Gingerly, she placed her hands upon its face.

She felt a flutter at the top of her head and then registered something akin to the tinkle of tiny bells. "Where do you wish to go?" the crystal seemed to ask.

"Why, I'm not quite sure," thought Schizandra, startled.

"That's ok," said the tiny sounds inside her head, "we know where to send you. Turn right and walk until you see a large crystal with smoky looking figures inside. That's a phantom quartz, but don't be scared. Their information can only help."

Schizandra did as the crystal instructed—easily finding her way to the next sentinel. Again, she felt compelled to feel its shiny face. This time, she heard deep chords within her, feeling a similar tingle in her brain, but also a sense of relaxation in her belly. "We are many!" sang the phantom quartz, "but we are kind. Turn right again then stay left at the fork. Should you forget, the Emerald Brothers will remind you."

Schizandra wandered until she saw a fork in the tunnel. "Left," she thought, glancing at two slabs of uncut emerald for confirmation. How delightful they looked! She found herself wanting to say hi, and even before the desire completed its expression as thought, the Emerald Brothers introduced themselves.

"We're very pleased to meet you," said one.

"We hail from Machu Picchu," said the other.

"The Beryl Family name."

"And balance is our game."

"If you feel off kilter or upset."

"Call on us and don't forget."

"Mercury's our special friend."

"Protecting journeys, end to end."

"*Fermion and Boson Beryl*," they announced in unison, "Are honored to make your acquaintance."

Schizandra giggled and her heart sang, "Thank you! I guess I should turn left now." She patted the Emerald Brothers goodbye and travelled on.

The tunnel widened into a large corridor with shimmering lights on each side. At first, Schizandra thought they were Christmas lights, but she soon recognized the work of millions of lightning bugs, all twinkling at once. In the distance she heard singing and could swear she smelled a hint of... *chocolate!* She continued walking, slightly faster now as curiosity urged her forward.

The singing became clearer, revealing itself as a sort of chant. Suddenly, a melodic voice commanded everyone's attention, and Schizandra could feel them listening. Whoever spoke must carry real authority! The girl waited and now heard birds and other jungle sounds. It seemed so very odd to hear birds in an underground cavern, and she thought she heard water, too.

Where *was* she? Unlike other areas, this part of the passageway offered no crystals to guide the way. Her father's voice told her to keep her eye on the destination, but curiosity said stay. She wanted to see the musical speaker, smell the jungle plants, and talk with the macaws. Besides, she didn't *know* her destination, so how could she keep her eye on that? She inched closer to slivers of light surrounding a rectangular slab of rainbow obsidian.

To Schizandra, the door simply looked shiny and black, but rainbow obsidian it was. Mexican Indians believed their gods inhabited this stone when they came to earth. They worshipped rainbow obsidian as heaven incarnate. Just then, the door flew open. As simulated sunlight splashed it, the obsidian released its rainbow display. Though dazzling, the door could not compete with she who crossed its threshold. Schizandra gasped as sunlight displayed a radiant woman in purple robes, daintily gliding towards her.

"Who, in the name of Belisama Mama Quilla, are you?" The woman's lilting laugh belied the intensity of her stare. "Ah," she said, after a moment, "your name is Schizandra."

The girl stood perfectly still despite her racing heart.

After shutting the door, the beauty yanked Schizandra into the shadows and said, "I need you to come with me, but no one can know you're here."

The woman searched her bulging pockets. "I've got nothing to tie you with," she confessed. "I'll have to trust you. But one scream—" She removed a small knife and ran it along Schizandra's chin. "And Queen Frauke will slit your throat." The knife was sticky and smelled like chocolate.

Trembling, the mute prisoner managed to send one clear thought to the queen, "I can't speak!"

Frauke laughed rather wickedly. "So you're a natural. Well that just figures! Come on," she said, prodding Schizandra, "we need to go."

Chapter Eight

MARK STEERED HIS GREEN JEEP Cherokee around the graceful curves of I-17 North. With two choppers down, his company had given him three days off in the middle of a seven-day shift until they could finish their preliminary investigation. Not exactly standard procedure, but the events of January 9, 2001 had pretty much blown away the standards. Two emergency autorotations in one day and both on Bells. Odds of the Jetranger's catastrophic failure of the short shaft were slim enough. But immediately followed by a 407-gearbox failure? It was no "Flight 19," but it seemed eerie nonetheless.

Navigating the turns, Mark pondered Arizona's diverse terrain: desert scrub, majestic pines, canyons, mesas and red rock. The giant cacti called saguaro could store water in their expanding ribs. One didn't see them in neighboring New Mexico. They were as signature Arizona as Tombstone or the Grand Canyon.

Mark had never *driven* to Sedona before. He usually took I-17 all the way to his company's home base in Flag. The choppers ran from Flagstaff Regional Medical to SRM and back to Flag all day long. With seven days on and seven days off, he could afford a double life. One in Phoenix and one in Flag: that came in handy with multiple girlfriends. Unusual circumstances surrounding yesterday's crashes had led the FAA to launch an official investigation. His first—and hopefully only—interview would take place this afternoon at the Sedona Airport Restaurant.

He took the exit toward Sedona/Oak Creek Canyon and turned left on Route 179. The topography loomed above him now, and he could see why people enjoyed this drive. The whole experience had more intrigued than scared him, and he found himself suddenly curious about Sedona's "energy." Maybe there really was something special if that girl couldn't leave town. Wanting the full experience, he had even booked a massage session with a local healer named Bhakti. Set for three o'clock that afternoon, the appointment allowed plenty of time for the FAA and maybe even some window shopping.

An old girlfriend had taken some massage classes and claimed people stored memories in their body tissues. She was just about the sexiest thing he'd ever laid eyes upon, which meant at the time, she could have told him anything and he would have pretended to agree. But now he wondered.

What about that Cherokee in Daleville, Alabama during his Fort Rucker days? He smiled. *Good ole Mother Rucker!* Mark had been leaving a bar with a rowdy cadre of other flight instructors, clearly part of their group. Still, the Indian singled him out. The Cherokee said to him, "You have always been a warrior." That phrase resonated in his bones and for a moment, he flashed to an ancient scene: him, in Native garb, holding something in his right hand, spinning it above his head while he hollered.

"Do not drive tonight." The Cherokee had dropped into his reverie. For reasons still unknown to him, Mark had decided not to drive that night, and two of his fellow flight instructors had traded their pilot's licenses for DUI's. When it came time for Operation Desert Storm, the Army left those two behind, while Mark got to fly Apaches with the scouts.

Had the memories in his cells saved his military career? Mark rarely spoke of such things, but they did stoke his curiosity. Something about yesterday's double malfunction reminded him of that Mother Rucker encounter. Both events seemed unusually loaded.

He wound through the Village of Oak Creek and into Sedona proper, passing the *Center for the New Age* and *Crystal Castle* on his right and some spendy looking place called *Tlaquepaque* on the left. Traffic was like Mardi Gras without the booze. He crawled up the incline, dodging tourists who wandered into the street without looking either way. *You know it's bad when a pilot's the most grounded one on the road*, he chuckled.

For thirty minutes, he had tried to make it the quarter mile to what locals called the "Y," where 179 meets Highway 89A. He had moved faster through an L.A. rush hour. Despite Sedona's obvious commercialism and only two main roads, he had to admit, the scenery was stunning. Red rocks formed a cocoon, wrapping their quiet presence around the buzz of "higher consciousness" and the ka-ching of timeshares.

Sandstone towered over wooden stores and juniper bushes. From the giant red sentinels had sprung tales of Sedona's "magical energy." Some areas seemed to concentrate the power, and these had gradually become known as *vortexes*—nearby Airport Mesa among them. A few New Age seekers had grown to four million tourists per year, followed by souvenir shops, time-shares and competition. Every metaphysical bookstore and rock shop claimed "the highest vibration in Sedona."

Finally at the stoplight, Mark turned left and headed to the airport. Good thing he had allowed extra time for the drive—he would make his one o'clock meeting with only seconds to spare. As he climbed the airport's 4,830 foot elevation, he passed markers for trails leading to the Airport Mesa vortex. *Maybe before his massage.* If he was going to explore Sedona, he planned to treat her like a woman and do so thoroughly.

It felt strange to park his truck in the lot instead of landing a helicopter. He hopped out of his Jeep and entered the restaurant. He quickly spotted the FAA official, sat down and ordered a cup of coffee: black. He'd never understood the whole cream and sugar thing.

<hr />

Forty minutes later, Mark left the Airport Restaurant feeling more mystified than ever. Those officials wanted a left brain explanation, but nothing satisfied. The whole situation reminded him of the Bermuda Triangle, except nothing like this had ever happened in Sedona.

Best he could tell, it was either a freak series of coincidences, or it had something to do with the girl. Someone or some*thing* just didn't want her to leave. He was glad they decided to keep the girl in Sedona because, honestly, he had a bad feeling about taking off with her again.

He checked his watch. 1:45. He left his car in the restaurant lot and ambled to signs for the popular Airport Vortex. Following a group of Japanese tourists up the red rock path to a panoramic mesa, Mark wondered what to expect.

He climbed to the edge of a cliff overlooking the verdant canyon and giant red rocks. To his right and in the distance sat Bell Rock. Everyone knew that one. Suddenly, the wind picked up, throwing his buzz cut on end. The gale grew so strong that Mark needed to focus all his attention on not falling off the cliff.

Despite the fifteen other tourists, he felt alone—almost in a different dimension. The howling wind sounded like radio static and, instinctively, Mark tried to "tune in." He listened keenly to the whoosh of air, his senses taut and ready as when flying. "Close your eyes," said the roar.

Without fighting it, Mark let his eyelids drop and suddenly, he was underground. Silence. And then the image of a girl. *The* girl. From yesterday. Holding both hands on some kind of huge flickering crystal. Something shiny now. The gleam of a knife. Still no sound, but the *feeling* of a scream. The feeling of water. A sense of drowning. Mark gasped for air, and the wind stopped. He opened his eyes.

"Mother of frickin' God," he thought. "What the *hell* is going on?" He had had premonitions before, usually about himself, but occasionally about strangers, too. He called it "being in sync" and figured the universe just needed a messenger sometimes. It had come in handy, typically involving a phone call to check in on an old friend, or approaching and then listening to someone at the bar.

This was different. The girl seemed to be reaching out to him from somewhere else. She wanted help. She wanted ... her grandmother! Mark had no idea how he knew this, but it resonated in his bones. The girl in the coma was in trouble. Somewhere, someone or some*thing* was holding her captive, and she wanted to escape.

His cell phone rang. "This is Mark," he answered.

"Yes, hi, Mark. This is Bhakti. I'm just calling to confirm your massage at three o'clock this afternoon. For some reason I had a feeling you might not make it."

Startled, Mark looked at his watch again. 2:42. He had been gone nearly an hour.

"Hello?"

"Uh, yeah, I'm here," said Mark, not sure what that meant anymore.

"Do you need directions?" asked Bhakti.

"No, I'm, I'll be fine," he said. "I'm really looking forward to meeting you." And suddenly, he was.

"Your shoulders are tight," said Bhakti, as she rubbed eucalyptus and clary sage into Mark's back. "What do you do for a living?"

"I'm a helicopter pilot." He waited for Bhakti to melt like every other woman he knew.

Unfazed, she said, "All that vibration takes a toll on your muscles."

Her fingers seemed to glide underneath his right shoulder blade. "Let me know if I'm pushing too hard," she said. "You've got some trigger points here. Been doing some stressful flying lately?" She knew exactly where to go.

Mark chuckled. "Yeah, you might say so."

She moved her thumbs up along both sides of his spine. As his sacrum released, he felt his body settling deeper into the table. The face cradle made it difficult to talk, but he found himself wanting to share more.

"Yesterday, my chopper malfunctioned." Bhakti's hands moved along his spine and over each shoulder. "Our rescue went down twenty-five minutes later. I just came from—"

"Oh my God!"

Bhakti's hands stopped. She rested them on his back for a full twenty seconds then doused him with extra lotion and essential oil. He heard her inhale fast and he took a long breath too as lavender wafted through the face cradle. "Sorry about that," she said, back in rhythm. "You're one of those pilots from the Parker case, aren't you?"

"What, did you read about it in the paper?" he asked. Mark felt drowsy from the lavender. The heels of Bhakti's hands worked his back and shoulders.

"Hmmm," she said, "this side doesn't wanna open up. I'm gonna try an ancient energy technique called Reiki on it. Just let the energy move you so your body can heal itself. I sense old trauma here, maybe not even from this lifetime."

"Really?" asked Mark. He felt too sleepy to smirk, but she had stoked his curiosity. "What are you picking up?"

"It's best if you just relax into it. Try not to think too much."

Mark recognized the command behind her suggestion and felt himself drift away on puffy clouds of colored lights. Greens and turquoise.

A misty entrance to something dark and underground:

Firelight playing on red walls. Watching a man he knew was his father painting sacred symbols in a cave. Noise at the entrance. The ritual abolished!

Men, clubbing his father in front of him, a helpless boy. The men leaving and Mark picking up one of their discarded clubs, swinging it above his head and screaming. Running after the men and swinging the club so hard it dislocated his right shoulder and killed them all. Continuing to swing wildly, even after his shoulder left its socket.

The chief, finding him sobbing over his father's body. The tribe, honoring him as the great warrior for whom they had prayed. A young boy, thrown into the world of men by the murder of a shaman.

Tears streamed down Mark's face as he felt the release of centuries of grief and shame. Bhakti crooned, "It's OK to let it go."

Chapter Nine

C OME ON," FRAUKE SAID, "WE need to hurry."

Schizandra stood mesmerized by the scene before her.

"Oh, right, you've never seen a hydroponic garden before. Well, here it is," said the queen, gesturing to her right. "We don't need much soil, and these underground streams are so mineral rich we don't require fertilizer. We feed two hundred thousand people from these three acres."

Schizandra continued to stare, unable to comprehend such lush greenery inside a cave.

"We're on level four of five," said Frauke, "dedicated entirely to our gardens. Everything's organic, and the light here comes from the love in people's hearts. We have masters blessing the food every moment that it grows. Just wait 'til you taste the vibration! It's heavenly—nothing like your genetically engineered stuff above."

"If this is four," Schizandra wondered silently, "then what are one, two and three?"

"We don't have time for that," Frauke snapped.

"What's level five?" Her telepathic question escaped before she could rein it in.

"That's the deepest level—where the king lives—and he's still waiting." The cacao had begun to wear off, and Frauke felt on edge. Not to mention she found the girl's presence here unnerving. The last time an Ancient's prophecy had come true, she'd found herself married to an amphibious upstart.

Schizandra's arrival seemed like an even bigger deal. It had been spoken of for centuries before Frauke's birth. On her hundred-fiftieth birthday, Frauke had learned that she would usher a chosen one into the underworld, but with three hundred and eleven years of anticipation, her excitement had considerably waned.

Frauke could read Schizandra's thoughts about her. "I am *not* afraid of the king!" she shot back. "Why, I was queen even before that little frog man was born."

"You call your king a frog man?"

"OK, look, you're very good at what you do, whoever you are, but if I wanted someone to analyze my feelings about the king, I'd, I'd, well," said Frauke, out loud now, "I could do it on my own!"

"Just asking," came Schizandra's thoughts, "it seemed unusual is all. No need to get all hostile about it."

To Schizandra's surprise, Frauke wiped a tear from her pretty features and averted her eyes. "You're a prisoner here, but your heart is soft. Why aren't you angry with me?" Frauke asked, silently.

Schizandra's heart opened wider and she no longer felt afraid. "Because," she radiated, "you need my help."

Frauke narrowed her long-lashed eyes and said, "You know I'm queen, right?"

Schizandra nodded.

"Then, shouldn't you show me more respect?"

"I more than respect you," exploded words from the prisoner's heart. "I *see* you." Schizandra suddenly felt free! Her chest released and she could finally breathe without obstruction.

"Nonsense," said Frauke, adjusting her cloak and patting her long, ebony hair. "What are you, fifty years old?"

"Fifty years old!" laughed Schizandra.

"What's so funny?" The queen looked confused.

"I'm thirteen. How old are you?"

"I'm not telling," said Frauke, pouting. "Why don't you guess, miss know-it-all?"

"Um, nineteen?"

"Close," Frauke smiled.

"Four-hundred-sixty-one years old!" Schizandra's brain exclaimed. "Oh," she paused, suddenly getting it, "you're joking. I didn't realize you could joke this way."

"You can't."

"So you're really not kidding?"

"Nope," said Frauke, "I look pretty good for my age, huh?" She winked.

Schizandra's mind began to swim. *But.No.Melissa.Crazy.Mu.Daddy. What? Where am I? This isn't funny. Wake up, wake up wake up wake up! I can't wake up.* She squeezed her eyes shut and clenched her fists. *When I open my eyes, I will be in my little bed in Melissa's house. No, I will be at the kitchen table, feeling the hard oak beneath a bowl of vegan chili with vegan cornbread crumbled on top. And I can smell it, and I can taste it, and I can feel it, and I know that I am there.* She couldn't believe how wonderful it all felt.

Frauke giggled. "You're in Mu," she whispered. "Open your eyes."

"I'm not, I'm not, I'm not, I'm not!" thought Schizandra, even as her heart jumped with curiosity. *"Mu?"* The question trumped her other thoughts. *"I'm in Mu?"*

"Well, what's left of it," said Frauke. "Please open your eyes." The queen gently smoothed Schizandra's curls and smiled fondly in spite of herself.

The girl opened her left eye first and carefully absorbed the scene. "This is *not* what Daddy told me about Mu."

"With all due respect," said Frauke, carefully cloaking the thought *which isn't much,* "your father had some additional things to learn."

"I guess so!" sighed the professor's daughter, shaking her head and opening her other eye, "but, why am *I* here?"

Frauke fingered a cacao pod and took out her knife.

Schizandra jumped back. Wonder became fear.

"No, silly!" Frauke laughed. "I want you to try this." She peeled the skin and split the bean in two. "One bite and you won't care why you're here."

Still wary, the girl refused the proffered cacao.

"Suit yourself," said Frauke, popping the other half between her lips and visibly relaxing. She shuddered. "My workers did *well* cultivating these! Mmmmmm-*mmm*!" She closed her eyes and jerked her chin for emphasis. "OK, we've dallied long enough. Chop, chop, Schizandra!" She snapped her fingers and started walking. Realizing her charge hadn't moved, Frauke turned around. "Come *on!* We have to see the king!"

The entire situation seemed so bizarre that Schizandra decided to go with it. Slightly smirking with disbelief, yet wondering what came next, she followed the queen, whose steps moved much faster than before. The cacao had kicked in!

"Hey, wait up!" gasped Schizandra, breaking into a jog.

"We're making up for lost time," said the queen.

"There's no such thing," Schizandra thought.

"What?" Now it was Frauke's turn to stop and stare.

"Time," she paused, "I don't think you can lose it."

"OK, smarty-pants, where'd you get that one?" asked Frauke.

"I don't know," thought Schizandra, truthfully. "It just popped into my head."

Frauke rolled her eyes. "You are going to *love* the king! Now come on. No more dilly-dallying. We've 'misplaced' several hours already."

Chapter Ten

MELISSA FELT GRATEFUL THAT MAIA had fit her in on such short notice. She had really wanted Bhakti's transformative touch, but right before Melissa's call, the gifted healer had booked today's only open session. Reluctantly, Melissa had agreed to call Bhakti's new office mate, who did have a three o'clock available.

Massage ranked among the very last things Melissa expected to do the day after Schizandra's incident, but this morning had brought such pain! Not wanting to leave her granddaughter's side, she had spent the night in a chair at Sedona Regional Medical. Her body felt like someone had clubbed her, leaving invisible bruises deep within the flesh. After two sleepless nights, her brain had fogged like a Magic Eight Ball. *Ask a question, shake it up. Wait. Wait: "Ask again."* Every nerve begged her to surrender.

She had buried a husband, a daughter and a son-in-law. She couldn't bear to watch her granddaughter die, too. Melissa understood why Schizandra might want to check out. Grief was brutal, and sometimes the midwife wished that she could close her own eyes to a world that allowed such suffering. But in her heart, she knew she needed to survive. Years of midwifery had taught her the importance of caring for herself in order to care for others. Her body needed help. With the right blend of cranio sacral therapy, aromatherapy and music, she would find a way to get through this. She was all Schizandra had left!

Except for Rosemary and Lobelia, of course—her twin sisters from Madison, Wisconsin. Melissa sighed into Maia's movements at the base of her skull. She should probably call them. The two spinsters had hardly spent a day apart. Indeed, they had always functioned almost as a single unit, leaving a younger Melissa to fend for herself as a girl. *Oh, you couldn't blame children, but still, sometimes the twins interfered more than they helped.*

"Ow, that's sore today!" Melissa squirmed even under the gentle touch.

"I'm sorry. Would you like me to lighten up?" asked the petite therapist.

"A little," said Melissa, longing for Bhakti's intuitive awareness of her trigger points.

"I know you asked for cranio work today, but I'm sensing you're even a little too sensitive for that. Would you like me to try something above the body?"

"I guess." Melissa felt disappointed at the lack of human touch but realized she couldn't handle even the slightest pressure.

As she lay on the table, she found herself comparing Maia to Bhakti. That figured, of course, since Bhakti had treated her for years, but Melissa supposed she should give Maia a chance. She closed her eyes and immediately opened them as she felt the gentlest touch on her abdomen. But Maia's hands remained about four inches above her body. Melissa smiled and relaxed into the treatment. *This might work after all.*

Sunlight gently sliced through the fog in her brain, reminding her of the Golden Gate Bridge in her native San Francisco. That's what she needed today: a bridge. From victim to support. She needed to stay warm and walk across that bridge. As the fog continued to clear, Melissa recognized it as a soft cocoon that had erased clamoring thoughts and honking concerns until she could reach this place. Poised above the waters of emotion and between two worlds, she could finally breathe.

"Take as long as you need," whispered Maia. "We've finished our hour."

Melissa felt slightly surprised that time had moved so quickly, and yet, it also seemed like she had slept for days. Her body awakened as from deep, restorative sleep, and she realized that her pain was gone. She smiled, snuggled under a fleece blanket, keeping her eyes closed to prolong the experience. The fog had cleared, and she could now return to Life moving all around her.

"Thank you," she murmured, slowly sitting up. She had stayed clothed in anticipation of cranio sacral therapy, and so Maia remained in the room with her. "That was wonderful!"

"I'm glad I could fit you in," said Maia. "Bhakti was worried about you."

"She's a sweetheart," agreed Melissa. "Did she tell you what happened?"

"Only that you really needed some bodywork today."

"Yes," said Melissa, suddenly wanting to confide, "my granddaughter's in a coma."

Maia touched her hand. Melissa could see the therapist's eyes tear up. "Oh, my God, that must be so hard for you to witness! She's your only grandchild, isn't she?"

"Yes, how'd you know?"

"I'm pretty intuitive," Maia said. "I'm actually getting a bit of a hit on her. Do you mind if I share it with you?"

Melissa inhaled quickly, as she remembered yesterday's foreboding Navajo. "OK," she said, "I guess I'm open to suggestions since the doctors don't know what to make of it."

Maia handed her a business card. *New Cycle Astrology in Uptown Sedona—40 Years of Inspiration and Experience.* Melissa raised her eyebrows, doubtful.

"I know the card's a bit cheesy, but I promise you this guy is *phenomenal.* I think you need him to do your granddaughter's natal chart."

"Her chart?" asked Melissa. "I'm not even sure I believe in astrology."

"I wasn't either," said Maia, "until I met Tom Brown. He will blow your mind! I'm not even kidding. He told me things about myself that I've never told anyone, and it really helped."

"Like what? If you don't mind my asking."

Maia looked like she might leap out of her chair and start dancing. "Three months ago, I was living in a trailer in South Dakota. Something told me to go online and look for an astrologer in Sedona. I did and *New Cycle Astrology* came up. Tom let me email him my details, and he did an astro report from my birth wheel to Sedona."

Maia caught her breath, barely able to keep up with her own excitement. "Sedona's really good for my progressive moon."

"Progressive moon?" Melissa raised her eyebrows.

"I didn't know what that meant either," said Maia. "Apparently, it's got something to do with your emotions. Anyway, Sedona's supposed to be really good for me."

"So you moved here, just like that?"

"Just like that!" Maia said. "I was ready for a change. It was like I was waiting for the universe to send me that little bit of guidance, and Tom delivered."

"So, I just email him?"

"Well, you're *here* so you can actually schedule with him in person. That's *so* much better!" said the petite therapist. "If you talk with him in person he can actually *show* you her chart, and he'll probably do some *tarot* for her, too. Ever had a numerology reading?"

"No," said Melissa.

"Well, *Tom* is *amazing*! I guarantee if you see him, you won't be sorry."

"That's quite an endorsement," said Melissa. "Has Sedona really treated you so well so soon?"

"Oh, my *God*!" Maia squealed and displayed a huge Herkimer diamond on her left ring finger. "I found my soul mate in a week!"

Melissa smiled, trying not to look as skeptical as she felt. She had heard it all before. People came to Sedona on a supposed calling, expecting "the universe" to care for all their needs. After struggling for six months, they either just squeaked by or fled, crushed by an economy as harsh as the desert landscape. A few people made it, sure. Like Bhakti, for example. Or Melissa herself. When she'd arrived in 1970, she had been the only midwife in Northern Arizona, and look how her practice flourished! She tried to smile as she said, "Congratulations."

"I know what you're thinking," said Maia. "You're wondering how I *know*. All I can say is that I *do*, and it's wonderful, and I am just so grateful to Tom for leading me down here so my life could begin!"

"I'm happy for you," said Melissa, sincerely. Despite the over-enthusiasm, Maia drew her in. Melissa found herself really hoping the healer had found true love.

"*Thank* you," Maia said, casting a furtive glance at the clock.

Melissa caught it. "I'll let you get ready for your next client. And thank you! For everything," she said, lifting the business card. "I'll consider it."

When Melissa opened the door, Bhakti was just saying good-bye to her client, a ruggedly handsome man who appeared in his mid-forties. Bhakti looked startled to see her.

"Mark, could you hold on for just a moment," she said, "I wanna say hi to Melissa."

"Oh, that's OK, we're done here, aren't we?" he asked, still a little disoriented from his massage.

"If you could wait—just—a minute," Bhakti said, holding up her index figure in a playful manner. "Melissa!" She ran over and hugged her friend and client, then whispered in her ear, "You have got to meet this guy."

Melissa's heart crept into her throat and she hung back.

"I promise you won't regret it," Bhakti said, dragging her by the hand.

"Mark, this is Melissa. Melissa, Mark. You two need to go out to dinner or something."

"What?" They asked, simultaneously.

"Melissa," Bhakti turned to her friend, "do you trust me?" Her eyes penetrated Melissa's face.

"You know I do, but—"

"Mark, you and I just met, and believe me, I *never* do this, but you *really* need to take this woman out to dinner."

Mark eyed Melissa. She squirmed under his gaze, feeling like a piece of gum he had just discovered on his shoe. She wanted to say, "No, thanks," and she was sure he did, too.

He looked as surprised as she felt when he said, "I'd be honored if you'd join me, but you'll have to choose the place."

Stunned, Melissa rummaged for a plausible decline. She thought she'd found one until her mouth spoke: "I'd be delighted! You can follow me. I drive the silver Jaguar."

Bhakti smiled and ushered them away. "I need to get the room ready for my next client. Love and blessings to you both." She closed the door behind them.

"Haru!" said Brielle, surprising the chess champion after practice. She and Angie followed him in their cheerleader uniforms.

"C'mon, wait up!" called Angie.

Haru stopped and eyed the girls suspiciously. "What do you want with me?"

"Look," Brielle said, "I know we haven't exactly been the nicest to you over the years, but you're in Shazzie's biology class, right?"

"Uh-huh," Haru nodded, sensing a ploy.

"Well," said Angie, fluttering her eyelashes, "what happened yesterday?"

"Nothing," he said, "she just collapsed. Have you heard anything?"

"No, silly," said Angie, "that's why we're talking to you."

Brielle elbowed her.

"Ow!" Angie pouted as her friend stared down Haru.

"At least Angie tells the truth," he said. "If you're looking for more information, I don't have it."

"We're just worried," said Brielle, "same as you. Shazzie's our friend."

"I know," said the Japanese-Navajo, recognizing the futility of his crush. If they hadn't been lab partners, he wondered if Shazzie would have ever even spoken to him.

"So," Angie said, "you can't tell us anything we don't already know?" She smoothed her chin length hair behind her ear and flashed green eyes at him.

Haru shook his head. "Not about Shazzie. I'm really worried about her."

"So are we," Brielle said. "I heard a helicopter crashed taking her to Flag."

"*What?*" shouted Haru, spilling his books and then his pens as he tried to retrieve the books.

Angie giggled. "Ow!" she exclaimed again.

"My dad said it was on the news," Brielle said.

"Exactly what was on the news?" asked Haru, blushing.

"Two emergency helicopters crashed in Oak Creek Canyon yesterday," said Angie, making a face at Brielle.

"No one was hurt," her friend continued, "but the news said one of the passengers was a thirteen-year-old girl. We figure that *had* to be Shazzie!"

Haru's heart sped up a notch, but he managed to retain his books and pens this time. "Are you sure?" he asked.

"Well," the girls said in unison, "no."

Haru wrinkled his forehead and scrunched his nose, deep in concentration. Kids made fun of him when he did this, but it helped him think.

Angie wisely kept her giggles to herself.

"I'm going to try something," he said. "Do you know where she is?"

Brielle shot her friend a look to keep quiet, and Angie raised her eyebrows in mock defense.

"It seems like she's in Sedona," said the perky blonde. "I heard an ambulance couldn't make it out of town either."

"So… she's not supposed to leave," Haru said, wrinkling and scrunching more. He fiddled with the black pearl in his pocket and closed his eyes. Suddenly, he opened them wide. "How much time do we have?"

Angie looked at her watch. "It's 4:15, and my mom's picking us up at 4:30. Practice ended early today."

"Alright," Haru said, "that will have to do." He looked around to make sure no one had noticed their unlikely meeting. "Follow me."

Chapter Eleven

I NEED TO MAKE ONE STOP first," Melissa said, as she and Mark approached her car. "We can reschedule if you want, but I won't be able to concentrate or eat until I check on my granddaughter."

Something in Mark's stomach churned. This just kept getting worse. Her granddaughter? How old was this lady? He almost bowed out, but that would have looked too obvious, and, in spite of himself, he *had* just invited her to dine with him. What the hell was Bhakti thinking? No wonder Sedona had a reputation for kooks!

"No problem," he said, "do you need to make a call, or should I follow you somewhere?"

"You can follow me," Melissa said, preoccupied, "if you're sure you still want to have dinner together."

Mark smiled and shrugged. "Your friend Bhakti seems to think we should."

"Yes," Melissa said, "she's never done that to me before."

"Great, now I feel like some sort of punishment. Kiss the frog!" Mark chuckled nervously.

Melissa smiled and touched his arm. "I'm sorry," she said, "This has been a really difficult week! If Bhakti weren't so insistent, I would've taken a rain check. It's got nothing to do with you."

Mark's heart jolted when she touched him. *Nothing to do with you?* That was his line. Melissa slid into her Jaguar. *Nice wheels.*

"We're just headed to Sedona Regional Medical," she called out the window.

Mark climbed into his Jeep and followed Melissa. And then it hit him! When they pulled into the parking lot, he jumped out of the Cherokee and grabbed Melissa's arm. "Your granddaughter's the girl from the helicopter, isn't she?"

Melissa extricated her arm. "Please let go of me. I asked them to keep details off the news. Did Bhakti tell you? I knew this was a bad idea," she said. "Please, go back to your truck and leave me alone. You're—"

"I'm," Mark interrupted, then paused.

"You're?"

"The pilot."

Melissa caught her breath. He sensed she stared at the blond stubble on his chin to keep from making eye contact.

"I'm sorry," she said, "it's just—"

"I understand." Mark inhaled slowly, reaching into Melissa's eyes with his own. "Want some company in there?"

Melissa started to shake her head no then changed her mind. "That," she sniffed, "that would be nice." She smiled as they exhaled together.

While waiting for Dr. Swinburne, Mark told Melissa about yesterday's adventures. The unusual nature of the malfunctions. The ambulance's flat tire. She, in turn, told him what the mysterious Navajo had said.

"So, you don't know this guy?"

"No more than I knew you at Bhakti's."

"Sounds like some kinda Sedona wack job to me," he said, troubled despite his bravado.

"I don't know," Melissa said, shaking her head. "I want to believe that's true. More than anything! But you have to admit, this whole thing is weird."

Mark couldn't argue that. He glanced at his watch: 4:28. This had been one heck of a two-day stint. He debated whether or not to share his vortex vision with Melissa. He felt guilty withholding, but she already had so much to ponder. He decided to compromise, saying, "I'm sure she misses you, wherever she is."

"I don't know," Melissa said. "Sometimes I think none of this would have happened if I had just stopped riding her about her name."

"What *is* her name?" Mark said, suddenly curious.

"Schizandra Ginger Parker. We named her after the schizandra berry, as her mother intended, and kept Ginger in honor of her mother's sacrifice." Melissa paused and then said quietly, "Ginger died while giving birth to Schizandra."

Mark shook his head. "So where's her father?"

"He died on December twenty-first."

"Car accident?"

"No."

Mark took her hint and redirected the conversation. "That's an unusual name."

"For an unusual soul. Schizandra the berry raises energy and helps the body heal itself."

Mark watched Melissa. When she smiled, her eyes glimmered like periwinkle and violet pools. Her pupils were large and dark.

"It's an adaptogen," she said, "which means it can heal just about anything. Adaptogens are magical and rejuvenating."

He smiled. "Sounds like Schizandra could use a good dose of herself."

Melissa looked at him. "You know, you're right," she said. "But I suspect we could all use a good dose of ourselves. My sisters are always saying that: 'The only way to heal is to embrace who we truly are.' In Schizandra's case, that's doubly important. You see, she truly *is* a healer."

An athletic looking doctor met them in the waiting room. "Mrs. Vreeland, good to see you again," he said, extending his hand. He turned to Mark, "And you must be Mr. Vreeland. Glad to meet you."

Melissa corrected his mistake: "Uh, no, Dr. Swinburne. This is a, a friend, my friend Mark—"

Realizing she didn't know his last name, Mark grabbed the doctor's hand and said, "Adams. Mark Adams. Nice to meet you." They shook hands warmly. "How's Schizandra?" he asked.

Dr. Swinburne looked at Melissa for permission. She nodded.

"Well, the good news is that all her test results look normal."

"OK," Melissa said, "so what's the bad news?"

"The bad news is that she still hasn't regained consciousness, and we're running out of capacity to care for her here. If she doesn't wake up soon, we'll need to rethink moving her to Flag."

"You really think that's necessary?" Mark asked.

"I don't see any other way," the doctor said. "Mrs. Vreeland, the fact is, your granddaughter's not responding to our efforts. If she stays unconscious much longer, we'll need round the clock care, someone to stretch and strengthen her limbs, special treatment of the skin to prevent bed sores, urinary catheterization. We've already attached a temporary ventilator and feeding tube. We just don't have the facilities here to handle this type of long-term intensive care."

"What about home care?" Melissa asked.

Dr. Swinburne shook his head. "I can see your heart's in the right place, but I just don't think you understand all the implications. Without proper care, she could flatline, and we're talking non-stop care. One person simply couldn't do it alone! Even with a partner," he glanced at Mark, "I'm afraid it's just not feasible."

Does that doctor really think we're together? Mark had never dated anyone over age thirty-five. He glanced at her again.

She looked flustered. "I'll have to call my sisters," she said. "They always know how to handle these situations."

"Are they neurologists?" Dr. Swinburne asked.

"In a manner of speaking," Melissa said, "they practice reflexology."

Dr. Swinburne looked concerned and eyed her carefully. He turned to Mark. "She needs rest. All this stress takes its toll on even the strongest constitutions."

Melissa whispered through a tense smile, "Dr. Swinburne, whatever their foibles, my twin sisters do know a thing or two about healing. If you can't help my granddaughter, I'm sure not ruling out alternatives!"

"She has until tomorrow afternoon to wake up," the doctor said, "twenty-four hours. I wish I had better news."

"Are you sure there's no way you can keep her here a little longer?" Mark asked, "I know SRM's not meant for long-term care, but you *know* it's an exceptional situation. I mean, in all my years of flying I've never seen two helicopters and an ambulance bust up over a single patient."

Melissa's eyes watered as the doctor said, "I'm sorry, but my hands are tied on this one."

"Why?" Mark pressed, "Can't you just give her another week?"

The doctor shook his head. "Even if we had the room, she doesn't present with a normal coma. When Schizandra screams or has other changes in her breathing, we've got to know we have staff on hand to treat her. Unless she wakes up, we'll need to get her situated somewhere else before the weekend."

Mark offered his hand. "Thank you, Dr. Swinburne. We appreciate your care."

When the doctor left, the pilot turned to his crestfallen companion. "Now look, I'm gonna hold you to that dinner date. Why don't I bring us back some food? We've got lots to talk about."

The two girls followed Haru behind the school. Right now this exotic boy intrigued them. Haru shaded his eyes as he gauged direction by the sun. "OK," he motioned to Brielle. "You sit here." He pointed to a large slab of red rock on her left then looked at Angie. "And you go ahead and sit here." He motioned to a dusty area between two lamp posts, about three feet away from Brielle. "I'll sit over there, but first I need to call in the elements."

Angie looked excited and asked, "What kind of elements?"

Brielle said, "You know, Angie, the *elements* like at Hogwarts!" She smiled and her eyes grew big.

Haru said sternly, "No talking. We only have a few minutes before Angie's mom gets here, and I've never done this on my own before. I don't even know if it will work. I just need you both to sit there, and when I sit down, we'll all close our eyes and see what happens, OK?"

The girls nodded and took their spots, still watching Haru. Facing East, he stood with his feet shoulder width apart and spread both arms wide. "Spirits of the East," boomed his normally shy voice, "We honor you." He turned ninety degrees to his right then announced, "Spirits of the South, we honor you." Again, he turned ninety degrees and held out his arms. "Spirits of the West, we honor you," and after one last quarter-turn, "Spirits of the North, we honor you."

He looked up to the sky and raised his hands, saying, "Father Sky, we honor you and ask you to illuminate our journey." Looking to the ground, he finished, "Mother Earth, we honor you and ask for your protection. Take us deep within your womb. Show us your secrets so we will know what we need to know."

The girls sat mesmerized. As Haru joined them in his spot, a large white ring appeared around the sun, and the wind picked up. He nodded to Brielle and Angie then closed his own eyes.

Triangles and star tetrahedrons whizzed by their heads as they descended step by step into the elemental forces of a steam cave. Haru led the way with the girls tightly holding hands behind him. It was dark, but the walls flickered with distant firelight. They could hear and almost taste the water from a volcanic hot spring. Scents of heavy minerals and damp earth thickened and calmed the air.

Haru reached into his pocket and removed the black pearl. He set it on a makeshift altar of limestone surrounded by steam. An offering. He motioned his head to an entrance at the rear of the cave, and the girls followed.

Haru raised his hand and pressed his back against the moist wall. Brielle and Angie moved into shadows near the entrance. Someone was singing and laughing on the other side.

"Nestie! You always tickle me with your tales!"

Thump, thump, thump.

"But how can *I* help the girl? You know I'm loyal to m'queen."

Thump, thump, thump, thump!

"Poor queen! She doesn't have so many friends you know. Do you really think, Nestie, that Schizandra can help? Why, she's not even from this side o' things!"

A rapid thumping ensued, prompting the voice to chirp, "Ay, Nestie, I sense some listening ears as well."

Haru grabbed Brielle's free hand and pulled the girls quickly after him. Running through the steam cave, they felt the wet air part before them, climbing, climbing, climbing, the air growing thinner and dryer with each breath until finally, they opened their eyes behind the school, panting fast. Their three-part circle had closed in and they found themselves holding hands as they stared at one another.

"She's there!" gasped Angie.

Haru nodded.

Brielle and Angie looked at each other and then stared back at Haru. Gradually, they became aware of a car's horn in front of the school.

"My mom!" said Angie, scurrying up. She and Brielle waved good-bye to Haru, who remained too stunned to say a word.

Chapter Twelve

MELISSA LOOKED AT HER GRANDDAUGHTER. Schizandra was the kind of girl that everyone liked but no one knew. She could easily blend into others' expectations, becoming whatever they needed or wished to see. Her face had seemed as calm at her father's funeral as it did while lying in this coma.

Like a director of ceremonies, she had hugged professors distraught by their young colleague's demise and recited a flawless yet moving eulogy. Everyone knew how much she'd loved her father; they were notorious best friends. Schizandra just stepped so fully into her role that no one thought to question it. Every mourner accepted her nurturing with gratitude and love. She comforted everyone else so well that the guests literally forgot to care for a thirteen-year-old orphan. In retrospect, it was sad, but also strange.

Melissa stared at her pale, fairylike features and wild hair. She wondered how often that cute exterior belied what surged within. She had certainly misjudged her granddaughter on a few occasions. The midwife swallowed hard as she remembered Monday's fight:

"I will not pervert a perfectly beautiful name by calling you 'Shazzie.' And, no, your teachers will not call you 'Sandra.' 'Sandra' is not your name."

"But Gram—Melissa! *Everyone* calls me 'Shazzie'!"

"Maybe everyone in Chicago, but you don't live in Chicago anymore. You live in Sedona, and your name is Schizandra. That is what you will be called."

"But I hate my name!"

"Then you will learn to love it."

"No, I won't! I hate my name! And I, I hate you!" Schizandra slammed the door and grabbed her 10-speed off the porch.

It all seemed so silly now.

Mark interrupted her reverie by knocking at the doorway. "Vegan burrito for your thoughts?" He glanced at Schizandra. "Any change?"

"No," Melissa said. She continued her thoughts aloud now that she had someone to share them with. "I feel like I should understand her, but we haven't talked beyond logistics. She refused to discuss her dad's death, and I wanted to give her space to grieve."

"I'm sure you did the best you could," Mark said.

With the bag of food looped around his forearm, he pulled two plastic chairs closer to Melissa's seat. He sat down and smiled compassionately, handing her a wrap and a bottle of water from *Mayan Taco*.

"Thanks," she said.

He placed a carton of tortilla chips on one of the chairs between them so that they could share. "Welcome," he said, lining up four to-go containers of sauce. "And you're right. That place has quite the salsa bar."

They both started eating.

After awhile, Mark said, "A buddy of mine got shot down once. We found him, all blood and starry eyes. Dropped into a coma before we could get him back to base. When he woke up three days later, he said he'd gone fishin', caught more mackerel than an Alaskan—" He stopped himself and eyed her tofu burrito. "Sorry. Guess you're not much into fishin', huh?"

"No," she said, "but I appreciate what you're trying to say."

They talked about her diet. Melissa explained to him that she had gone vegetarian in the sixties with Roger and everyone else in San Francisco. Before he got drafted, they'd protested the war together, and it just seemed logical to minimize violence in every way they could. Pregnant by the time Roger left for Vietnam, Melissa had missed out on the heavy drug use and free love, but she began to realize just how much that era still affected her life.

When Mark humorously mentioned the way her lifestyle must have struck Schizandra, Melissa giggled, "Oh, my goodness! I really *am* an old hippie, aren't I? Compared to San Francisco, Sedona's conservative, but coming from her father's academic mindset … poor child! It must seem like another planet. I'll have to keep that in mind when she wakes up. Sometimes life just takes over and we lose touch with things outside our everyday world."

Melissa hadn't intended to become a walking stereotype. She explained how a battle with what turned out to be fibromyalgia had forced her to give up dairy and devote herself to yoga. She didn't care what other people ate or did for exercise. She just wanted to keep the pain at bay. As a midwife, she couldn't bring herself to eat eggs. Again, nothing personal—they just didn't appeal to her. Mark apologized for his joke, but she thanked him for the reality check.

By the time they finished talking, Melissa knew why Mark had joined the military—to help pay for his sister's college education—and why he'd stayed so long—because it gave him a chance to fly. He surprised the midwife with tales of Leonardo da Vinci's helicopter designs and some metaphysical thoughts on flying. She would not have pegged him for someone so interested in other cultures, but his world travels had shown him firsthand what she just read in books. She also liked that he honored Roger's ultimate sacrifice. Mark had seen casualties, and he shared his own perspective.

When Melissa mentioned the astrologer, he surprised her again. She would have expected an Army officer to scoff at that sort of thing, but Mark had apparently known someone "who did people's charts." Melissa suspected this "someone" was an ex-girlfriend. A twinge of disappointment surfaced but quickly receded as Mark told her the value he'd found in his own mini-reading. He raised some interesting points, and Melissa decided to call Tom Brown when she got home.

Schizandra tried to make sense of Frauke's revelation: *Mu.* She was actually in Mu. All those years of begging Daddy to tell her it was real, somewhere beyond imagination, and now here she was.

She tried to remember everything her father had shared about the Motherland. He said it was an ancient continent in the Pacific Ocean. During the Ice Age, much of the ocean had frozen into glaciers, so water levels stood much lower then. Parts of California, Hawaii and other Pacific islands had once formed hills and mountains of a huge landmass. Legend had it that all cultures had begun in Mu.

As Schizandra wandered through the tunnels now, the paths themselves began to feel familiar. Her body nudged her into déjà vu. She noticed drawings on the walls, like cave paintings she'd seen in history class, with one important change. Her hands remembered *drawing* these. As she and Frauke passed a spiral, Schizandra felt her fingers mixing colors and painting them in swirls. She followed her palm's urge to press itself against a handprint on the wall.

A perfect match. It sent shivers up her spine.

Her hands continued sharing. She flashed to a scene in Ancient Egypt. *Her right hand holding down papyrus; her left recording tales from distant lands.* Those Egyptian relics her dad found when he met her mother in Sedona: it seemed to Schizandra that not one but *two* great islands had sunken to oblivion—Mu in the Pacific and *Atlantis* on the other side. Daddy told her he'd made up these "myths," but now she wondered. Did the secrets of Ancient Egypt really come from Atlantis? And did Atlanteans come from Mu?

The memories in her hands traveled up her arms into her heart, expanding through the tunnel as she walked. The fireflies' flickers became candles: many flames, then one. Her eyes remembered staring at that flame until her heart absorbed its light, bouncing and dancing with the fire. It warmed her from the inside out. *She was male this time, high in the mountains of Tibet, one of many monks staring at the flame. Becoming the flame.*

The flame intensified.

Schizandra's mind felt bigger—and she tried to rein it in. Her body was solid, but she stretched through time, and her eyes saw things she knew she could not see.

Chapter Thirteen

MELISSA UNROLLED HER YOGA MAT, stood up, and closed her eyes. She took a deep breath and noticed the slight agitation in her chest. Nothing serious: just a feeling. She stepped onto her mat and stood in Mountain Pose, feet shoulder width apart reaching deep into the ground. She imagined herself connected yet rising tall from the earth, a rock of strength supporting the life around her. Inhaling, she raised her arms to the sides and above her head. On the exhale, she pressed her palms together, pulling them down to Prayer Pose in front of her heart.

The phone rang. *Oh, let the machine get it.*

"Melissa, it's Mark. Are you there?"

The aspiring yogini paused.

"I'm about to head back on I-17. Just wanted to let you know that I meant what I said at dinner. If you need anything. *Anything.* You let me know, ok? I enjoyed your company today."

The machine's light flashed its message, and Melissa returned to Mountain Pose. She continued her round of Sun Salutations and had just stepped into Warrior One when the phone rang again. She smiled and felt her chest warm. As she folded back into Downward Facing Dog, the machine clicked on.

This time, a woman's voice came through, "Melissa, darling? Pick up if you're there."

In the background: "We know you're there."

"Oh for Heaven's sake, Rosemary, just spew it out! Here's the phone, you can tell her yourself!"

"Melissa, dear, Lobelia and I are here. In Sedona. Please pick—"

Melissa grabbed the phone. "Rosemary?"

"She's on the phone!" yelled Rosemary to her twin.

"Melissa, dear!" Lobelia's voice boomed past Rosemary and into the receiver. "Why don't you come pick us up? We've had a terrible journey. Just terrible. Three people on the plane vomited and that shuttle up here was most terribly curvy. I almost vomited myself. ... Give me that phone, Rosemary!"

"Melissa, what Lobelia's trying to tell you," Rosemary said, "is that we've come. We're in Sedona."

"I don't understand," Melissa said. "What do you mean, you're in Sedona?"

"Just what she says," Lobelia shouted. A bit of a struggle ensued, which Lobelia evidently won. She replied directly into the phone, "We booked a last minute flight from Madison to Phoenix and then took the shuttle from the airport. We're waiting for you at Motel 8."

Melissa started to protest, "Lo— Ro—! This just really isn't a good time for me. If you would have called first, I'm sorry, I just, I can't, I'm—"

"Well, spit it out," Lobelia said. "Are you telling your two seventy-year-old sisters who've journeyed halfway across the country to see you, that we can't stop in to help?"

"Help?" Melissa asked.

"Remember that story our mother, oh, Rosemary, you always tell this one better," said Lobelia, handing the phone to her sister.

Rosemary said, "It was actually Great Grandmother Althea, dear sisters, who intuitively knew when healing was required, but we all have that sense to some degree. Melissa, we don't know what's going on with you, but you need us, and so we're here. Now, would you please pick us up at Motel 8? We're freezing! Whoever thought some place in Arizona would feel colder than Madison!"

"You're at Motel 8?" Melissa asked, "In West Sedona?"

"Yes, our little lemon balm," Lobelia yelled in the background, "and did she mention we're freezing?"

"I'll be there in fifteen minutes," Melissa said. "Why don't you wait inside?"

<hr />

Melissa threw on an embroidered poncho and faux suede boots then jumped into her Jaguar. Except for birth events, she hardly ever drove at night. Sedona's light ordinance kept the streets unusually dark so that folks in Flagstaff's Observatory could better see the stars. Odd that one town would decrease safety for the sake of another's views, but, there you had it! The heavens looked spectacular. Tonight's large moon helped a little with the roads.

She turned right and made her way to Motel 8. The Sedona-Phoenix shuttle ran bihourly from the airport, allowing non-drivers like Rosemary and Lobelia an easy route to Red Rock Country. As she pulled into the parking lot, two white haired ladies hurried from the lobby, each pulling a miniature purple suitcase.

"Melissa, dear!" launched Lobelia, a short woman stuffed into a royal blue coat almost as wide as she was tall. Size five feet in bright red heels seemed too petite to carry so much weight, yet she moved lightly, bouncing like a flower in a windy field, her fat rolls wriggling and shaking as she pulled her suitcase to the car.

"Not this old thing! Rosemary, can you believe she drives a car like this? Oh, Melissa, whatever will we do with you?" Lobelia's face peeked through a halo of pin curls, as her alto voice echoed through the parking lot, charging it with a sense of expectation.

With perfect posture and nearly six feet tall, Rosemary stood before Melissa. The rail thin spinster shook her head. "Melissa," she said, warmly, "how *wise* you look! The desert has certainly aged that skin around your eyes. I'll remember to let you borrow our Black Velvet crème." She turned to Lobelia. "Look at our little sister all grown up. You'd never know she's sixteen years our junior!"

Melissa groaned. This was why she never phoned them. "Do you need help with your suitcases?" she asked the unlikely twins. She hoped small luggage foretold a speedy visit.

"Why yes, dear," bellowed Lobelia, "you'd never guess how much these little satchels hold! We ordered them online at the Magical Emporium. I've stuffed three week's worth of clothes into my bag. It's like a vegetarian buffet at China Star! Where *do* I manage to fit it all?" she asked.

Dressed in a leopard print trench coat and red hat, Rosemary put away her own suitcase. "Now Melissa, remember, we're here to help. You just tell us what you need."

Melissa sighed. "I was going to call you."

"We know, dear," said Lobelia, starting a coughing fit as she entered the backseat of the Jag. "Oh, my *lungs*! This desert air will never do. What is that smell? *Sage*? My heavens!"

"How you live in the desert simply boggles the mind," Rosemary said, climbing in the front seat. "I can feel my skin cracking as we speak. That poor child moving all the way from Chicago to Sedona! Lobelia and I would have welcomed her in Madison, poor dear. How is she?"

Melissa cringed as she buckled her seatbelt and started up the car. "Schizandra's having some struggles right now," she said quietly.

"Spill it, sister!" shouted Lobelia. "Feed us all the details. We will gorge ourselves on details until the truth expels itself. Then we'll clean up all the mess."

"Lobelia," Rosemary snapped, "must everything be gorged and spewed? Can't we just have a simple conversation? I recall when we were—"

"Enough!" said Melissa, soft, yet firm. "Schizandra's in a coma, and she has eighteen hours to awaken. If you came here to help, then help. We can visit her tomorrow." She needed to make sure she didn't miss her turn. Even with a near full moon, these streets were dark. In a moment, she turned left on Juniper Drive.

She pulled into the driveway, exited the Jag and popped the trunk. Despite Melissa's irritation, the twins' arrival brought relief. The two women had thrown a lifetime of passion into their work as reflexologists. They could do things with feet that few people believed possible. Working in tandem—each on a single foot—Rosemary and Lobelia had enticed more than one soul back from the brink of death. Melissa was counting on their expertise.

Schizandra wasn't sure she liked these feelings. How could a thirteen-year-old girl know details of a secret meditation in Tibet or alchemy techniques from Ancient Egypt? She didn't remember learning about anyone named Hermes Trismegistus in school. Why did she suddenly know he wrote *The Emerald Tablet*?

She pinched herself to see if she had fallen back asleep. *Ow!* She was definitely awake. Frauke seemed preoccupied with her cacao addiction, so she hadn't picked up on Schizandra's "memories." The girl didn't know what else to call them. Scenes revealed themselves not just visually, but in her body. Sometimes she felt like an old man with a long beard. Other times her belly seemed large with child. One impression kept returning:

She was female and middle aged, although she sensed lifespans were much longer in Atlantis. She wore a long teal gown with some sort of band around her forehead. A crystal hung down between her eyebrows. She was working inside a Temple Beautiful perched on top of a hill overlooking the sea. A warm breeze blew through alabaster pillars and the air smelled fresh. She felt happy and alive.

She held a clear crystal in her right hand and pointed it at various points on the head and body of a woman lying before her. The woman had come to her for help, wanting to purify her mind and spirit. Schizandra sang to her in strange, melodic tones, and the woman's face began to change. It looked younger and more relaxed. When she opened her eyes, the woman glowed. She hugged Schizandra and they shared a sacred moment, high above the sea.

Chapter Fourteen

YOU CAN SHARE THE GUEST room," said Melissa. "The daybed has a trundle." She set a pile of lavender-scented towels on an antique white dresser. "Bathroom's down the hall, and yes, Rosemary, I have a full filtration system in the house. The water here is normally quite hard."

"Aren't you going to show us the rest of your home?" Lobelia coughed.

"Yes, do," said Rosemary, "so far it reminds me a bit of Great Grandmother Althea's. There's a presence here."

"That's Schizandra," said Melissa. "She leaves a residue."

"Anything we need to purge?" Lobelia asked.

"No," Melissa said, smiling, "I've grown used to it. I think they like her at the Medical Center, too—even though they don't know what to do with her."

Rosemary jumped in. "Melissa, dear, do you mean you haven't placed that child in a *hospital*? Whyever not?"

"We don't have one here in town, and they've had trouble moving her from Sedona."

The twins shook their heads and pursed their lips. "Wild West, indeed!" "That would never have happened in Madison!" As they neared Melissa's room, Schizandra's grandmother suddenly felt an uncontrollable urge to sob. Grief mixed with hope seeped through her lungs, eyes, nose, and throat, and left her keening at the threshold.

"That's right," Lobelia said, "let it out."

"I don't understand!" Melissa sobbed. "This is so unlike me. Rosemary!" she cried, "you *know* I'm usually so calm!"

The thin twin turned on the light. "What's on your window?"

All three sisters stared. With red rock dust on the inside of Melissa's window, someone had painted a square, cross-like symbol about five inches wide, with a circular hole in the middle—right in the center of her window.

"That wasn't here when I left," whispered Melissa, scanning the room.

"Holy Mary, Mother of God," mouthed Rosemary, uttering a prayer she'd picked up during their Catholic experiment.

Lobelia grabbed a smudge stick from the dresser and began swatting the air. "Out!" she said, "Out of here! Intruders! I will eliminate anything unclean from this house! Get out while you can!"

Rosemary stayed her sister's arm. "Quiet, Lobelia," she said, "we've seen this before."

"You have?" asked an incredulous Melissa.

Lobelia looked just as surprised as her younger sibling.

"Think," said Rosemary, "Machu Picchu, August 1987."

Lobelia's eyes looked empty.

"Oh, come now, Lobelia! Have you really forgotten?"

Her twin still looked blank. "As you well know," Lobelia said, "I can barely remember what I ate for breakfast. You know with me it's in one moment, out the next. Stop playing games, Rosemary. Tell us what you mean."

"It's the Chakana!" said the reedy spinster. "Don't you remember? I know I do, clear as day."

"And that's why you're the family historian," Melissa said, "but seriously, what are you talking about? I'm afraid I see no connection."

Mark wound his way down I-17 South. He watched the moon play hide and seek in his rearview mirror. Full with a white halo, it looked huge tonight. It disappeared behind curvaceous mounds, teasing as he moved. This whole area lay under water at one time, as evidenced by the rolling hills and rounded rocks. Under moonlight, the harsh desert became soft and fluid again, undulating as Mark drove home.

He pondered the strange woman from earlier that day. Melissa. Something about her felt familiar. Quite a coincidence their meeting at

Bhakti's. He tried not to think about crying at his massage. Bhakti seemed cool with it, but that was definitely not his usual M.O. Memories of the cave floated to the surface. He nudged them away. Instead, he wondered about the girl. Schizandra, the healing berry. Why had she contacted him, and more importantly, did she need his help?

Joni Mitchell's *All I Want* drifted across the radio waves.

For an older woman, Melissa had quite a bit of spunk. Mark chuckled as he remembered how she'd put Dr. Swinburne in his place. He wouldn't want to be on the receiving end of *that* whisper and stare. *Those eyes! Gray at first, then glinting almost purple as she stared. Periwinkle, violet. Reminds me of forget-me-nots. Reminds, forgets. Forget-me-not.*

He passed Black Canyon City on his left. Not much of a city, really. More like a one-stop town with good hamburgers. He'd be to Carefree soon and then home to Phoenix.

"You really think that drawing's of extraterrestrial origin?" Melissa asked.

Rosemary smiled. "We listen to Art Bell on *Coast to Coast*, right, Lobelia?"

The other twin had folded her generous arms under her face and slumped snoring on the table.

"Sometimes I wonder if I'm the black sheep or the only sane one of our family," Melissa said. "You're serious, though, aren't you?"

"Never more so," said Rosemary, nodding. "*Someone* has left you a message, and if memory serves me, a rather good one."

"You know what it means?"

Rosemary nodded again. "The Chakana, also called the Andean Cross, was sacred to the Ancient Incas. That hole in the center stands for Cusco, Peru, the naval of the Incan Empire. The three steps on each arm of the cross each represent a different tier of Incan Life, known as the three worlds: *Hanan Pacha*, the world above—including gods of the sun, moon and stars—*Kay Pacha*, this world—representing this life—and *Uqhu Pacha*, the world below (representing death). Each of these worlds has an animal totem: the condor, the puma and the snake, respectively. In Machu Picchu, the temple of the condor uses the Chakana in its very architecture! Remember all those steps in photos of that area?"

"But what's the Chakana doing on my window?"

"That's why I mentioned extra-terrestrial origin," Rosemary said. "No signs of forced entry to your home. You can't remember giving a key to anyone but Schizandra. A perfectly symmetrical image in something that looks like red ochre. How else do you explain it?"

"I don't *have* an explanation," said Melissa, "but why ET's?"

"Oh, ET's, spirits, what's the difference, for heaven's sake?"

"Please, Rosemary, I'd really like to hear whatever you can tell me."

The spinster smiled. "Alright, if you insist. It's *nice* to have someone listen for a change!" She eyed her snoring twin. "The Chakana evokes the Southern Cross constellation. The four points denote compass directions, and a total of twelve steps mark off the twelve months of the year. That constellation was holy to the Inca. In fact, you can divide the Chakana into overlapping square sections, with the major Incan deities, cosmological objects and male and female positioned within."

Rosemary's eyes twinkled as she recited learning from younger years. "Personally, the Chakana has always reminded me of that ancient conundrum of 'squaring the circle.' They wanted to create a square with the exact same area as the circle."

"Is that so hard?"

"Impossible!" Rosemary said, shaking her index finger for emphasis. "Mathematicians can approximate the area but never find an exact match. It's got something to do with the number *pi* being a 'transcendental number.'"

"Are you talking sacred geometry?"

"Oh, yes," Rosemary said, "in all its implications."

"Such as?"

"Well, for starters, Carl Jung became obsessed with the idea. For him, squaring the circle symbolized the paradox of male and female coming together as one. It defies logic that we can and defies logic that we can't. All the while, though, we keep on trying."

Melissa smiled.

Rosemary winked and grinned wide enough to reveal dimples in her gaunt cheeks. "If I didn't know better, I'd say you met someone today and some other beings helped to orchestrate that meeting. Oh, my stars!" said Rosemary, yawning. "Listen to me! I forgot about the time difference. Good night, Melissa." She nudged her twin. "Wake up, Lobelia! It's time to sleep."

After they left, Melissa stared at the oak table with its purple placemats. *Lots to talk about.* She turned off the kitchen light and walked into her bedroom. Her white duvet cover and shag throw rug seemed to glow above the hardwood floor. She had left the blinds open and could clearly see the mark filtering moonlight on her bed.

Chapter Fifteen

SCHIZANDRA YAWNED AS SHE FOLLOWED Frauke. Forcing her legs to march onward, she thought, "It feels like we've been walking for hours—*millennia*. Wasn't she in a hurry to see the king?"

"I heard that," Frauke said. "Truth is, we could have arrived much faster, but I need to strategize."

Schizandra gathered this wasn't the entire truth. She sensed the queen had "issues." Possibly big ones. "Can I help?" The prisoner yawned again. "I'm *tired*." She wanted another focus than her avalanche of visions.

Frauke giggled. "You're not supposed to be able to whine telepathically! Besides, you only think you're tired." She shook her head, obviously tickled. "In Mu, we only sleep to dream. You remember feeling tired and so you think it so."

"Huh?" Schizandra closed her left eye, considering her captor's words.

"It won't make sense with *that* eye closed," Frauke said. "Close the other one. Then you'll see."

Curious, Schizandra followed the queen's instructions. She noticed the swirling effect of fireflies lighting the tunnel and to her left, a slab of royal blue stone.

"That's Azurite," said the queen. "Go ahead and touch her—with both hands."

While the girl held the stone, she closed her eyes and felt a pulsing in her forehead. The striking color seemed to permeate her brain, turning her mind to indigo. As Schizandra breathed, her thoughts cleared and she knew what Frauke meant.

She also knew that the queen felt unworthy of the king's attention. That he saw Frauke more clearly than she saw herself and that he insisted the queen live up to her full potential. For these reasons and more, Frauke tried to avoid the king whenever possible.

Schizandra's limbs suddenly stiffened. She panicked, recalling her earlier paralysis. Concentrating on the blue stone calmed her enough to remember Haru's words from her dream: "You have to use your mind! If you can talk with it, you can do other things, as well." She focused on his words swirling in the blue, and gradually relaxed. She could move again.

Cool!

"I thought you'd think so," said the queen. Smiling, she removed a cacao pod and her little knife. This time, Schizandra wanted some.

"Just a little," Frauke said, "it's potent."

Schizandra put a slice of cacao on her tongue and slowly chewed. It tasted like chocolate! As the creamy fruit slid down her throat, her vision changed. Nothing tangible, but the world looked different, realigned.

Suddenly, she had a strange realization. It felt like she just knew, without even trying to think about it:

After twenty-six thousand years underground, Frauke's kingdom has fallen into obscurity, nearly forgotten by those who walk the Earth.

This queen has an important role to play, but she's forgotten her lines through centuries of silliness. The Ancients and king have tried to cue her, but the queen has waited backstage for far too long. Amusements meant to pass the time, long ago became her script.

Schizandra snapped back to herself. *That* was weird! Almost as weird as those ancient memories. She needed to focus on something else. "Would you like help with your strategy?" she asked.

Frauke swallowed another bite of cacao. When she came back to Earth, she looked at the girl with love. Schizandra smiled back.

"Your strategy?"

"Strategy?" the queen asked, riding bliss. "Oh, right! Yes, now that you mention it, darling, I suppose it could use a little tweaking."

Schizandra looked at Frauke then closed her eyes so she could concentrate. She projected energy from her heart and began sensing the queen as a blind person might run hands over a stranger's face. She had never done *this* before either! Schizandra felt her heart extend through her arms into energetic fingertips that could feel and gather information beyond her eyes. Their sensitivity surprised her. She found that she could reach inside the queen's body, touch a point and feel a corresponding flicker of pain or elation in her own body.

Frauke's throat felt like a song. The belly and feet—light. The eyes— slightly constricted around the temples. Schizandra's energy touched

Frauke's heart. She sensed sadness there, coupled with deep longing. A spark of joy, followed by shame. Frauke's heart reached back towards Schizandra and carefully checked for weapons or manipulation. Finding neither, the queen's heart lingered, quietly enjoying the connection.

"What kind of strategy would you love to have?" Schizandra asked, opening her eyes.

Frauke blushed, tucking her energy back inside itself. "Oh, never mind!" she said. "We need to get going."

"They love you very much," said the girl.

"Who?"

Schizandra closed her eyes and focused on that special spot behind her forehead. "Mikhail and ... I'm not sure what to call him. It looks like he's holding an antique brass bowl and a wooden stick."

"Pschhh!" Frauke said, but her heart perked up. "That's the king."

"And your little yellow friend—"

"Sephora!" The queen's heart fluttered with excitement. "How is my dearest?"

Schizandra tuned in to the hummingbird, which seemed quite lively for one who weighed so heavily on Frauke's heart. "She's fine."

"Really?"

"Oh, yes," Schizandra said, "very joyful with her rabbit friend."

Frauke wrinkled her brow for a moment and then smiled. Schizandra noticed that the queen's chest felt lighter "despite this confusing news of Nestor." As the queen understood it, healers did *not* have friends. Frauke assumed the girl had made a mistake.

Schizandra noticed these thoughts and more. She felt sorry for the queen. Frauke was very beautiful and very gifted, but she had lots to learn about life and love. All the crystals and chocolate in the world couldn't change *that* fact.

"Up and out!" Lobelia sang, peeking around the door frame.

Melissa stirred. She was dreaming:

A snowy owl spread its wings above the raven. Darkness and light. Flying now, reclaiming territory. They grabbed claws, fighting and spinning through the air like a giant yin and yang. Turning and turning. Navajo eyes staring into hers, hands upon her shoulders, the child is cursed, things fall apart, the center—

Melissa jolted herself awake.

"Good Morning!" Lobelia projected her voice from the diaphragm like an opera singer.

Melissa stared at her—gradually recollecting yesterday's events. She looked at the window. The mark remained—silhouetted by the desert sun.

"Up and out! We've got a busy day. According to my calculations we have less than eight hours to rouse Schizandra."

Melissa shuffled into the kitchen. This was definitely a Yerba Maté morning. Rosemary had already brewed the tea and handed her a cup. Melissa stirred in some soymilk and joined her sisters at the table. The twins were halfway through the *Red Rock News*.

"There's a nice photo of Monday's lunar eclipse," Rosemary said.

"Hmmfph!" said Lobelia. "The Arabs rejected Clinton's Mideast Peace Plan this week." She coughed then continued, "Ariel Sharon says 'The Oslo agreements became null and void the moment the current Palestinian violence started.' He also says the 'Oslo agreements no longer exist, period.'" She shook her head. "Our boys are still in Kosovo, but you'd never know it here."

"I know," said Melissa, "that whole region's so volatile. One of my clients gave birth two days ago, and her husband's in Kosovo."

Lobelia clucked and folded the paper.

"Military, just like Ginger's father, hmmm," Rosemary said.

"He had a name!" Melissa slammed down her mug. "You two have never supported that marriage or my family. Roger was drafted, not a hawk. He died serving as well as our government would let him. Do you have any idea how difficult it was to raise a child alone?" She caught herself.

Of course they didn't. Rosemary and Lobelia had longed for children but never found a man who measured up to the other's standards. Childless and single, they had devoted themselves completely to the art and science of reflexology. Melissa wondered when they'd stopped hoping for a child. Perhaps they hadn't stopped. Maybe they had hoped Schizandra would fill that void.

Despite the challenges left by Roger's death, raising Ginger had been the most amazing experience of Melissa's life. Each month, the midwife ushered new souls into this world, but no one could ever replace her own flesh and blood. It was Ginger, after all, who had inspired her to begin such a career. After birthing her own baby, Melissa had immediately thought, "I want to help other women do this! It's so real, so relevant, so *exciting*! There's nothing like it in the world." Her sisters would never know that joy.

"We need to focus on Schizandra," said Melissa.

"Alright, cough up the details, sister."

"Lobelia, honestly, must we begin informational bulimia so soon?" Rosemary asked.

"The girl's in a coma," replied her twin. "Do we or do we not need information to bring her out?"

Melissa interjected, "I'm afraid there's not too much to share. From what I've gathered, Schizandra lost consciousness Tuesday morning in biology class while they were dissecting a frog."

"So she passed out," Lobelia said.

"That's initially what they thought, but she hasn't awakened since. So far, every test has come back normal."

"So why isn't she awake and why isn't she in a proper hospital?" Rosemary asked.

"Well," Melissa took a deep breath, "apparently, the tests are the only normal part. Her symptoms seemed unusual, so they tried to MedEvac her to Flagstaff that morning. I say tried because two helicopters suffered rare malfunctions with her on board."

"What kind of rare malfunctions?"

"It's complicated. Mark explained them to me, but for sake of simplicity, let's just say that two helicopters and an ambulance experienced statistically improbable events that kept her from leaving Sedona."

"Who's Mark, and what do you mean 'kept her from leaving Sedona'?" Rosemary asked.

"Spill it, sister." Lobelia snapped her fingers.

Rosemary rolled her eyes then stared at Melissa.

"Mark's the pilot from the first helicopter."

"And you know him how?" Rosemary's dimples threatened to show themselves.

"We met yesterday," said Melissa. She hated when the twins focused their attention on her. That laser precision so useful in locating reflexology points bore into her soul, delving for secret connections and hidden triggers.

"Interesting!" Rosemary said. "Was this, by chance, a highly synchronous and unexpected meeting?"

"As a matter of fact, it was," said Melissa, quickly changing the subject. "As for Schizandra leaving town, well, it doesn't seem likely. After the helicopters crashed, the ambulance got a flat tire when it tried to leave Oak Creek Canyon. At Mark's suggestion, they finally sent her back to Sedona in another ambulance, which traveled fine in that direction."

"Is that everything? Why do I feel like something still wants to come out?" asked Lobelia, probing.

Melissa gulped the last of her Yerba Maté. "I delivered a baby boy and then saw a Navajo on Tuesday. The Navajo said, 'The child is cursed.'"

"Anything else?" said Lobelia.

"I asked if it was the boy I'd just delivered and he shook his head no. Then he said, 'Sins of the father,' and disappeared without a trace."

"Without a trace?" Rosemary's dimples disappeared.

Melissa felt stupid, but they wanted all the information. "A raven flew by my head, kind of aggressively and fast, and, well, it occurred to me, oh, it's silly, but it occurred to me that it might have been the Navajo."

"Ohhh-kay" Rosemary said, "anything else?"

"Oh, and someone gave me this card yesterday." She reached to grab her purse off the counter and handed the twins Tom's card.

"*New Cycle Astrology?*"

"He comes highly recommended. An intuitive woman suggested I have him read Schizandra's chart. She claimed to have 'gotten a hit on' my granddaughter." Melissa expected some eye rolling. For as much as the twins entertained conspiracy theories, they tended not to support what they considered pseudo-sciences. Melissa had never quite understood the evaluation process, but she suspected astrology fell into the hogwash pile.

Lobelia surprised her by saying, "You should go. Call him today while we're working on Schizandra. She's only got two feet, and I assume she's not pregnant."

"Oh, goodness, no!" Melissa said, "Why, I don't even think she's had her first menses yet!"

"As I suspected. Why don't you go see what this Tom fellow can tell you? You may be able to help her more by doing research than spending your day with us. Rosemary's not far off in her interpretation of that window message."

"I thought you were asleep," Melissa said.

Lobelia winked at Rosemary, "Little honey bee's got a bit to learn, doesn't she, sis?"

"Oh my stars, don't we all!" replied her twin. "See what Tom has to say. You don't need to tell him much. Just give him her birth date, place and time and let him do the rest. If it sounds like Schizandra, we'll accept his input. If not, nothing lost. You can meet us at the Medical Center when you're done. Do we need to make special arrangements for a visit there?"

Melissa nodded. "I'll call you a cab and let Dr. Swinburne know you're coming. Then I'll head Uptown as fast as I can. I called Tom last night. He's got an opening in forty-five minutes."

Chapter Sixteen

A TAN AND GREEN '87 IMPALA station wagon lumbered its way onto the gravel driveway of 3216 Juniper Drive. Lobelia waved her arm as though hailing a cab in downtown Madison. Even through her thick blue coat, her arm continued to bobble as she and Rosemary hurried to the car.

"Good-bye, Melissa! Remember to request a tape of the reading. Lobelia and I will want to hear all the details."

With her arms snuggled under a lilac chenille poncho, Melissa cut a striking figure on the porch. Her tan, moon shaped face looked almost Native this morning, except for violet eyes that stared serenely at her sisters. She waved and called through crisp morning air, "You have my cell if you need anything. I'll get there as soon as I can after Tom—cassette in hand."

"Have him feed you as much information as possible," bellowed Lobelia, as she closed the creaky door. "You can always toss up what doesn't resonate."

The cab driver watched Rosemary shake her head in the rearview mirror.

"Where to, ladies?"

"Sedona Regional Medical, and young man, please remember to turn on that meter!" Rosemary noticed that he hadn't done so.

"Yes, ma'am," said their dreadlocked and patchouli-scented driver. "Live here?"

"No," Lobelia said, slipping into work mode, "we're here to initiate a healing."

"Been to the vortexes yet?"

"No," said Rosemary, "we just arrived last night, and we've got our hands full today."

"Well, if you get a chance, you should really try the Airport Vortex.

Some people think it's overrated because all the tourists know about it, but it's still the best one, in my opinion. Of course, I'm a Gemini, so I like the uplift ones. We Gemini's like our air, you know!" He laughed and then looked serious, making eye contact through the rearview mirror. "Don't try Boynton Canyon if you're depressed. That one's sure to bring you down to the depths of your soul."

"Young man," said Lobelia, "you locals attribute far too much influence to those vortices."

"*Vortexes*," he corrected her. "I've lived in Sedona for sixteen years. The iron in the red rocks aligns with the iron in a person's blood. It took me awhile to get used to the energy here, too." He chuckled. "It does affect people differently. Maybe that's what you mean. Some people feel juiced—like a total head buzz. I've heard newcomers giggle the entire cab ride without knowing why. Others develop a ragin' headache! We get four million tourists per year and lots of transients." He paused. "But it takes a special soul to stay."

"So our sister claims," Rosemary said, as they passed Kokopelli Suites. "She's lived here since 1970."

"Who's your sister?" the driver asked. "Thirty-one years is a long time, and we've only got about ten thousand fulltime residents. I bet I know her."

The twins looked at each other and shrugged. He seemed safe enough.

"Melissa Vreeland," said Rosemary.

The cab driver tilted his head to the right, either deep in thought or in search of channeled information as he traveled west. "Where does she read?"

Lobelia snorted.

"She's a midwife," Rosemary said.

He paused again. Just as Lobelia coughed and nudged her twin, he said, "Oh, that's right! She delivered my niece and nephew. Awesome lady! I knew I knew the name. She calmed my sister-in-law down, and if you knew my sister-in-law, you'd know what an amazing feat that was! Melissa Vreeland is like, the hero, in my brother's household. They moved back to Tucson shortly after my niece was born six years ago, but they still talk about their midwife. Tell her the brother of Ron Melampus says hello. We met just briefly right after the birth. So, that was her on the porch? I *knew* she looked familiar. Killer eyes."

"We'll remember you to her," said Rosemary.

"I'm Carter, by the way. Awesome encounter, ladies! We're all one, you know?" He turned into the Medical Center and asked, "Front entrance ok?"

"Yes," said Lobelia. She looked at the fare and gave him a ten. "Keep the change."

Carter turned around, brought his hands to Namaste and bowed his head: "Blessings."

"To you as well," said Rosemary, softening as she closed the door.

The white haired twins turned to face the Urgent Care entrance. "Let's do this!" shouted Lobelia, throwing up her arms as they crossed the threshold.

Melissa turned east towards Uptown. Sedona didn't have a downtown, but the restaurants and shops in Uptown certainly drew the tourists. Quintessential Sedona: a mixture of Wild West, Mexico, Navajo Nation, old money, and the Age of Aquarius. Melissa rarely ventured there anymore—not since West Sedona had started offering more shops and services. With the increased traffic from visitors viewing the backdrop of so many Westerns, it just seemed easier to stay put.

An unexpected wave of nostalgia crested as she crossed the Y and entered Uptown. Melissa remembered how perfect Sedona had felt right from the start. Sunrise: watching the looming red rocks turn violet, yellow and then finally red again—feeling so safe in that grand display of beauty. After Roger had died in '68, she had stayed in San Francisco for two more years. His parents gifted Melissa the expensive car they bought for Roger. A misplaced token of faith that he'd return alive. Imported from England, the 1967 Jaguar Mk 2 was the first of its kind to offer non-leather seats, which had especially appealed to the peace-loving couple.

She angled the Jag into a spot. Before getting out, she removed a tissue and blotted her lips, leaving two berry colored lines around the fold. Pushing the tissue back inside her purse, she left the Jag and locked the door, ready to enter *New Cycle Astrology*.

"I assure you, young lady," Lobelia proclaimed, "we know what we are doing. Now, up, out!" She made a shooing motion with her hands. "We require full concentration here. If you're not going to nourish this process, then kindly expel yourself from the room."

Amelia said, "This is highly unconventional. Does Dr. Swinburne even know you're here?"

"Melissa Vreeland phoned him this morning, and he authorized our visit," said Rosemary. "Why don't you check your records?"

"I know he authorized a visit," the nurse said, "but you're asking for more than a visit! Just what do you plan to do with this patient?"

"This patient," boomed Lobelia, as the heart monitor pulsed behind her, "happens to be our grandniece Schizandra. My esteemed sister, Rosemary," she nodded at her willowy twin, "and I have practiced the ancient art and science of reflexology for nearly fifty years. I dare say you could absorb a thing or two by watching us, but take your pick. If you cannot assimilate this process then do remove yourself. We have enough on our plate without your poor combination of doubt and distraction."

Rosemary added, "Try to recall the first part of the Hippocratic Oath to 'do no harm.' Reflexology works *with* traditional medicine. We're not trying to supplant it. We simply stimulate the body's own recollection of health. There are thousands of nerves and major meridians in the feet. If we touch her soul by jogging physical memories, so much the better. Cells remember trauma, and in her case, time is of the essence."

"Well," said Amelia, skeptical but curious, "as long as things stay gentle and non-invasive." Then she added, "I'd love to watch."

Lobelia coughed. "*Well!* Now we can all breathe easy."

Rosemary carefully removed the hospital booties from Schizandra's feet.

"Left?" said Lobelia, holding the girl's foot in both hands.

"That feels right this time," Rosemary said. "Perhaps we'll switch, but let's get started." The twins began by warming each of their grandniece's feet. "Her circulation feels ok now," said Rosemary.

With that, fingers and thumbs began their search for knots—any hard nodules in the soles to indicate blocked Chi. The sisters massaged each big toe. The stems corresponded to Schizandra's neck; the fleshy part connected to her pituitary and pineal glands; the tips linked to her whole brain.

Schizandra stumbled and caught herself, throwing her hand into a swarm of fireflies dancing by the calcite wall. They scattered themselves in a dizzying array of flashing lights around her head.

"What's wrong?" asked Frauke.

"Ohhhh," Schizandra said, "I feel strange. So tired. I don't think I can walk anymore."

"Nonsense," giggled the queen, "you only think you're tired! Remember, you're in Mu now. We only sleep to—"

"No," thought the visitor, "this is different. It's like my body's got a mind of its own. My toes tingle, and the top of my head feels prickly, and suddenly—" Schizandra paused.

"Suddenly what?"

"I really want my mom!"

"Your mother?" said the queen. "Well, where is she?"

"I don't know," she cried. "She died giving birth to me. I never knew her." The girl's chest heaved with a grief she had never even noticed before.

"You're talking out loud," said the queen, eyes wide.

Schizandra stopped crying for a moment then returned to the gaping hole at the center of her heart. She keened. Her wails crescendoed through the tunnel.

"What can I do?" asked Frauke, wringing her hands and trying not to reach for her cacao.

"I want to go home," the girl sobbed. "Please, I want you to take me home."

Frauke touched her shoulder then lifted Schizandra's face to look at her own. She gazed into the visitor's teary and pleading eyes. Schizandra's heart responded with a jolt of hope. This queen ruled a magical land. Surely, she could find a way to take her home! But Frauke shook her head. "I'm sorry, darling. I wish I could, but I just can't do that. We need to see the king."

The queen lifted the prisoner's arm around her neck and half dragged Schizandra forward. Each sob wracked Frauke's body as the girl buried her face in the queen's velvet robe. Fireflies returned to their spots along the tunnel walls, highlighting the sad procession.

Schizandra's weeping gradually subsided, but her body hiccupped from exertion. She looked ahead and planted her feet firmly on the ground, her right arm still supported by Frauke's neck. "I don't even know what 'home' means anymore."

Frauke stroked the girl's chocolate curls and cupped her cheek. "You'll find it, sweetness. Someday, we all will."

Chapter Seventeen

MELISSA OPENED THE DOOR TO *New Cycle Astrology*. A thin, bearded man, somewhere in his sixties, greeted her. Despite white hair and a balding pate, Tom exuded enthusiasm and youth, reminding her a bit of Maia. His presence made Melissa smile and for the first time, she actually began to anticipate the reading. *What if he could share valuable information? It was certainly worth a shot.*

"Thanks for squeezing me in on such short notice."

Tom smiled. "It was quite the synchronicity. I never answer calls after hours, but for some reason I left my cell phone on last night. You caught me at the perfect time."

"Well, I appreciate it," she said.

Tom opened the door to his private office. Several silver-framed computer printouts of astrological charts hung on the wall. A marble bust of Pythagoras and a framed concert poster for Pink Floyd's *Dark Side of the Moon* completed the decorations. He motioned to an indigo velvet armchair. "Please, make yourself comfortable. Would you care for any water? Or tea, perhaps? You look like a tea drinker."

"Anything herbal would be lovely," she said. Still draped in her lilac poncho, Melissa snuggled into the chair.

Tom returned with two cups of vanilla Rooibos. He seated himself in a carved wooden chair across from Melissa. The astrologer tapped his deck of cards and displayed a piece of graph paper with numbers penciled in careful formations—triangles, rectangles, squares—connected by lines that looked like a flow chart or numeric family tree. He clicked on a tape recorder.

"Let's make sure we've got this right," he said. "Schizandra Ginger Parker. S-C-H on the first name, right?"

Melissa nodded yes.

"November 1, 1987 at 9:09 p.m. in Chicago, Illinois." Tom's slight

Midwest accent warmed as Melissa nodded again. "We're going to start with the very purpose for which the soul came into this life. We find this by employing the Pythagorean process of triadic inversion." He pointed to the marble bust. "Are you familiar with Pythagoras?"

"A little," she said, "but I might need a quick refresher."

"When most of us hear the name Pythagoras, we think of the Pythagorean Theorem. You know, that equation we learned in high school geometry and hoped we'd never see again." His laugh surprised Melissa— breathy and rapid, but engaging nonetheless. "Well," he said, "Pythagoras was a spiritual man—very cool guy. He studied the heavens and also did some amazing things in the fields of astrology and numerology—what we call *sacred* geometry."

Melissa nodded, wanting to get on with her granddaughter's reading. She had told Tom as little as possible last night, trying not to influence his interpretation.

"Pythagoras was a vegetarian," Tom said. "The Goddess Demeter— Persephone's mom—prescribed him a fleshless diet rich in honey. For some reason, I thought that might interest you."

"I'm vegan," she said, "but, right now I'm just anxious to get started."

"Right!" Tom inhaled fast then exhaled deeply. "The Pythagorean process of triadic inversion. We're looking at things from the perspective of the soul. The soul's contemplating this mission before it even incarnates. At this point, it's a 'theoretical entity.' We're going to take the triadic inversion of the date of birth and the triadic inversion of the birth name."

He removed the top card from his deck and placed it face down in front of Melissa. "Now, when we do that with this soul, we get the same number both ways."

"Is that unusual?"

"Statistically significant, but I do see it happen sometimes with *evolved* souls. In Schizandra's case, both the birth name and the date of birth triadically invert to a sixteen."

He turned over the card. A scroll reading *16—The Tower—16* crossed the bottom of an ominous drawing: on a gloomy night, two lightning bolts struck a cone shaped, gray tower. From its heights, two people plunged to their deaths.

Melissa shuddered. "What's this triadic inversion process mean again?"

Tom explained how a soul contemplated its potential life before incarnating. According to Tom, life did not begin with birth, but well before. Souls looked at goals and decided which ones they would address in any given lifetime. Then they chose exactly the right time and place to enter third dimensional reality in order to meet those goals. Schizandra's soul wanted to emphasize things associated with the number sixteen.

Some of this sounded new to Melissa. She at least passively believed in reincarnation, but a soul basing its life around a sixteen? She found that hard to fathom. She had heard of sacred geometry, yet Tom was strictly talking numbers. She tried to stay with him and gathered that in numerology, numbers meant more to Tom than they did to her.

"The sixteenth card, which illustrates this soul's goal, is the Tower. In tarot symbolism, the Tower represents human endeavors and achievements. It also signals a drastic shift in the overall course of evolution. Schizandra's an older soul who's developed a tall Tower—lots of achievement in her other lives. But," Tom paused, "we're entering a whole new world—a new *reality*. Everything she's done and developed was for the *old* world."

Schizandra smiled at the queen's kind gesture, but Frauke's talk of "home" gave little comfort. Schizandra knew her home was gone for good. Her father had shaped her entire world. When he died, everything she knew went with him—her friends, her home, her school.

Her grandmother's house felt as strange as these caverns and the chocoholic queen. Melissa was one of those New Age freaks she and her dad poked fun of. The day before all this weird stuff happened, her grandmother had banned the use of nicknames. Just like that. Melissa's roof, Melissa's rules. End of discussion. It seemed so unfair. No one *ever* called her Schizandra. Changing her name destroyed the only remaining tie to the life she knew.

Schizandra couldn't even eat the things she used to eat. Melissa was vegan and ran a "cruelty-free" household. No eating or harming animals. No meat, no cheese, no leather, and no animal testing. That meant she needed to change shampoo and soap as well as food.

Once, she caught herself enjoying vegan chili. She stopped when she remembered her dad's chili, full of beef and topped with loads of cheddar cheese. Melissa's chili reminded Schizandra of her life now. It was missing the best ingredients.

Tom cocked his head to one side. "What do you know about the Mayan Calendar and the unfolding of things on this planet?"

"A little," Melissa said, intrigued but wary.

"Well," he said, "shortly before Schizandra was born on November 1, 1987 ... back in August of '87, we reached a point on the Mayan Calendar called the Harmonic Convergence. According to the Mayan Calendar, energies would become as dense as they could possibly get and then they'd turn around back towards the light, becoming more and more ethereal. The Mayan Calendar actually ends at the Harmonic Convergence."

"I thought the Mayan Calendar ended in 2012."

Tom shook his head. "That's what most people think, but it's not quite accurate. You see, the Mayans had an understanding of astronomy that we've only recently regained. They knew about *galactic* timing. In 2012— on December 21, 2012, to be precise—our sun reaches the Galactic Equator."

Melissa tried to wrap her mind around that one. *Galactic Equator?* She knew about Earth's Equator, but Tom meant the central circle of the Milky Way. He, and apparently the Mayans, believed this moment in time and space would mark an important shift:

"It takes twenty-six thousand years for the sun to complete that orbit, and we are in the fifth—and last—Mayan cycle of those orbits. One hundred thirty thousand years ago, at the beginning of these cycles, evolution took an interesting turn. According to fossils with traits such as high, rounded skulls, small brow ridges, a vertical forehead and a pronounced chin, *Homo sapiens* first appeared in Africa about one hundred thirty thousand years ago. With the end of the fifth cycle, we're approaching another key moment in evolution. *A brave new world!*"

Schizandra doubled over in pain, grabbing her abdomen.

"What is it?" the queen asked.

"Agggh!" Schizandra screamed. She inhaled through her teeth, clamped them shut and tried to pull the pain somewhere else. "It hurts right here." She pointed to her lower abdomen then grabbed the area directly above her tailbone. "And here. Ow, it feels like someone's twisting a dagger in the base of my spine."

Frauke tried to remember some basic healing techniques she learned from Nestor. She placed her left hand on the girl's sacrum and her right hand just below the neck. Her hands burned! "You sure have a lot of energy," she said.

Still hugging her belly, Schizandra climbed down onto her knees and folded forward, curling herself into a tight ball on the cavern floor. She rested her forehead on the ground and tried to breathe. It wasn't easy. Sweat poured from the crown of her head, and each time she inhaled, she felt like her heart would burst. Every breath brought more pain, and Frauke's hands felt hotter and hotter with each passing moment.

"It's too much," Schizandra gasped. "It hurts too much!"

Frauke felt her own energy contract with a sense of inadequacy. Was she helping or not? Schizandra read her mind and sent a telepathic message back: "I know you want to help, but I think you're making it worse. I'm too hot. Your hands are too hot! I just need to be alone right now."

The queen pulled her hands away and felt ashamed. She tried to focus on the girl writhing at her feet, but a sob threatened to escape her own throat. Here she had put herself out there, offering what she could, and she appeared to have made things worse.

"Stop feeling that way!" Schizandra screamed. "This is not *about* you. I can feel what you're feeling, and you're making me hurt more."

She crumpled tighter on the ground then turned her head to peer up at Frauke. "Your shame feels like you're tugging on me—" Another wave of nausea and stabbing pain silenced the girl as she pushed her forehead into the ground. It hurt to talk, but she felt like yelling. "That shame feels— like you made—me swallow—a rusty—anchor," she gasped, "and you're pulling—on the line.—That anchor's—ripping—out—my guts."

She paused for a few moments but started again before Frauke could say anything. She did *not* want to hear the queen right now. "If you can't help me," she said through gritted teeth, "please, just go away."

Frauke tried to swallow her shame instead of projecting it onto the girl, but it didn't feel any better in her own stomach. She lifted Schizandra by her armpits.

"Ow!" the girl yelled. "What are you doing? I told you to leave me alone."

"I can't do that."

"Yes, you can." Schizandra wrestled herself away from Frauke and tried to move to fetal position, but the queen lifted her up again.

"We need to go," Frauke said firmly. Her heart grew stronger as she followed it.

"You can't take me home. You can't heal me. You can't leave me here. What *can* you do?" Schizandra screamed through tears of pain, quickly morphing into rage.

"I can take you to someone who knows what to do."

"Who? That rabbit? Where's your rabbit now?"

"No, not Nestor," Frauke said quietly. "This isn't easy for me to say ... ." The queen's humility caught Schizandra's attention, and her eyes stopped launching hatred. Frauke continued, "I think I know why the king was calling for me, and I'm sorry I delayed so long."

"What's your king got to do with me?" Her pain remained, but it had become slightly more bearable as she rose and started talking. "I thought he was just some sort of frog man."

"I'm sorry for that, too," Frauke said, beginning to slip into shame again.

"Owww!" Schizandra doubled over but managed to hiss, "I told you not to do that! If you wanna kill me—get it—over with. Stab me with your knife, break my neck—but please—" She grimaced again. "Get on with it."

Frauke tried to sidestep her own emotions, but they chased her. Schizandra rolled her eyes in agony and frustration. "Stop thinking everything revolves around *you*. Tell me what you meant to share about the king."

The queen composed herself, and the girl's pain crashed and receded. "He will sing for you," she said. For once, Frauke hoped her husband's hype was well-deserved.

Schizandra glared at Frauke. "I'm dying, and you're gonna take me to a *concert*? Your king will *sing* to me? What kind of world do you think we live in?" she asked. "This was fun at first, but I am so over all this woo-woo stuff. Just get me out of here."

Frauke grabbed the girl's forearm and marched her forward. When Schizandra continued to fight for freedom, the queen popped her once in the neck. The girl immediately slumped unconscious.

"Sorry, sweetness." Frauke pulled her charge to a dark spot in the cavern, and huffing, said, "I promise this ... is for ... your own ... good."

She might have sounded confident, but Frauke felt her heart inside her throat. She removed the black pearl necklace. Rolling a pearl between thumb and index finger, she shook her head. She was used to people indulging her every whim. Keeping the necklace hadn't seemed like such a big deal, but oh, Goddess, had she ever messed up this time! Tears misted her eyes as she felt shame resurging in her gut.

Schizandra moaned.

Frauke realized she needed to move quickly. She had to get Schizandra to the king, but she needed to deliver that necklace *before* they met the king. Closing her eyes, the queen evaporated, leaving the girl in a silent and empty tunnel.

Chapter Eighteen

THE MAYA CALLED THIS TIME of a little more than a quarter century between the Harmonic Convergence and 2012, 'The time of no time.' We're not *in* the new world yet," Tom said. "This is the time of no time. Us older folks who knew the old world have begun to realize: *that world we grew up in?* We are definitely not in Kansas anymore! Schizandra's part of a batch of souls who rode in on that wave of change. It's a unique batch of souls."

"Aren't all batches of souls unique?" Melissa asked.

"Good point," Tom said, "but this batch even more than usual." He explained that the planets Saturn and Uranus exerted opposite influence. Normally, they worked in separate spheres, but every forty-five years, Saturn and Uranus came together. Souls that arrived during those times experienced dramatic inner tension.

Tom returned to the Tower card and its implications. Because of that Saturn-Uranus placement, Schizandra had come in predisposed to inner conflict. The Tower symbolized evolution, so Tom predicted she'd have major issues with change. Part of her would blast through limitations while the other part would cling to the old ways she had mastered so well in earlier lives. Most people struggled with change to some degree. For Schizandra, courage and resistance dueled in epic proportion. The battle inside raged so fierce that it would play itself out on the cosmic stage.

"Schizandra's soul's done a lot of big time evolution. She's had lots of very spiritual lives, but in those lives that spirituality helped her to put up with all the old world's bullshit—how to cope, how to transcend it." Tom chuckled. "Do you practice yoga?"

"I do."

"Well then," he said, "you know what I mean. Yoga's a spiritual tool for that old world. It helps us navigate distractions and persecutions, find a calm center from which to engage the old world. The new souls coming in here recognize that the old world's kaput."

But the would-be yogini did *not* know what Tom meant. Sure, things had changed since 1987, but change formed the very essence of life. This reading seemed way too general. Tom asked if she'd like more tea. Melissa shook her head no.

She was just about to end the reading when he asked, "Was there a problem with the birth?"

━━━◆━━━

Hovering above a dead oak tree near Glastonbury, England, a disembodied spirit said, "You bet there was a problem with the birth." His voice howled like a gust of wind, and nearby birds took flight.

He liked this tree. Centuries ago—back in 1111 A.D.—he had orchestrated quite a scene from here. It hadn't finished exactly as he'd planned: the human race survived. But the violence and betrayal of that moment had left a deeper scar on humanity than the death of Christ. No one dared record events of Winter Solstice 1111, so a group healing had never taken place through Bible studies or support groups. The participants had all scurried away in shame, binding their greatest strengths and gifts for all eternity.

Until now. He was aware of Schizandra Ginger Parker and what her birth had signified.

"Another chance for humanity, nothing short of a bloody miracle!" His voice shrieked across a barren landscape, forcing squirrels into tunnels and tourists back inside their cars.

Through Remote Viewing, he had watched the girl's mother die in 1987. That death had seemed to stifle any chance of the girl awakening to her destiny. Schizandra had turned her intellect to Spelling Bees and learned to silence Extra Sensory Perception. She blended well—an elixir of life disguised as empty calories and diet soda pop. All that changed with her father's death and the subsequent move to Sedona.

He did not like these changes. Every so often, a chance for evolution came, but fear and resistance quickly shoved it down. Souls *still* cowered from the Inquisition's witch hunts and burning stakes. If he couldn't destroy humanity, at least he could bully it into submission. Convince its leaders that natural radiance was wrong. Persecute those who dared to reach and live beyond the "norm." Ban books. Question sanity.

But Schizandra threatened it all. Already, thousands of healers from around the globe felt their hopes lifted by her very existence. If she stepped into her power, she would rally them together. Their collective vibration would begin to shift—permanently. Planet Earth would respond to all that love and launch itself into the next dimension.

He could see it now and yowled into the wind, "She must be stopped."

———

Melissa sat up straighter but said nothing. Her eyes grew wide.

Tom continued, "Any birth defects? How did that birth process go?"

"Why do you ask?"

"Well," Tom said, putting on his glasses and pointing to a spot on one of the computer generated charts, "we've got this extremely tight Sun-Pluto conjunction. The Moon or the ruler of the Sun in extremely tight conjunction with the Sun often indicates problems at birth. Schizandra's a Scorpio, and Pluto rules Scorpio. The ruler of Schizandra's Sun Sign—Pluto—sits in extremely tight conjunction with the Sun. Here's Pluto."

He pointed at the chart again. "Look how close it is—same degree, just minutes away. Very often when that happens, we see difficulties at birth."

"Her mother died of a rare complication during childbirth," Melissa said. "Are you telling me that was 'in the stars'?"

"Not in the sense of causation, but yes, in the sense of influence," he said. "Were you related to the mother?"

"My daughter," Melissa said, "I was her midwife."

Tom exhaled a long sigh. He extended his hand and touched Melissa's, searching her face. "Would you like me to continue, or has this become too painful?"

Melissa's mouth lifted into a half-smile. "Honestly? I feel a bit relieved. I mean, it's still a horrific turn of events, but to learn that something external validates my sense of inevitability, well…that helps a little. Please," she nodded, "continue."

———

The spirit above the tree could feel lives synchronizing. Order from chaos. Sense from madness. It sickened him to the core of his being.

He continued to howl. The wind he generated slashed apart frozen branches. It severed power lines. Several fires started from thunderstorms. As sparks flew into the air, a few people heard his call. Some congregated around the dead tree, still black from a lightning strike on the darkest night of 1111AD. Others felt his voice inside their heads, self-righteous and demanding: "Schizandra Ginger Parker must be stopped."

He told them she was an abomination to the Spirit—the darkest abuse of power. Her siren song would lure seekers with its beauty then smash them against the very foundations of reality. He lied, but his listeners swallowed his words as drowning victims gulp water before attacking a would-be rescuer.

"Destroy her!"

The warning rippled out across the world. The biggest fanatics made plans to reach Sedona in whatever way they could. A thirteen-year-old orphan garnered no sympathy. They would sacrifice the girl.

"OK, so that birth date happens to triadically invert to a sixteen," Tom said. "This soul came in here and will take some hammering at first. Using the imagery of the card, this soul calls in the light in the form of a lightning bolt, which hits the Tower. The date *and* the name both invite the light then get struck by lightning and knocked out."

The astrologer explained that the soul that would eventually become Schizandra had spent many previous lifetimes honing skills. Schizandra's soul had mastered the old world so well that it could move through this world on autopilot, yet her soul craved massive change. It had grown way too comfortable to make an easy shift.

Tom pointed to the ominous Tower card. "She'll get that stuff knocked out of her. This male figure represents the conscious self, and the female figure's the unconscious self. Notice that *both* have fallen from the Tower."

He reiterated that the triadic inversion of the date of birth—in Schizandra's case, a sixteen—marked the very purpose for which the soul had come into this life. The sixteen meant evolution of the species. Schizandra's soul had incarnated to help humanity move to the next level. According to Tom, souls came in here with more than just a goal; souls arrived with personalized instructions: a "Soul Path" that revealed itself through the given name at birth.

"Guess what?" Tom asked.

Melissa leaned in as he slapped the table. "Schizandra's Soul Purpose and Soul Path are the same number! *Very unusual.* Having that sixteen in both positions exponentially intensifies its influence. We're talking quantum leaps! Mother and Father Archetypes plunge from the Tower to their deaths."

Melissa swallowed hard. "You know, Tom, I think I'll take that cup of tea after all." As he left the room she tried to calm her pounding heart.

Lobelia pressed the center of Schizandra's left foot. "Have you felt the adrenal point? No doubt that's where most of this originates." The girl's contorted face visibly relaxed as the sisters pressed her corresponding points. Even the heart monitor responded.

"That's incredible!" Amelia said. "What did you do?"

"We've relaxed her adrenal glands," said Rosemary. "Sometimes a mere rebalancing of them sparks an awakening, but poor Schizandra's got her work cut out for her."

"I'm going to touch the pineal point," Lobelia said. She pressed the center of the girl's big toe, and Schizandra squeezed her eyes shut as though trying to block out light. "Interesting!"

"Not really," said her twin, "if I recall correctly, the pineal gland marks our spiritual center. It calls in the light, even pulses sometimes during spiritual awakenings. Perhaps our grandniece isn't ready for such brilliance."

They held the big toes for another thirty seconds until Lobelia suddenly exclaimed, "It's grief! That's what's blocking her. Let's check on the lungs."

They moved their hand placement to the top of Schizandra's feet, just above the toes.

"As you suspected," Rosemary said. She turned to Amelia and explained, "Grief resides in the lungs." Rosemary's face fell serious. "This poor child has really been through it, hasn't she?"

"Out with it," said the stout old twin, "come, Schizandra, you can let this go."

They held the lung point for a few moments. Tears started trickling down the girl's still unconscious face. Weeping silently, she filled the room with pathos—a tragic heroine among props of life support. The twins continued to treat Schizandra's lungs until her breathing returned to optimal range.

"Lobelia, are you sensing what I'm sensing?" Rosemary asked. She pressed the arch of Schizandra's right foot.

"You mean her solar plexus?" Lobelia pressed the same point on the left foot. "Unbelievably blocked! We've got to give her some release. It's taking so much longer than usual. Passes then blocks again."

Lobelia had moved to the inner foot, directly below the girl's left ankle. "I think there's something going on in the uterus," she said.

"Oh, yes," said Rosemary, "her Chi is blocked almost everywhere. It's like we clear one area, and the blockage just moves somewhere else."

"Menstrual cramps or pending miscarriage? What's your guess?" Lobelia asked.

"Likely menstrual, but with kids these days, who knows? Amelia, have you tested her for pregnancy?"

The nurse looked away and quietly said, "Actually, we did test her, but we don't make a big deal of that unless we need to. Parents, you know: they never want to think it's their child engaged in those behaviors. But no, she's not pregnant."

"Odd," Lobelia said, "she seems blocked here, but in such a full way it almost reads like a pregnancy. She's completely bloated!"

"Remember, that's her second chakra," Rosemary said. "It could be related to all sorts of birthing—creativity, her own birth trauma. Poor child, losing her mother that way. I cannot believe that with us so close, Philip never let us see her. For all we know, Schizandra's an artist like her mother and that dreadful academic tried to abort the gifts right out of her."

The girl twisted herself as though in pain.

"Let it go," said Lobelia.

Schizandra moaned.

"I think that's enough there," Amelia said. "Her heart rate's up. Why don't you go back to that adrenal point that calmed her down?"

———◆———

"When you look at a chart like this, you think, oh this is drastic." Tom raised his hands in mock distress, inhaled a nervous laugh and imitated pre-incarnate souls:

"*Gee, maybe I'll take two or three lives to work on this issue, and these other issues, oh, I'll take seven or eight lifetimes to work on those.* But older souls will say, *Oh screw that!*" He tapped Schizandra's natal chart and deepened his voice for theatrical effect. "This chart says, 'git her done.'"

In his normal voice, he continued, "Early in life she'll get some great awakening. Cool thing about this, though: once she makes that shift, she can move on to the *integrated* application of the sixteen."

"So there's a positive spin to this gloomy card?"

Tom nodded. "So many tarot cards look negative because traditionally humans have *resisted* working with these energies. They don't want to change."

Melissa nodded. She pondered how much pain resistance caused—especially in labor. When a woman brought a soul into this world, the worst thing she could do was try to halt the pain. She needed to paddle out, surf it and move on to the next wave. Stopping labor pangs was like trying to halt the ocean. Melissa told clients to focus on their breathing because the breath affirmed *this too shall pass.*

She felt Tom staring at her. "Please," she said, "continue."

Tom smiled. "So, the sixteen: one plus six equals seven. In all the numerology systems, seven is the sacred number; however, the way Robin Wood draws this—"

He removed the next card from the deck and turned it face up for Melissa: same scroll as the Tower card, except this one read 7—*The Chariot*—7. The card pictured a blond man playing the lyre. He rode in a chariot drawn and a blue canopy with white stars covered his head.

"Just sort of lighten your gaze and see that starry canopy as a living portal," Tom said. "Can you see it?"

Melissa nodded, stretching her imagination.

"The Chariot—or, as I prefer to call it, the 'Starry Canopy'—looks like a nice piece of cloth with stars sewn on it. Keep looking at the Starry Canopy as a portal."

Tom explained what he meant by "integrating the sixteen." With numbers of two or more digits, a numerologist had the option of reading them as is or adding the digits together to make a single digit. *Integration* meant that a soul had learned all the lessons associated with the energy of an unreduced number. A soul could also integrate by embracing the total energy of the reduced number. In Schizandra's case, the seven meant a cosmic portal through which she could access all kinds of spiritual information.

"The energy of the seven integrates the sixteen," Tom said. With the theme of human evolution reducing to that cosmic portal, Schizandra's process of integration offered potent possibilities.

"When she integrates the sixteen, she'll become a living portal for all that stuff coming in from the celestial realms. Her incarnation *is* the portal," he said. "I'd imagine something in her DNA has built up for millennia and it all got downloaded into her. Something very special intends to come through this being."

⋯⋯⬥⋯⋯

Melissa considered herself progressive, but sometimes Tom went too far! Her granddaughter was a person, not some prophesied *being*. She might need to fast forward this part for her sisters. If Mark hadn't convinced her to keep an open mind, she might have already stopped this reading. She figured that if a self-described "adrenaline junkie" could sit through an astrology reading, then she could, too—especially if it helped her help Schizandra.

Melissa wanted so badly to support her granddaughter, but she wasn't sure she knew how. Those concerns had raised themselves even before this reading. She felt sorry for teenagers these days. Hormones posed enough of a challenge, but in 2001 the world moved fast. Kids faced all sorts of pressures that Schizandra's mother never met in the early 80's. Melissa feared she might have lost touch with today's youth. Her days of mothering had passed with Ginger. She knew birth, and she had certainly witnessed a lot of death, but that middle ground, oh, she hoped she could guide a girl into womanhood.

Tom just added several layers to her confusion. *Cosmic portal? DNA?* Melissa wanted to tell him to end the reading, but curiosity got the better of her. Though what he'd shared so far made little sense to her, too many bits and pieces resonated for her to dismiss everything. She had never studied astrology or numerology, so all of this seemed new to her. Bizarre? *Definitely.* But had anything about the last few days seemed normal?

⋯⋯⬥⋯⋯

Tom continued, "Children with a seven birth path automatically qualified for the Sacred Mystery School of Pythagoras. He felt they were meant to learn the cosmic secrets. Once Schizandra gets that sixteen integrated and becomes the living portal, she'll no longer experience those drastic things you see in the Tower card. It's more like the energy of *aha!* The cosmic download. Her energy will want to cry out *Eureka!*"

Tom slapped the table twice. "Once she gets that sixteen integrated, it becomes the seven, which means she *is* the living portal, which in turn,

111

allows all that downloading to take place. Schizandra becomes a living *aha*!"

He slapped the table once more and smiled.

"The living *aha* happens especially when we have a strong emphasis on the ninth house. With the Moon in the ninth house, especially a *Pisces* Moon in her ninth house, a lot of people will view her as a walking spiritual encyclopedia. She doesn't need to carry that knowledge around with her, although she probably has a lot of it. Instead, she becomes this *access point*. Even though she's never heard of something, she can directly channel it. Once she gets over this hump, she'll be a real dynamo. She'll take a huge download of some kind, get short-circuited, come out of it and be amazing."

Melissa took a deep breath and pursed her lips. Tom shifted his papers then suddenly looked concerned. "I'd keep an eye on things right now."

"What do you mean?" she asked.

"Well, we just had this lunar eclipse. Let's see," he consulted his tables. "It happened at 4 a.m. Greenwich time on January ninth, so that actually means it was on the evening of the eighth for us. The lunar eclipse started in her twelfth house and it just passed over … Hmmm," Tom stroked the gray hairs on his chin. "The lights are on, and there we go."

"What does it *mean*?" Melissa asked, frustrated with things she did not understand.

Tom looked her squarely in the face. "It means that everything in the whole chart gets triggered."

Chapter Nineteen

H ARU RAISED HIS HAND AND asked for the hall pass. *"Est-ce que je peux aller aux toilettes?"*

"Oui, mais, s'il vous plait, c'est quoi la date?" asked Mademoiselle Franco in an overly annunciated drawl.

"L'onze janvier," said Haru.

"Merci, monsieur, et très bien. Voici." She handed him the hall pass and then chirped. *"Allez-vous en!"*

Haru didn't need to use the bathroom. He just wanted to stretch his legs. Watching Louis Malle films and talking about Mademoiselle Franco's love life didn't seem like learning. Plus, he felt too concerned about Shazzie to sit still. He had dreamt of her last night:

She stood in front of him, screaming for help and reaching for his hand, but Haru's own hands were tied. He wriggled his shoulders and tried to slip his palms through knots, but nothing worked. Meanwhile, someone started dragging Shazzie by the feet. She stretched her arms as far forward as she could, reaching for his hands. Whatever swung her did so in patterns. He watched Shazzie's fingers claw the dirt as her captor whipped her back and forth: a circle within a square and then a jagged edge around them both. When Shazzie finished the outline, she and her captor disappeared.

Haru stood there with his hands behind his back, pondering the image:

Telescoped up, it would make a stepped tower. Pressed flat, it became a rabbit hole. He relaxed his eyes and let them pulse from circle, square to cross—in and out the layers. The center drew him in ...

Shaking himself back to present, Haru wondered how long before Mademoiselle Franco would miss him. He walked through the empty corridor. Once she started talking about her boyfriend—*son petit chou*—the teacher could sometimes go the whole class without noticing a student's absence. Provided no one else needed the hall pass and no teachers saw him, he might have twenty minutes.

Under a fluorescent ceiling, he wandered between walls of brown lockers. He closed his eyes and kept on walking. He counted how many lockers he could pass before reopening his eyes. Six seemed average, but once he managed to walk the length of thirteen lockers without running into anything. He liked the feeling of awareness in the dark—sensing his way through space without his vision. Haru continued this game of pacing, intuiting when to turn right at the end of the hallway but opening his eyes to maneuver the stairs. He hadn't "blind tested" those quite yet.

He feared hurting himself less than he feared having someone see him trip. The young Japanese-Navajo had always been clumsy, bumping into the wrong people at the wrong time, sending books and lunch trays flying. It felt like obstacles just appeared in front of him. But the jocks and bigger kids never seemed to understand. Instead, they roughed him up, pushing him between each other and asking how he liked people crashing into *him*. Even the girls pretended to drop stuff and then accused him of looking up their skirts when he crawled to find their things. Laughing, their boyfriends would rough him up some more.

Haru's teachers liked him well enough, but Shazzie was the first student in a long time to treat him like a friend. Even though she had only been in school a week, Biology didn't feel the same without her. He had felt so happy to have a partner. All the other kids had paired up at the beginning of the school year, leaving him behind. Haru liked Biology—really he liked all sciences—and hadn't previously minded working by himself. He did most things alone. After working with Shazzie, though, that class had become special. It felt void without her.

Plus, ever since his dream about Queen Froggy and the frog king, the idea of dissection bothered him. He found himself apologizing to his refrigerated "specimen." Sometimes when he closed his eyes, he would see a beautiful, dark-haired woman in a purple robe and have the crazy thought that she *was* Queen Froggy in human form. It bothered him to think he might have hurt her.

Haru decided to head back toward class now. In case he got a funny feeling about Mademoiselle Franco, he wanted to stay close enough to reappear. After climbing the steps, he again practiced walking with his eyes closed, mentally counting lockers as he moved. At sixteen, he got a funny feeling—but not about Mademoiselle Franco.

He felt his hair lift with goose prickles and wondered how far it stuck out now. His hair acted like whiskers sensing his surroundings. Something had definitely changed. The air smelled musty, and he lost his balance on the slippery floor. His hair told him to stop walking. Suddenly, Haru felt more afraid to open his eyes than to keep them closed. He could feel someone staring at him but resisted looking at her. He knew it was a her, even without checking.

"Hi, silly," said a perky, female voice.

Angie? Haru opened his right eye just a crack, but it was enough. No more lockers and no hallway, just as he feared. He felt a sinking feeling in his gut, and the cavern where he stood began to spin.

"Silly boy," said the voice, more melodic this time, "why don't you open both your eyes? I have something for you."

Haru took a deep breath. *It wasn't Angie.* On the silent count of three, he slowly lifted his eyelids.

"That's better," giggled the dark-haired woman in a purple cloak. Somehow, Haru had known it would be her.

"What do you want with me?"

The brunette beauty pouted. "Don't you like my visits?"

"I don't even know if you're real," said Haru.

"What does *that* matter?" Frauke laughed. "Besides, this time, *you* called for *me*."

"I did?"

"Well, not exclusively, but you must admit you do enjoy my visits." She fluttered her long eyelashes, and Haru blushed. First Angie and Brielle, and now this, this fairy queen, or whatever she was. His mom had always told him he would grow into his charms, but he didn't expect it to happen this fast. *It wasn't unpleasant—just odd, could take some getting used to. Not to mention the crazy part!*

"Oh, come now, darling, admit it! You like me. You really like me!" said Queen Froggy, whoever she was. Her face clouded as Haru continued to ponder his feelings before answering.

"Fine!" she said, pulling out a knife. Haru stepped back, and Frauke laughed again. "Silly boy!" She removed a reddish oval pod from her cloak then scraped away its paper skin. With her mouth full, she moaned, "Oh, thank Goddess, this is good!" Her eyes glazed over and she smiled warmly.

Haru backed away another step.

"Ungrateful darling, I have a gift for you. Put out your hands."

Déja vu startled him as he remembered last night's dream. He hid his hands behind him then realized that's exactly what he'd done in dreamtime. He opened his hands in front, palms up.

"Good boy!" said Frauke, her voice slippery and strangely musical. She dropped the black pearl necklace in his hands. "You'll need these later."

Haru ran his fingers over the smooth black stones—just like the one he'd found in his hair! He stared in wonder, marveling at their similarity.

The woman suddenly snapped at him, "Isn't it enough that I gave it to you now?"

"Wh-what?" asked the astonished boy.

"No one needs to know about yesterday, OK? I gave the king my word, and now it's done. *Le Fin! Fait accompli, oui?*"

"Ooo-way," said Haru, stifling assessments of who seemed crazier. This lady was clearly coo-coo, but he, Haru Begay could see her and sometimes even spoke to her. He put the necklace in his pocket, wondering if he would find it later. When he looked up, Queen Froggy had disappeared. In her place remained the same symbol from his dream, drawn in red rock dust.

Again, Haru followed the design. His eyes played with the forms—grounding with the square, opening with the cross, diving into center. His mind followed. Haru ached for Shazzie. Seriously, he felt like crying, right here in the middle of—

Regaining peripheral vision, he noticed lockers again. Students poured into the hallway to the clang of Period Three. How long had he been gone? Hundreds of footprints covered the corridor with dust, completely obliterating the cross. His mind wanted to protest, but instead, he reached inside his pocket, feeling extra weight. Sure enough, he removed a string of black pearls. *You'll need these later.*

When Tom returned with Melissa's now-steeped second cup of tea, he found her pale and disconnected. She needed to process this information, weed through the New Age psychobabble and find the seeds and fruits of truth.

"Would you like to ask me something? You look concerned," he said.

Melissa debated how much to tell him. She still didn't know if she believed in astrology. "I'm not scared," she said. "I just," she inhaled deeply. "I guess I'm just not sure how much to trust what you say."

To her surprise, Tom cracked up, laughing in rapid exhales like the Breath of Fire. "You're not the first and you certainly won't be the last to tell me that," he chuckled, shaking his head and wiping a gleeful tear from his eye. "We've still got more time, or we can stop right now."

Melissa pulled her energy inside, weighing her options. Finally, she reasoned that she owed it to Schizandra to explore all avenues, regardless of her own opinions. But should she tell him about the coma? She decided to hold off awhile longer. "OK," she said, "let's keep going."

"Alright," said Tom, "so, she's plunged from her carefully constructed Tower, and astrologically, it would be normal for her to go down into some sort of metaphorical cave. Ever read Joseph Campbell?"

Melissa shook her head. "No, but my sister Rosemary probably has. Go ahead. She wants to listen to the tape."

"We're talking about the hero's journey into the cave. The hero—or in this case, heroine—can never be the same again. She'll have this turning point." He watched Melissa, but she had completely regained her composure. "The best tool she can use would be the thirty-two—sixteen plus sixteen—the card of *liberation*." He removed the next card and turned

117

it over. "The thirty-second card of the deck is the Six of Wands."

Melissa looked at the card: a blond haired man rode triumphantly on a white horse, apparently in procession. Five tall wands stood in the background. He held the sixth wand, wrapped in ivy that secured a white flag depicting a brilliant yellow sun.

"The thirty-two closely aligns with liberation," Tom said. "*Freedom!* The founders of this country were all mystics. They used astrology and numerology as well. They realized that they had an astrological window of opportunity. In that window they chose a very specific date: 7/4/1776, which adds to, guess what?"

"A thirty-two," Melissa said.

He continued, "In zodiacal numerology, the number thirty-two holds Scorpio energy."

Melissa swallowed the rest of her tea and put down her cup. She folded her legs into half lotus pose on the chair, spread her poncho over her knees, and stretched her neck high. She listened attentively. The astrologer linked a bunch of Schizandra's other numbers to Scorpio energy, too.

"Scorpio always means business," he said. "Take the numbers twenty-three and thirty-two, for example: very similar, except twenty-three is Aquarius energy—fun, open, cool. Turn it around, and thirty-two is deadly serious. It's like 'Don't tread on me.' I like to say that thirty-two is twenty-three with an attitude."

Tom laughed. "Thirty-two wants the same freedom as the twenty-three, but it means that it would rather *die* than not have that freedom. The essence of the thirty-two—the people who wrote the Declaration of Independence—they meant business. Patrick Henry meant it: 'Give me liberty or give me death.' 'Live free or die.' In 1776, they meant it."

Schizandra was a very old soul who had acted as a background player for most of her many lives. She had mastered all the skills necessary to support others. This lifetime would require her to take a strong leadership role. Tom reminded Melissa of the schizandra berry's adaptogenic nature. Like her namesake, the midwife's granddaughter could adapt quickly, providing exactly what people needed in order to free themselves.

On the other side of the Equator fog rolled over the shores of Peru's Lake Titicaca. A crowd began to assemble. Nestled at 12,530-feet in the Andes Mountains, this highest alpine lake on Earth formed a mini-ocean complete with salt water. Those who gathered let its waves nip their heels as they awaited long lost colleagues. Orbs of white light danced around the group of men and women. One by one, these orbs materialized into figures of unclear heritage. Some looked Japanese; others wore the long blond hair of Vikings. Some had the distinctive brown skin of the Tibetans; others appeared as Australian Aborigines. Many carried themselves with the solid stance of Native Americans.

Within moments, thousands of men and women had arrived by light, lake, or crevice in the rocks—an international crew that seemed more alike than not when viewed together. Their differences melted into similarities: height between five-foot-two and five-foot-five; faces of indeterminate age; long fingers; lightness of energy and weight. Their arms and hands gestured wildly, but only laughter broke the silence. These people seemed to communicate with thoughts and feelings instead of words.

Together a man and a woman raised a staff and thumped it on the ground in order to draw the crowd's attention. The woman spoke aloud, "Greetings, friends!"

The audience beamed at her, and she continued, "Indeed, a time of joy the likes of which we have not seen for thousands of years. In ancient times—"

The crowd giggled its amusement.

With radiant cheeks and eyes, she resumed, "In ancient times—which many of you remember so clearly—the spoken word was sacred. And so, we return to the spoken word in honor of this moment. We have gathered here today in a sacred place at a sacred time. A time of hope. A time of renewal. We have gathered to celebrate the replanting of the Garden."

Eyes crinkled into smiles and overflowed as long-fingered hands clapped their cheers. The woman's partner thumped his wooden staff on the ground in order to refocus the audience.

Their speaker continued, "What we have whispered and wondered for millennia has finally come to pass. Schizandra Ginger Parker has crossed the veil."

Applause led to another tapping of the staff.

The woman's face turned serious. "She has crossed the veil, but, dear ones, that marks only half the journey. Mother Earth has gone thus far before. Many times. Always, forces of resistance have withered hopes of our return to Paradise. There will be fear this time as well. And anger.

And the digging of heels into barren soil. To grow beyond the lies, we must return to primal seeds for healing on all levels." She spoke softly, but the syllables carried their own strength into the crowd. *"Ra Ma Da Sa, Sa Say So Hung."*

The group joined her, murmuring the ancient chant. They sang louder to the tune of *Pachelbel's Canon*, and their voices rose and fell like a lullaby to Schizandra and Mother Earth. The man planted his staff on the ground once for each little seed of sound. *"Ra Ma Da Sa, Sa Say So Hung."*

The lake calmed. One by one, the visitors disappeared. They dove into water, walked through solid rock or floated away on orbs of light, scattering seeds from whence they came.

Tom moved on to what he called the Life Lesson Number, the most important number in numerology. In Schizandra's case, it was a thirty-seven.

"I call this the Reserve Tank," he said to Melissa, *"the energy that's way deep down inside.* Most people don't access this until they go way down. What's there, when all the chips are down? Schizandra's Life Lesson: she must learn to access herself *without* getting knocked down. Life Lesson is the most important process in traditional numerology."

By comparing numerology, astrology and what he called *zodiacal* numerology, Tom noted ongoing themes in Schizandra's chart. Independence recurred, as did that Scorpio influence. "First of all, Schizandra's a Scorpio. Her Venus is in Scorpio, her Moon's in Pisces, and her Rising Sign is Cancer. This comes from her astrological chart. You might have noticed that these are *all* the water signs. This soul loves water."

"Does that mean she hates the desert?" Melissa asked.

The astrologer paused and took a sip of Rooibos. "She'd have some struggles with Sedona, for sure! Her favorite place would probably be somewhere like Hawaii or Fiji, some tropical island completely surrounded by water."

"What about Lake Michigan?"

"Chicago would work for this soul. She'd feel at home near any large body of water, the larger the better!" Tom looked into Melissa's eyes and said, "But water also represents our emotions."

He turned over the next card. A bearded man sat on a lotus-petal throne, carefully balanced on a rock jutting from the stormy sea.

"The King of Cups is the thirty-seventh card of the deck. The suit of cups rules the water signs. Water represents our emotional nature, and this is the king of water. The Key to our Ascension lies in our *emotions*. See how we're tying this back to that Tower card?"

Melissa shook her head. "I'm afraid you've lost me."

Tom reminded her that the Tower card marked Schizandra's very reason for incarnating: to trigger evolution of the species. Ascension meant *spiritual* evolution, because when human beings evolved, they would move to a higher vibration, higher dimension and higher plane of existence; they would *Ascend*.

He explained that the physical body could not accomplish this task on its own. The physical body would follow along, but it required a trigger from someplace else. The mental body couldn't handle this sort of download either. The mind's spam filters would reject it like an oversized email from an unknown source.

"Ascension's a matter of the heart," Tom said. "We've got the King of Cups here—firmly and calmly enthroned, but his throne sits out there in the middle of the waters. This is a man completely in touch with his feminine side."

The key for Schizandra making this work mirrored how Jesus managed to calm the stormy seas. Tom did not mean repression; he meant appropriately *invested* emotional control. "You'll never repress the ocean," he said, "but you can learn to calm the seas."

This Ascension process would only occur in a calm and loving heart. Schizandra had plenty of love, but the calm part would challenge her passionate Scorpio nature. Scorpios could become vicious if they felt threatened. In order to overcome that tendency she would need to find a still point within her heart. The unique aspects of her natal chart, numerology, and DNA had all converged in order to transmute the human species through the emotional realm. Schizandra was about to become a living, breathing Holy Grail.

Amelia had just left for a bathroom break, leaving the twins alone with the following instructions: "You can hold that adrenal point, but promise me you won't try anything fancy while I'm gone. Otherwise I'll have to ask you to leave." Rosemary and Lobelia had agreed and worked in silence until they heard the door behind them.

"I'll take over from here." They jumped at the sound of a male voice.

The twins turned to face a short man in a buttoned white lab coat. He darted for Schizandra's bed without reading her chart. Bending over their grandniece, he prepared to lift her from the bed. As he slipped his left arm under the girl's neck, Lobelia reacted. She threw her bulk in the way and pushed him back, knocking him off balance. The man's pointy teeth flashed.

"Out with it!" she shouted. "Exactly what do you think you're doing here?"

"We haven't met," he said, as he regained his footing. "I'm Dr. Swinburne, Schizandra's physician. I need to take her away." His right eye twitched as he spoke.

"What do you mean 'take her away'? Does she need more tests?"

Rosemary moved closer. "If memory serves me, she's got 'til 4:30 to awaken." She could see his long fingers poised in anticipation of the grab.

"I've got strict orders to move her sooner," he said, peeking around Lobelia's girth.

"Prove it," Lobelia said.

"I'm her *doctor*," he said. His breath came fast now between those pointy teeth. "I don't need to prove anything." He dodged Lobelia and lunged towards the bed.

The twins glanced at each other.

Rosemary whispered, "I don't remember Melissa saying anything about a tic."

"I don't remember *anything*," Lobelia said, as quietly as she could, "but something's not sitting right."

Rosemary nodded.

When the man's fingers touched the girl, her heart rate accelerated, nearing the danger zone. The machine worked overtime, and the twins knew they needed to act fast. He was pulling her from the bed! Lobelia grabbed him by the back of his lab coat and yanked as hard as she could. It ripped.

She gasped as a three-foot-long black tail flicked out at her.

"Out of here!" she shouted, "*Intruder!* I will eliminate anything unclean from this room! Get *out* while you can!"

He snapped her with his tail.

"Jesus, Mother Mary and Joseph," whispered Rosemary.

The imposter hissed and dropped the girl on the bed. His arms twitched as though struck by lightning. A moment later, he spun his head and hissed in Rosemary's face.

"*Sweet Jesus!*" she murmured, reaching for Lobelia's hand. The man bared his teeth at Rosemary and twitched again.

The sisters stared as he evaporated into thin air. Only the beeping of Schizandra's heart monitor made them aware of their own pounding chests. Together they resettled their grandniece on the bed. Rosemary smoothed the girl's curls before joining Lobelia at her feet. This incident had sabotaged all their previous work. By the time Amelia returned, they were fighting for Schizandra's life.

"I first encountered this process in an old Kaballah writing," Tom said. "They called it the Fatal Flaw—one we won't integrate early in life. Another person called it the Achilles' Heel, and someone else called it the Greatest Challenge."

Melissa nodded, and he continued, "I like to call it the Golden Key. If it's your Achilles' Heel if you don't incorporate it, then what happens if you do?"

Tom turned over the cards. The first showed an angel blowing a trumpet against a light blue sky. A white flag with a red cross hung from the trumpet, and naked gray forms, presumably dead people, jumped out of coffins, throwing their arms to the heavens. The bottom of the card read in all capital letters: JUDGEMENT.

The second predominantly yellow card depicted a naked woman rising from a black pot. In contrast to the way women usually hid their private parts, she lifted her arms to the sky. On this card, one could clearly see the woman's breasts and pubic hair. She had no shame of them. A bird's head hovered above the woman's, and its yellow feathers doubled as rays of the sun. The scroll across the bottom read *20—Judgement—20.*

"The first card comes from the Rider-Waite deck," Tom said. "Normally I use Robin Wood's versions, but I wanted to show you how these numbers remain open to interpretation. Schizandra's Golden Key is a twenty. Earlier, I mentioned the twenty as a Scorpio number. Lots and lots of Scorpio energy."

Melissa stared at the cards. The images moved her heart.

"The number twenty represents a call from darkness into the light, depicted here by Gabriel blowing the trumpet and people coming out of their graves." Tom pointed first to the Rider-Waite card and then to the other card. "Robin Wood pictures it as the phoenix rising from its ashes. Once Schizandra gets knocked out of her Tower, she will get pounded into the dark. Then she'll be called out of the darkness and back into the light. St. John of the Cross called this process the Dark Night of the Soul."

Melissa shuddered. She had learned some of that lesson herself.

"St. John of the Cross said, 'The endurance of darkness is preparation for great light.' If you want to become a complete vessel for the light, guess where you're going? *All the way down into the darkness.* Kahlil Gibran's got those wonderful lines about sorrow carving the path for joy. Whenever the Dark Night of the Soul shows up as a Golden Key like this, it shows up early in life. As I said, I'd keep an eye on things right now, because we just had that lunar eclipse."

Melissa glanced at the clock. 11:11.

The disembodied spirit above the dead oak tree howled in frustration, "Idiot! Next time I'll have to do it myself."

His anger raged even colder because he had been unable to incarnate since the time of Christ. He wanted so badly to influence events on this planet, but the lack of body forced him to rely on others: incompetents like this cat man who couldn't even accomplish a simple kidnapping.

The cat man pleaded for mercy, but the spirit's wind ripped through his flesh. Two weeks from now, tourists would find a skeleton coiled in fetal position. Scientists would consider it evidence of *ancient* sacrifice— unaware of how fast hatred and disgust could age a body.

Tom flipped over two more cards to illustrate the twenty. Beneath a full moon, a young woman with long, black hair held a book in her left hand and a crystal ball in the right. The scroll at the bottom read 2—*The High Priestess*—2. The other card showed a young blond man dressed as a harlequin playing the flute. He danced on the edge of a cliff. The scroll read 0—*The Fool*—0.

Tom launched into a discussion of masculine and feminine numbers— way too esoteric for the midwife. This numerologist could talk! And talk.

From what Melissa could surmise, Schizandra's twenty held maximum feminine potential because the two and zero combined the prime feminine number (two) with the Source of All That Is (zero).

"Schizandra's a walking goddess," he said, "but first she needs to get through this stuff."

"So how does she get through it? She's really going through something right now."

"I'm not surprised," he said, "because she didn't leave herself an out."

"Meaning what?"

"She came here determined to get her Life Lesson, no matter what. That King of Cups Awakening the Heart card, evolution of the species through the Tower," Tom clucked his tongue, "yep, she's gonna do this no matter what the human part of her wants to do. In fact, if she decides she wants to go out and end it all, other souls will go into her body. You'll have all these entities around the body saying, 'Don't kill the body. We will take over the body.'"

He tapped Schizandra's chart and said, "This mission will get done through this body. There's no way I know of for this physical body to die."

"Oh, my God," Melissa cried. "Is this true? Because the reason I called you. Oh, my God!"

She sobbed then collected herself enough to update Tom on the deaths, the coma, the Navajo's curse, and the deadline for awakening.

Tom looked into Melissa's eyes and smoothed the girl's chart. "That kind of journey is normal for this soul. We live in bodies designed to renew themselves. There's no reason for us to age, get sick and die, except that we believe the old programming. Schizandra's soul came here to give us a new paradigm. A new world without the old rules. We're talking Immortality."

"So you think she'll pull through?"

"She'll live long and fly high. Nothing can stop her."

Melissa nodded. *"But will it be her?"*

Chapter Twenty

S CHIZANDRA LAY SLUMPED IN A pitch black ditch. Unlike the night before, she felt no fear of the dark this time. She stared into the void and felt ... nothing. Black surrounded her. Not like a blanket, not like a monster, not like anything at all. Black absorbed her, swallowing each thought the moment it occurred. An image of her father came—bald and suffering through chemo, but he disappeared. Daddy pounding the table when she acted like her mother: nothing.

Nothing moved through her, erasing memories one by one. Every image, every feeling, every hope: she held onto nothing, and nothing held onto her. Schizandra's world slipped away. A vast desert spread across her heart. For less than a moment, she almost realized what they meant by "valley of the shadow of death," but that thought aborted before it fully formed. Only death remained. Not an event, not a moment, not a transition—just the *absence* of life.

No water ran through this desert. No wind. Only a vacuum that sucked her dry and inside out, then spat her into Monday afternoon. Once again, she stood at the vista on Airport Road, gazing over West Sedona from four-thousand feet above. As the sun dipped behind Coffee Pot Rock, the full moon began its slow ascent over Uptown. The spheres moved in tandem like arms of an ancient scale.

Her grandmother would say the vortex drew her there, but Schizandra knew better. It wasn't some airy-fairy, New Age hippie "Airport Vortex." It was the airport itself: her fantasy of flight. The fact that somewhere— however inaccessible to a Sedona schoolgirl—there was another, *normal* world. A world where psychics were the freaks, not the standard. A world where banana peels thrown outside did not survive intact for *two full years*. A place whose front yards did not need six-foot ditches to hold the floodwater when it finally rained. A place where everything wasn't *red*.

Schizandra hated the desert. She biked to the airport to let her thirteen-year-old mind coast above this tiny town and find its way back to the heartland of America. Not the East. Not the Wild West. The Midwest. *Chicago.* She missed the Lake. Pausing at the overlook on her way to Sedona Airport, she managed to fight her tears this time. To the left, two couples smiled at her, then marveled at the beauty stretched before them. "Do you live here?" asked one of the men, eyeing her bike.

Schizandra nodded, and the two women grew giddy. "Alfred," said one, "Did you hear that? She *lives* here. Oh, darling," she turned to Schizandra, "do you know how lucky you are? We come here every single year." She poked her husband in the ribs and sighed, "But Fred thinks it's too isolated. Can you *imagine*? Oh, I'd give *anything* to live here!"

Schizandra smirked as the woman spread her arms wide, embracing "the face of the American West."

Tourists!

"That dead father you planted in Chicago," the other woman asked, "will he bloom this Spring?" She was black and appeared to have four arms. Two of her hands grabbed Schizandra's shoulders. The girl stepped back, teetering on the edge of the cliff. With her two left arms, the crone shook a necklace of skulls. Fifty human jaws chattered with the movement. The woman stood naked and alone, her black breasts sagging under so much death.

Schizandra screamed as the hag laughed. Her cackle destroyed the panoramic view. Without warning, biplanes crashed and red rock crumbled. The black force danced like Kokopelli on methamphetamines. Toothless and maniacal: a shadowy hunchback whose feet created gale force winds. Blood tumbled from the corners of her mouth as she shrieked, "Full fathom five, thy father lies. He *lies*!"

Schizandra tried to steady herself, but the wind dislodged her. Swinging in wide arcs, she dug her fingernails into dust whenever she could reach it.

"Look at this wasteland!" screeched the hag. Vultures played on wind and prayed for carrion. "You miss *the Lake*? Watch what grows from desert clay!" The monster grabbed Schizandra's ankles and spun her round: circle, square, cross; circle, square, cross; circle, square, cross. A tornado churning faster and faster, tearing earth and clutching roots as they whirled their way down, down, down the rabbit hole, down and back to ...

Nothing.

Frauke smiled at the prisoner who had somehow become her friend. "Thank Goddess for that carotid baroreceptor so I didn't have to hurt you. Just a quick knock out while I ran my errand. C'mon, let's go!"

Schizandra didn't stir.

"OK, silly, I'm serious, we need to go now. The king won't wait much longer."

She poked the girl, but nothing happened. Frauke kneeled in front of her, peeling up Schizandra's eyelids. "Wake up! Sweetness, c'mon wake up! Ohhhh," she rang her hands, twisting nervous fingers around themselves. "Schizandra!" she moved from spoken words back to telepathy, but still no response. The queen waved her hands in front of the girl's face, hoping wind would revive her.

Nothing.

She remembered a nearby pool of water. *Worth a shot.* Frauke dragged her charge to the pond and gathered Schizandra's curls into a ponytail with her left hand. Carefully, she dunked the girl, pulling her face back fast. Water trickled over closed eyes, and the queen started to cry.

"Wake up!" Again and again, she dunked Schizandra's head. "Wake up, why do you go on sleeping?"

In her grief, Frauke began to sob hysterically, releasing her hold of the girl's hair. While the queen wept, Schizandra floated face down in the glassy pool.

Mark had thrashed all night. He awoke thinking of the girl and her mysterious grandmother. He could not get that woman out of his head. His usual black coffee burned all the way down this morning. It sloshed during arm curls, and the caffeine made him jittery. During his fifty morning pushups, Melissa's face appeared beneath his own. Her violet eyes smiled up at him as he pressed and rose above her. He stopped without finishing and paced about the room.

Maybe he should run, burn off some energy. Today was one of those rare overcast Phoenix days. Moisture might do him good. He grabbed keys, headset and an arm band radio then sprinted downstairs.

As he ran, the concrete felt good. Solid. He welcomed jolts to his knees and lower back, hard earth pushing against his stride. Pink Floyd's *Eclipse* blared across the radio waves.

Passing Sunnyslope High, Mark realized that for the first time since high school, his right shoulder felt fine. Since yesterday's massage, twenty-five years of pain had disappeared. *Coincidence?*

Homeless women whistled at him as he flew down Seventh Avenue to Central. He headed east-southeast and hit his stride at mile three. Four miles east of Sunnyslope, Mark turned onto the canal by Granada Park, just east of the highway. Traffic sounds flowed above his steady breath. Compared to Saturdays when friends met here for workouts, Granada Park looked empty on a Thursday morning. Mark's radio picked up static, so he adjusted the dial. Joni Mitchell again. *Woodstock.* The park offered two manmade lakes for migrating birds, swings for kids, and David Phelps' bronze sculpture of a man dragging his boat through the desert.

Flowing easily now, Mark envisioned his route: east-southeast from here through the classier parts of Phoenix, past "The Biltmore," then around the south end of Paradise Valley to Arcadia and back. His legs moved fast along the canal.

A few minutes later, he noticed a giant javelina ahead of him. "That's odd," he thought, "why would Phelps put a huge, bronze statue here?" He kept running until he felt the eyes upon him. That was no statue.

"Go home," said the eyes. Mark turned around. Like wild boars, javelina could be vicious, especially during the day. They had big tusks, which they weren't afraid to use. This was the biggest javelina he had ever seen. "Go home." He felt the eyes upon his back.

Suddenly, yesterday's Airport Vortex vision returned. The girl screamed into his brain, and then he saw her, floating. He picked up the pace, stretching his stride and breathing hard. As he passed Granada Park, a raven swooped so close to his forehead that Mark had to swat it with his hand. He'd never seen one of those in Phoenix before, and this did not bode well. He kept running. He wished he had told Melissa about the vision yesterday.

Mark wondered what his role entailed. He retraced steps, sprinting to Central towards Sunnyslope High. The homeless women smiled.

Mark ran faster as Depêche Mode crooned *Behind the Wheel.* Pouring sweat and breathing hard, he turned left into his apartment complex. His heart kept pounding as he walked around the lot. Did that girl really need his help? What about Melissa? He ripped the headphones from his ears, tired of someone else's answers. He could see her violet eyes staring at Schizandra. Salt ran down the back of his throat.

He ran upstairs to shower, his mind made up. Quickly toweling off, Mark dressed and climbed into the Cherokee. He repeated yesterday's drive, leaving the radio off this time. Two hours later, he turned onto 179's red rock curves, making his way to the Village of Oak Creek. He passed Bell Rock. A bit later, he spotted *Javelina Cantina*, noting it was one of the favorites Melissa mentioned last night. He turned left, heading towards the "Y." As he passed *Center for the New Age* this time, something told him to stop. He pulled into the gravel lot and climbed out of the car.

When he opened the *Center's* door, wind chimes, two streams of sandalwood incense and a giant carved yellow Buddha greeted him. He looked at the Buddha's sticker: *$3500.* An amused Mark shook his head. To his right hung glamour shots of psychic readers and massage therapists; on his left, a stairway and a dozen greeting cards, one for each astrological sign. The theme song from *Roswell* floated through a stereo system with good bass, and a sign pointed left for Aura Photos.

He approached a large glass case housing necklaces and rings. A cash register sat at the far end of the counter, ready for impulse buys. Crystals and stones of all sizes, shapes and colors filled the space around him. The room vibrated more than a hovering Hiller. Mark smiled and looked around. *Where to start?* Three women descended upon him at the same time, but he barely noticed. He needed to find something.

From the lowest shelf, a gray stone caught his eye. He picked it up and examined a perfectly formed brown cross raised from the surface. "Is this natural?" he asked the women.

"That's staurolite," said the tallest of them, "also known as 'fairy cross.' Yes, it's natural. That one comes from Brazil. It protects children from cramps and brain tumors. Also paralysis and any disease of the central nervous system."

"*Really?*" Mark asked.

The women all nodded, staring at his chiseled arms and face.

He set the rock on the case by the cash register. "I'll take it."

"We have cards with properties of all the stones and crystals," the short woman said, grabbing a shoe box that had reincarnated as a file drawer. "Here," she handed him a two-by-three inch card. "'It brings the wearer back to reality and helps treat schizophrenia.'"

Mark glanced at the paper. "So all these rocks do something?"

The women smiled and nodded. The middle one touched him lightly on the arm. Mark moved away to look for another stone. "What about this purple one?" he asked.

"That's sugilite," the tall woman said. "It has a calming effect, eases pain and treats the nervous system."

The short one reached for a card and handed it to him. "It's also associated with the end of the world!" she said. "Sugilite mitigates destructive powers of cosmic radiation. We believe it rose from the center of the earth to offset the current forces."

"Hmmm," Mark said.

"Should we set it aside for you?" asked the tall one.

"Guess it can't hurt," he said. He still wanted something else. *For Melissa.* The woman touched his arm again. This time, Mark moved to a stone across the store. "What's this marbled green one?" he asked, picking up a four inch slab.

"Malachite." The woman had followed him, as they so often did. "It's the stone of pregnant women." She smiled and leaned closer.

"Good for a midwife," he said, "I'll take it."

The short woman removed a tiny card and read, "'*The Egyptian Book of the Dead* says a goddess drops stars on the earth in the shape of green stones. Malachite works on the heart chakra and promotes understanding and spirituality.'"

Mark nodded absently. *One more.* He scanned the shelves. He had picked two for Schizandra and wanted to give Melissa two as well. A small, clear crystal beckoned him. Three inches long and an inch and a half wide, its back end made rainbows in the light.

"That's a Lemurian Seed Crystal," said the tall woman.

"I like it," Mark said.

"Twelve thousand years ago, during the last days of Lemuria, people decided to plant crystals seeded with messages of Oneness. Most of the Lemurian citizens left for other parts of the galaxy, but some went underground to inner earth. It's believed they still communicate telepathically with those who left."

Mark wanted to roll his eyes, but the crystal held his gaze.

The tall woman continued, "These special quartz crystals connect inner earth, the surface and the stars. They just appeared in Brazil last year."

"So Lemuria's a place?" asked Mark.

"An entire civilization, lost in the Pacific," the short one said, pulling another card. "Native Americans call it the Motherland of Mu. Crystals only allow themselves to be discovered when humanity can use their energies. Finding these Lemurians signals the coming of a New Age."

"What's the card say?" Mark asked.

"'Each Lemurian Seed Crystal connects with all the others. The grid lines represent encoded information.'"

"So, if I buy two of these, they're linked?"

All three women nodded as a second Lemurian chose Mark. "OK, I'm ready," he said.

"That comes to $232," the tall one said. "Should we wrap them for you?"

"All but this one," he said, holding the second Lemurian. "This one stays with me."

"The triadic inversion of the date of birth represents the soul's *reason* for incarnating: the Life Purpose. The triadic inversion of Schizandra's birthdate *without reducing* is two-hundred-thirty-two: the Scorpio." Tom tapped her chart. "Lots of Scorpio energy!"

"It's actually the thirty-two—'liberation card'—expressed through that number two card, the High Priestess. Add together two plus three plus two, and it reduces to a seven, that Living Portal. *Her purpose for incarnating.*"

"So that Living Portal business pops up everywhere."

Tom nodded. "The Super Conscious, called the Destiny Number is the full name: Schizandra Ginger Parker. When we add up her full name at soul level, meaning the S is actually the nineteenth letter of the alphabet... "

His voice continued. Melissa tried to follow—really she did—but Tom flew on a trapeze far above her. He didn't seem to need a net. Or a partner. He could flip and swing and somersault on air. This whole reading had become a circus, now that she thought of it. Instead of clowns emerging from cars, numbers leapt from charts. Each appeared with its unique expression, but after awhile, they all looked alike. Their unfamiliar faces became one "strange" instead of many individuals.

"In Schizandra's case, the Soul Level Destiny Number *is* the Life's Purpose," Tom said, "which means *nothing* can stop her from achieving this. Drum roll, please!" He improvised on the table.

"Achieving what?" she asked.

"First, she must experience true freedom and then express it through the energy of the High Priestess. Two's a good arbitrator, bringer of tact and diplomacy. When a message comes through the two energy, the High Priestess softens whatever she brings through. Schizandra can make that 'live free or die' energy more accessible for people without her courage."

As Tom spoke about quantum leaps, Melissa realized that she herself lacked Schizandra's courage. Shooting from cannons was not the midwife's style. *She* preferred *Cirque du Soleil*.

⸻◆⸻

Sobs wracked Frauke's body as Schizandra turned blue. The queen felt a nudge at her back and then loud thumping, which she mistook for her own pounding heart. A yellow flash caught her eye and then, "M'lady, m'love, Schizandra!"

"Sephora!" squealed Frauke, opening her palms, but Nestor demanded attention first.

"Remove the girl," ordered the rabbit. "Now."

Frauke covered her cheeks and closed her eyes. "Oh, my Goddess. What have I done?"

"Enough," Nestor said, "and not nearly enough. Remove the girl. *Now.*"

Frauke pulled Schizandra by her pony tail and Nestor thumped rapidly on her chest. The girl spit water, choking herself awake. Sephora fluttered back and forth above her face, trying to catch her eyes, but they remained glazed.

"Reviving her will require a story," said Nestor, telepathically. She looked at Frauke. "Sit. I will relay the tale while Sephora acts it out. Following her movements will help Schizandra's synapses reconnect. And you—" she thumped at Frauke, "now do you believe me that shame distracts? You're distracted to the peril of humanity. Wait without reflection, for *you* are not yet ready to reflect."

Frauke hung her head.

"Don't cry, m'queen," warbled Sephora, kissing Frauke's tears. "We loves ya and now ya gets a story. It's alright, Nestie speaks directly w' the Ancients."

"Since when are you two so chummy?" asked Frauke. "Healers don't have friends. They're much too serious for that."

Nestor thumped. "Never you mind, Frauke. 'That which you see is not: and for that which *is*, you have no words.'"

Frauke sniffed. "You sound like the king."

"As well I should," Nestor said. "He *loves* Kabir. Speaking of the king, we must prepare Schizandra for their meeting. Shall we begin?" Frauke nodded and the rabbit thumped a mock drum roll: "Sephora, we're on! You will dance as I relay our tale."

———

"Hold it, hold it, hold it," said Rosemary, pressing the K1/Solar Plexus point in the middle of Schizandra's left foot. Lobelia pressed K1/Solar Plexus on the right foot, and the tall twin turned to the nurse. "Just give us thirty more seconds."

"I'm going to call Dr. Swinburne," said Amelia. "She's about to flatline."

"That's what we're working to prevent!" Lobelia shouted. "Now, out! Out with the doubt! We're working here."

"We need to concentrate now." Rosemary stared into Amelia's wide eyes. "Twenty more seconds."

The twins closed their eyes and focused all their energy on a point at the bottom center of the balls of each foot. By blasting a current of bioelectric energy to Schizandra's kidney meridian, they hoped to reverse her sudden plunge. After releasing the grief from her lungs and some of the anger from her liver, the patient's vitals had surged into stronger territory. She had rested peacefully until that *imposter* incident. Less experienced reflexologists might have panicked, but Rosemary and Lobelia had both reached for K1 at the same time.

The only major meridian point on the bottom of the foot, K1 allowed the twins to access Schizandra's kidney meridian. Like an underground spring, the kidney channel anchored energy drawn into the lungs, housed one's Essence, and formed the basis for the soul's strength. The life force energy known as Chi gathered and regenerated in the kidney meridian. If that channel weakened, vitality would leave—sometimes permanently. The twins knew they needed to hurry.

Amelia had just picked up the phone when Schizandra's vitals returned to normal. Lobelia whooped and Rosemary's dimples reappeared.

"That was close," said Amelia, putting down the phone. "How'd you know it would work?"

"We made the connection in 1970 during a yoga retreat in Varanasi."

"We did?" Lobelia coughed.

"Yes," said Rosemary, "we did. It was 1970, on the banks of the Ganges. We dropped into *Mandukasana*—sometimes called frog pose—and all my perimenopausal pain just disappeared. Lobelia and I researched the pose and found it treats the kidney meridian. From there, we learned that in addition to housing our life force, the kidney meridian also controls birth, growth and reproduction. We looked up K1 in our reflexology manuals, and the rest is history."

"I just work on instinct," Lobelia said.

Wanting to halt another bickering match, Amelia said, "Do you think Schizandra's premenstrual? If so, this is some *serious* PMS."

"A woman's curse," said Rosemary.

"Period or not, she needs to rebirth herself." Lobelia made sweeping motions with her arms. "Speaking of which, where *is* our little midwife? That astrology reading's gone way past an hour."

Thinking of Melissa, the twins glanced at each other and silently agreed: *they would keep the imposter story to themselves.*

Tom pointed to a clump of letters and numbers on his graph paper. "When we play with the initials and what I call *finitials*—the last letters of each name—added together, we get a seventy-nine. The Soul's Dream means she wants to come in and *do* this thing." Tom explained that the Soul's Dream for Schizandra meant purification: following a spiritual path and becoming a portal.

He played with the seventy-nine, expanding it out to the one-hundred-sixty-nine, and distilling it down to the sixteen, which Melissa recognized from their earlier conversation about the Tower and human evolution. Of course, the sixteen further reduced to the number seven, that Starry Canopy or Living Portal. Each level revealed its own subtleties, and the whole process reminded Melissa of a pointillist painting. Viewed close-up, all these numbers stood alone like so many unrelated dots, but when she stepped back, a coherent scene appeared.

Tom flipped over a card with a one inscribed in a white circle. A gold coin with a five-pointed star floated above a garden walkway leading to a tower. "The sixty-ninth card of the deck is the Ace of Pentacles," he said. "The suit of pentacles corresponds to the earth signs. It deals with practical matters, like money and other resources. Some people call it the 'manifest your destiny' suit. On the Rider-Waite version of this card you can actually see that Hand of God coming out of the clouds."

Tom turned over another card whose bottom scroll read *1—The Magician—1.* A bearded man in a red cloak wore a deer head and antlers as a crown. Above his right hand floated a glowing infinity sign, and on the table in front of him lay a pentacle, goblet, wand and sword.

"See this?" Tom asked. "For the one-hundred-sixty-nine, we've got the Ace of Pentacles projected through the Magician. The Magician has all four suits on his table."

"He looks like a nice guy."

"And a powerful one," Tom said. "With that one-sixty-nine, Schizandra would love to come in here and *master* the art of manifesting. It's not about putting your nose to the grindstone the old fashioned way. It means, 'You're a divine being, part of the energy field. When you need to do something, resources just appear!' Lots of travel and lots of moving around for this kid."

Melissa smiled and he added, "The sixty-ninth card is the first one that reduces to a fifteen. It used to represent the Garden—as in the Garden of Eden. The Medieval Church bastardized some of the Tarot symbolism—*especially* the fifteen, which they turned into the Devil. The fifteen had previously meant living on Earth and enjoying the journey. God created the physical body and material realm to be relished, not suppressed. *A pure Garden of Delight.*"

Tom started to flip over a card then changed his mind. "I'm not even going to dignify this one with a viewing," he said. "*Labeling the Garden as the Devil.* Arggh! It just robs that whole intention! Look at the Ace of Pentacles." He pointed to the card with the gold coin. "See that Garden? As a species, we've forgotten how to recognize the Garden."

Melissa nodded and said, "So, the sixty-nine's a good thing?"

"Yes," he said, "it's an extremely good thing. But," Tom's face clouded, "when the sixty-nine expresses through the one, as in one-hundred-sixty-nine, it reduces to that Tower card: number sixteen."

He shook his head slowly then added, "That one-sixty-nine brings fantastic fun and love and beauty, but most people will take a huge knock on the head before they can fully manifest their Garden."

Chapter Twenty-One

(Nestor's story with interpretive dance by Sephora)

ONCE UPON A TIME, A magnificent king had a baby girl. He named her Dorinda, and he loved her very much. His wife fell asleep giving birth, so he knew he would have no more heirs. He also knew that in order for his daughter to reign as queen, she needed to prove herself worthy and capable of the task.

Therefore, even though it broke his heart to do so, he ordered his servant, "Take the child to Marketplace and leave her wrapped in a piece of linen embroidered with her name."

The king kissed his daughter and whispered in her ear, "As rain and snow come down from heaven, and return not without watering the earth and making it bud and bloom, *return*, my beloved. Return to me."

At Marketplace, a thin man and his dowdy wife kidnapped the child. At first, they thought she was an ordinary babe from a wealthy home. They planned to extort a ransom. Until they read her name. Instantly, they realized she belonged to the king, and they grew afraid. They knew they could not demand a ransom, and yet they feared the king would destroy them if they returned the child. Instead, they moved to a distant land, believing the king would never find them there. When they saw that the princess held no value, they despised her.

Dorinda grew, and her royalty showed. If the couple needed food, she covered the table with delights. If they complained of cold, the sun surrounded them. The child knew nothing of their hatred. She sang with the birds and swam with the fish. Frogs talked to her, and butterflies nested in her hair. The more love she felt, the more magical things occurred. And the more magic and beauty the child expressed, the more uncomfortable her "parents" became.

"Pascal," said her stepmother, pointing to a bouquet of daisies Dorinda had made from air, "the child's a witch!"

The short man shook his head and spat, "She's sick, Aradia. Mentally disturbed. And she's starting to infect you, too. I see no flowers. There *are* no flowers."

"I tell you she's a witch," said Aradia.

"She must be stopped."

One day, Aradia and Pascal drugged the princess and used vines to tie her to a tree. They left her overnight to be eaten by a bear. In the morning, Dorinda lazily awoke in the sunshine of her own soft bed. "Mother," she cried, "I had the most wonderful dream! I was sitting under a tree, and a giant bear kissed my hands and feet. At first, I thought he might devour me, but he just nibbled the leafy vines. After he ate, he grunted 'princess' and bowed his head."

"A bear, you say?" Aradia eyed the girl.

"Yes, Mother, the biggest bear I ever did see!"

"And the bear said, 'princess?'" Aradia's eyes grew fearful, and she fingered the cross around her neck. "This bear you dreamt, did it say anything else?"

"Oh, no, but then I had another dream, and in this dream I *was* a princess! I wore fine linen like a queen, and my cloak, it said 'Dorinda.'"

"As if *you* could ever be a queen!" said Pascal. "Who would ever follow *you*?"

"Animals follow me."

"A crazy dreamer who thinks she talks to beasts! You're lucky we don't tell the authorities on you or they'd lock you up for lying! Such tales!" Pascal shook his head.

Dorinda began to cry.

"You best forget those dreams," said her stepmother. "There's nothing good whatever came from dreams or magic. Devil's work, they are. As the Good Book says, 'Let no one be found among you who practices divination or sorcery, interprets omens, engages in witchcraft, or casts spells.' Dorinda, you play with fire."

When the child ran outside, Aradia and Pascal huddled in a corner and began to plot.

"We obviously can't leave her in nature. Nature loves her as much as she loves it," said Pascal.

"We could drown her."

"With what, a stone?" Pascal snorted and wiped his nose on a checkered hanky. "With our luck, the stone would help her float. This calls for something more than nature. We need something *super* natural. We must put her in a tower."

"What kind of tower?"

"An ivory tower—one too slippery and perilous to climb."

"Of course! An ivory tower!" Aradia cackled for twenty seconds. Then she looked puzzled. "Where will we find an ivory tower? We live in No Man's Land."

"She'll make one for herself." Pascal rubbed his palms together. "Leave everything to me. I know what to do."

Pascal approached the princess. "Dorinda, dear, you show such an aptitude for heights. I declare, your mind reaches higher than even the birds can fly."

"Really, Father? Do you really think so?" asked the girl.

"Absolutely. You have the highest mind I've ever seen in a child your age. That mind belongs in a higher place than No Man's Land."

"But I like it here."

"Nonsense, you just think you like it. Your mind needs height. If you sit here playing among the beasts and trees, you'll surely shrivel up and die."

"I will?" Her eyes went wide. "But trees grow tall. Why can't I just climb a tree? I like the animals and trees."

"I know you do, sweetheart." Pascal choked on a word he'd never used before, and then continued, "Trees are unpredictable. If you climb a tree you will fall, and I can't bear to see you rot among the roots."

"I won't fall. I climb trees all the time!"

For a moment, Pascal was stumped, but not for long: "You're wasting your talent. You need something loftier than a *tree*."

Dorinda smiled. "You really think I can go that high?"

"Of course you can, but it's a blessing and a curse. If you stay at this altitude, you will die a long and painful death. I myself once climbed to lofty heights and if I hadn't needed to care for you, I would have stayed on high," he lied. "I've slowly suffocated here for fifteen years. Don't tell me I've sacrificed for nothing."

Dorinda crinkled her brows and felt her chest constrict. It seemed difficult to breathe. Maybe he was right! "But what about my friends—the animals and trees?" Her heart imploded and she felt close to tears.

"Oh, honey, I know it's hard for you, but you're just not one of them. They're not your equals, not even the birds. If only you could find a tower. A tower is the proper place for you." He shook his head sadly, and said, "Only in a tower can you look down on birds. You think *singing* like them is fun. In a tower, you would have a bird's eye view of the bird's eye view! What could be better than studying what they see from a higher vantage point?"

Dorinda felt quite low indeed, like she was sinking into an ever deeper and darker pit. "Oh, Father, I feel so wretched now."

"That's life," said Pascal.

"I cannot stand such misery!"

"Your only hope is to find a tower that will let you in without great cost. Since you have nothing to offer, I will supply the coins." Pascal handed Dorinda a small leather pouch.

She looked inside. "*Gold?* You always told me we were poor."

"And so we are," said Pascal, "so we are. Now, go. Find a tower! It's your only hope."

Dorinda ran into the woods and prayed as her mother had taught her: "Jesus, I need a tower. I need a tower right now. Please, I need to leave this misery behind."

Dorinda prayed and prayed, but nothing like a tower appeared. Instead, she stumbled into a giant oak. She landed where its trunk split into two huge halves of tree. She looked up and desperately felt like climbing. She touched the solid bark in her hands and heard the hum of nature. As the tree cradled Dorinda's back, her stepfather's voice screamed inside her head, "Trees are unpredictable. If you climb a tree you will surely fall, and I can't bear to see you rot among the roots."

She forced herself to stand. The day grew dark, and still no tower appeared. Dorinda's doubts grew like weeds suffocating wheat. In the past, whenever she had needed anything, it had magically arrived. Maybe she no longer belonged in No Man's Land, just as Father claimed. Her chest felt tight, and she could barely breathe. Still, no tower, and things seemed to be getting worse. *A bear could eat her in the dark.*

Panicking, the princess gathered all her deepest, darkest fears—potent tales her parents had shared of misery, poverty and ghouls, of those who had chosen to follow what they loved and consequently vanished, no longer existing in this world! She combined the force of all such fears, rumbled it up her gut and extracted from her mouth a mass of lead. For a moment, she held the heavy ball. Then she hurled it as far as she could. A metallic taste remained, but Dorinda thought she felt better already.

She noticed something tall and white gleaming from the darkness where she had thrown the ball of fear. "A tower!" the princess sobbed with relief. "Oh, thank you, thank you, thank you!" she cried, tears streaming down her face.

"Stop that rain!" yelled a tiny voice below.

Dorinda, looked down at the foot of the tower. A little man, no higher than her knees, wearing a hat equally large and pointy to give the illusion of height, glared up at her. "Just what do you think you're doing here? This tower's not for you."

"Oh, but it *is*!" said the princess, speaking fast in her excitement. "I want to live in the highest tower in the land, and I asked and I prayed and I wanted it ever so badly, and now here it is—an ivory tower."

"Ivory towers are not for the likes of you," said the dwarf.

"Father said you would not find me worthy."

"Did he? And what, pray tell, does your *father* know of towers?" asked the little man in green.

"He lived in a tower once himself and knows that I belong there, too."

"Lies!" yelled the dwarf, in his squeaky voice.

Dorinda got down on her knees and folded her hands together. "Please, sir," she begged, "I must live inside this tower. If I don't, then I will surely die."

"Lies! All lies!" The dwarf shook his tiny fist, but seeing her determination, he said, "There is an entrance fee, which I will wai—"

"Father said you would require coins," she interrupted. Dorinda gave him her stepfather's bag of gold. The dwarf threw the bag on the ground, scattering its change.

"You cannot enter the tower without my word," he continued, "and once you're in, you will find it very difficult to leave. Are you sure you wish to go?"

"Of course," the princess smiled, "but don't you want the gold?"

"No," said the dwarf, "you have sacrificed enough."

Only then did Dorinda notice that the tower had no door. The dwarf waited while she considered the ramifications.

"Are you certain?" he asked.

Dorinda nodded.

From a miniature pocket, the dwarf removed a miniature proclamation. He blew a miniature horn, untied a miniature ribbon and in his tiny voice, he said, *"Accept!"*

Instantly, the princess found herself ensconced in the ivory tower. The room perched so high that the giant oak seemed like a broken twig, and birds flew far below. She saw the birds, just as Father said she would, but she could no longer hear their song.

"Wait!" she yelled to the dwarf below. He was a grain of sand, but she needed help. She had made a terrible mistake. "Wait! Don't go! Don't leave me here! I miss the birds. I want to sing!"

"You'll have plenty to watch and study," Pascal's voice bellowed inside her head. "Appreciate the opportunity, you ingrate. Without my guidance and gold, you'd be rotting at the roots."

"I love the roots!" she cried, trying to drown his voice with tears. "And the birds! I want to sing with the birds."

"You will never sing, at least not like a bird," sneered the voice inside her head. "The best you can hope for is a bird's eye view. Now *look!"*

Dorinda felt herself being pulled back to the window, closer and closer to the window, closer now, closer, looking at the birds below ... "Ha!" The sneering voice became a scream as the princess flung herself over the edge. She fell a thousand, thousand feet, and the wind ripped her dress and froze her eyes.

Dorinda lost consciousness before she hit the ground, so she did not know that an owl had caught her in its talons and eased her fall. Two elk flanked her sides and kept her warm, as she slept and slept. When the princess awoke, she could not see. Everything looked dark except a blinding light within her heart.

"Help!" she screamed. "I'm lost and I can't see! Please, somebody, help!"

No one answered, but the huge elk snuggled closer. She heard a distant sigh like "princess." Remembering the bear from her dream, she drifted off to sleep against the furry chests. When she awoke again, Dorinda felt refreshed. She opened her eyes to darkness, but this time she was less afraid. A small bird warbled on her finger. "Seewithart," he chirped, and as Dorinda sang with him, she recognized the words: "See with heart!" She smiled, and her bright heart opened wide.

Each day, more birds surrounded the princess, until soon the entire forest sang her song. Accompanied by nature's hum, Dorinda's words addressed each passerby. A woman stopped to marvel at the harmony, and the princess burst into a song made just for her. "You see so clearly," said the mother-to-be, feeling a life that surged within. "My child thanks you for your gift to us."

An old man with a sore leg collapsed nearby, wondering if he could make it home. As he lay on the forest floor, his sore leg began to tap, tap, tap, and before he could wonder why or how, he had danced the whole way home.

Word spread of the Singing Woman in the Woods. Some called her a Goddess, others a gift of God. Some said she was a bird herself, or a princess from a faraway land. A few called her Siren—a dangerous witch coaxing thousands to their doom. Most came to hear her song and learn to hum through life, but a few journeyed there to curse and scorn. Among those few, Dorinda's stepmother marched strong, determined to stomp out evil one footstep at a time. And so it came to pass that Pascal and Aradia learned of the princess' return.

Back in their cottage, Pascal yelled, "Aradia, calm down! You did *not* hear Dorinda singing fortunes in the woods."

"But, Pascal, I did! She couldn't see me because she's blind, but she sees ... other things. I think she knows I came."

"Nonsense!" He snorted into his checkered hanky. "She's blind, you say? We'll have to guide her back inside her tower."

"You and your stupid ivory tower," said Aradia. "She won't go back there. *Of that* I'm certain."

"Then we'll have to put her somewhere else," said Pascal, running gnarled fingers through a sparse goatee.

"She's a wretched blasphemer, that's for sure, but she's not bothering us in the woods. Maybe we can leave her there."

"Woman, are you mad? What happens when she remembers where she came from? Already I hear talk of a 'princess' in the woods. If she returns to the kingdom and claims her birthright, then you and I are ruined."

"Perhaps the king will forgive our transgression."

"Let's say he does *forgive,* as you say, our original transgression," said Pascal. "What about tying her to the tree that night? Convincing her to lock herself inside a tower? Making her so miserable she threw herself beyond the edge? You think your king will forgive all *that*?"

Aradia froze.

"Just leave everything to me," said Pascal. "I know what to do."

Late one afternoon, Pascal and Aradia walked into the woods. Pascal carried a shovel, and Aradia held her Bible and a giant sock. They slunk around the back of a crowd that had gathered near the singing princess. Women's eyes glistened with tears of joy, and strangers embraced and blessed each other.

"Charlatan!" muttered Pascal to Aradia.

"Shhh!" said Aradia, hoping to avoid a confrontation.

"I will not be quiet," said Pascal. "Look at her, giving the sick false hopes. Goldbricking like Cassandra in the woods. I bet she's not even really blind. It's part of her show to make people feel sorry for her and give her gold."

Aradia said nothing.

"It's disgusting," said Pascal, "the way she twits with lowly birds. I'm ashamed I ever fed her at my table."

"Father!" sang Dorinda. "Is that you? Father, I recognize your tone. Why don't you speak loud enough for me to hear your words?"

"I have nothing to say to her," said Pascal through gritted teeth. Anger turned his clenched jaws white. His cheeks burned red as the audience stared. He took out his checkered hanky and blew his nose.

Aradia said, "Pascal won't talk to you, Dorinda. He says you are a charlatan. You fool these people, but you don't fool him. He says you don't know how to sing, and you certainly don't know how to heal, so if you're taking gold from these victims, well, he hopes you meet punishment. You're a charlatan and a fraud, he says."

"And you, Mother, who do you say that I am?"

Aradia mumbled something incomprehensible.

"I don't understand," sang the princess in a clear, melodic line.

Aradia finally answered in crescendo, "I won't call you a charlatan, no, not exactly a charlatan. Who am I to understand or judge the things you do? I don't believe you are *entirely* evil. The Good Book says 'beware false prophets.'" She opened her Bible and read, "'Then you will stand outside knocking and pleading, *Lord, open the door for us!* But he will reply, *I do not know you.* You will say, *But we ate and drank with you, and you taught in our streets.* And he will reply, *I tell you, I don't know you …* '"

"Mother, is this who you say that I am?" asked the princess, her voice beginning to crack with shame.

The crowd scattered as the music stopped. This was a family matter, no concern of theirs.

Aradia said nothing, but Pascal continued murmuring to his wife. "Don't let her scare you. There's no such thing as witchcraft and there's certainly no value in your so-called faith. You drag that book and cross around as though they'll protect you from the likes of her. You don't need to protect yourself from her. She's not a monster: she's a fraud. A tricky girl with an OK voice who couldn't hack it in the ivory tower. How she gets all these suckers to pay for concerts, I'll never know. What's more, I'll never care. Now, get over here, Aradia. I need your help."

Dorinda sat at the base of the oak tree sobbing louder than the noise of any excavation taking place in front of her. Pascal wiped sweat from his brow and continued digging. "Aradia? Now!"

The princess looked up, and Aradia stuffed the giant sock inside Dorinda's mouth. Then Pascal knocked the princess with his shovel. Together they pushed her inside a shallow grave. They covered her quickly, leaving her to rot among the roots.

The magnificent king owned a crystal ball and when he saw what Aradia and Pascal had done, he said, "Enough is enough!" He ordered his servants to call all worthy knights, but no one answered the call. The king continued to send his messengers, hoping that one day someone would choose to accept the quest.

Two hundred thirty-two years passed by, and the king's grey beard caressed the floor. Then one day, a young man flew in on a horse named Bliss. The horse's wings made her difficult to control, but the knight had spent years learning to ride with Bliss and he would fly no other way. He asked to see the king, and the king granted his request.

"What brings you here, my son?"

"Bliss, my Lord. It seems I'm always following my Bliss." The handsome knight stroked his white-winged horse and smiled.

"You know not the reason you're here?" the king said.

"I certainly have enjoyed the journey," the knight said. He shrugged his armor and grinned.

"Well, it's enough to enjoy the journey," laughed the king. "Tell me your name, my son."

"They call me Sean of the Smiling Eyes, Your Majesty."

"And smiling heart, I'll wager too, riding along on Bliss."

"Ay, my Lord," Sean said, "I can't complain of the adventures."

"I want you to find a buried treasure," said the king.

"My Lord and Master, I am at your service."

The king told Sean where to find the prize: at the base of a huge oak in a copse of No Man's Land. He instructed the knight not to dig for the vessel himself. Patience would be required. According to the king, a precious jewel would eventually unearth itself. Then Sean of the Smiling Eyes would carry fortune home with Bliss.

The knight journeyed hard and he journeyed well, following always the lovely Bliss. At a giant, two-trunked oak in No Man's Land, the white-winged horse refused to move. Sean dismounted and let the ancient tree support his spine while he waited, contemplating roots.

Underneath that same two-trunked oak, Dorinda awoke with a sock in her mouth and mud in her hair. She lay covered in dirt, unable to move. Used to blindness, she remained calm in the dark, but her nostrils flared. Together they tried to extract one precious element from the soil.

Buried under seven inches of dirt, Dorinda *imagined* what she would do with air. To pass the time, she made a game of it. Breathe in through the right nostril. Pause. Breathe out through the left. Pause again. Breathe in through the left. Pause. Breathe out through the right. Pause. Feeling the space between imaginary breaths, she imagined oxygen going in and out and in, and her mind grew very still.

She felt the breath move from the base of her spine to the top of her head. Inhaling up, up, up to the brain. Exhaling down, down, down to the root. Up, up, up to the brain, now going down, down, and resting at the base. With her mind's eye, she traced a ball of light moving up and down her spine.

Above the grave, it began to rain. Sean of the Smiling Eyes danced to keep himself awake and warm. Underneath the earth, a drop of water found its way between Dorinda's eyebrows. She felt it cool and magnetic between her eyes, pulling her mind inside her brain. It was quiet there, like a glassy pool, and Dorinda hardly moved at all. Suddenly, a thousand white wings lifted from the pool. Through softened earth, the supine princess raised herself to sitting. The sock flew from her mouth like a flock of doves.

Young Dorinda opened her eyes and *saw*.

She climbed out of the dirt and dusted off her dress then straddled Bliss with Sean of the Smiling Eyes. Together they rode home. When Dorinda met her real Father, they leapt for joy. The king showed everyone how and why—even at his ripe old age—he remained the Lord of the Dance. Princess Dorinda became the Queen of Song. She married Sean of the Smiling Eyes, and they lived joyfully ever after in a kingdom decidedly *not* of this world.

As for Aradia and Pascal, they grew old and weary. Every night Pascal hunched over his bag of gold and watched a single coin evaporate before his eyes. Grasp and scream and pound though he might, Pascal was powerless to stop his gold from disappearing. One bitter night as the final coin faded away, Pascal died, clutching an empty sack.

Aradia fared somewhat better. When she realized that his money offered no security, she stopped listening to Pascal. Eventually, she left No Man's Land and wandered on her own for forty years. She tried to accept the things she had done and those she had left undone. Whenever she heard a bird, she remembered Dorinda singing fortunes in the woods.

Aradia read her Bible and prayed for deliverance: "Seek and ye shall find; knock and it shall be opened to you." One day, she found the narrow path and approached the gate. People call it a pearly gate, but when someone knocks, the gate becomes a mirror. When Aradia knocked and looked into the mirror, she screamed! Steeling her heart, she marched all the way back to No Man's Land, terrified of the beauty within.

Chapter Twenty-Two

TOM POINTED TO TWO SPOTS on the natal wheel. "Schizandra's north node sits in the ninth house. Her south node sits in the third house. I've seen many people with third house south nodes who stay in the same neighborhood where they were born and grew up." Tom eyed Melissa over the rims of his glasses. "In order for this process to work, Schizandra needs to get into the ninth house, which means travelling all over the place."

"Well," Melissa said, "she got ripped out of Chicago when her father died. Does that count?"

"Oh, yes," he said, "that counts!" He paused and adjusted his reading glasses. "Just out of curiosity, when did her father die?"

"December twenty-first."

Tom closed his eyes. "Winter solstice: the darkest night of the year. Was it just this past December?" he asked. "Y2K?"

Melissa nodded. "I guess her Dark Night of the Soul began on a truly dark night."

"Evolved souls do that," he said, "lots of patterns. But what I notice goes beyond the Dark Night of the Soul. *December 21, 2000. Exactly twelve years—to the day—before Earth hits the Galactic Equator.* Twelve signs of the zodiac, twelve disciples ... twelve's a very potent number."

Melissa smiled, wondering if Tom could possibly answer the big question: "So what do you make of *this?*" she asked. "Apparently, Schizandra can't leave Sedona. Two helicopters crashed trying to take her out of town."

Tom shook his head. "Remember I told you she didn't leave herself an out?"

Melissa nodded.

"Well, she can't leave now because she needs to complete this process. They say one year in Sedona equals ten anywhere else, so it's one of the fastest places to 'git her done.' Once she does, she can go all over the world. With her moon in that ninth house, she'll find a lot of joy in travelling. And not just little trips: this soul has a global path."

Melissa was just about to wonder how she would pay for all these trips when Tom said, "Once Schizandra finishes her initiation, she'll have the *Hand of God* reaching out of the clouds to give her whatever resources she needs. Not just dollars and cents: resources can be energies and abilities and anything else. 'Wanna go over there?' *Hey, here's a portal!* Schizandra's the only thing that can keep her from teleporting."

Melissa wrinkled her brow. "Teleporting?"

"Sure," he said, "haven't you ever gone somewhere in your mind?"

"Yes," she said, "but you don't just—"

Tom's eyes twinkled as he watched Melissa.

Schizandra still looked paralyzed, but her mind began to move. Listening to the fairy tale, she recognized parts of her own story. Dorinda's journey offered hope in a world where parents could leave daughters orphaned in strange lands. Maybe she was like Dorinda. Maybe she just needed to open her eyes and see a world of joy and song. Watching Sephora's dancing helped. Schizandra noticed that shifting her gaze could change her thoughts. If she started tunneling into despair, the motion of her eyes helped her brain switch tracks.

Here with Nestor, Sephora and the queen, Schizandra began to witness her childhood as passing scenery. She didn't have to derail in order to view events; the faster she moved the more she saw. And she didn't need to stick with trains. If she wanted, she could ride through life like Sean of the Smiling Eyes—following her Bliss. She could become the Queen of Song, or dance like the Magnificent King!

No one had told her fairy tales since her father got his cancer. As she listened now, Schizandra realized she missed the stories as much as she missed her dad. When he'd stopped telling them, parts of her died, too. She learned to call those parts "silly," "stupid" and "emotional." Without ceremony, she had buried them in unmarked graves.

Until Dorinda rose from the ground, Schizandra never knew she could revive her soul. Nestor's story kissed her like the prince in Sleeping Beauty.

"Does Schizandra like to dance?" Tom asked.

"I don't know," Melissa said. "Why?"

"Oh, just another cool thing."

He pointed to a triangle of numbers on his graph paper and described how he came up with them. His finger moved so fast that it left trails of light before finally resting on the triangle.

"This calculation represents the energy that can set the soul free while it still remains in the body."

Perhaps from all her years of yoga, Melissa understood. People normally needed to die in order to free their souls, but this special process would allow liberation *within* the body. Death was not required.

"The peak of this pyramid symbolizes that release: *the narrow way*," Tom said. "The soul gets released into the cosmos, has its peak experiences, returns to the pyramid and goes down and gets grounded in the base of the pyramid, back in the body. Schizandra has a thirty there." He flipped over a card and said, "The dance."

Melissa examined the card: on a wooden stage, a man wearing a white shirt and red tights danced with a beautiful woman in green. She pointed her toe as he held up her arm as if to twirl her, but all their feet touched the ground. Green hills rolled in the background, and a floral garland hung from the bottom of the stage. At the center of the garland a white circle enclosed the number four.

"When we run through the Major Arcana and dip into the Minor Arcana, the Four of Wands corresponds to the thirtieth card of the deck," he said.

Pointing to another equation, Tom's finger performed its magic again before flipping over another card. "When we take Schizandra's date of birth, crack it open and pour out the Essence, we get ... "

The same man from the Four of Wands: this time, he hung upside down from a branch connecting two trees. His legs formed a four as they wrapped themselves around the branch. The bottom of the card read *12—The Hanged Man—12*.

Melissa gnawed her lip, but Tom said, "I'd rather call this card the Mystic: someone who has perspectives not of this world. Way not mainstream. We're talking about a *highly* intuitive person." He explained that the Hanged Man/Mystic symbolized Schizandra's extraordinary gifts of intuition and psychic healing. Such gifts went far beyond the skills of others. Even Tom's.

He tapped the equation. "At her Core Essence, Schizandra holds insight so deep that nothing exists beyond that knowledge. She's the still point between the physical and mystical worlds." He looked at Melissa. "*But such wisdom always requires a sacrifice.*"

Frauke sobbed as Sephora bowed.

"Brilliant!" thumped Nestor. "Well done, my bird! Sephora, your movements have perfectly captured the tale. Why, the Atlantean Ballet had nothing on you!"

The hummingbird bowed again and warbled softly, "I saw Schizandra tapping her feetz like the man whose legs a'tapped him home!"

Indeed, Nestor's tale had performed its magic, rousing the catatonic girl. Schizandra yawned and stretched her arms over her head before wrapping them around her knees. She smiled at Sephora. "You were very good," she said, "but, Frauke, why so sad?"

The queen grew feisty. "Oh," she cried, "my heart just broke for that poor, poor girl with those wretched stepparents. Awful, just awful! Sephora, can you even imagine such a thing?" She turned to Schizandra and asked, "Is that what surface families are like? Wretched! Nestor, thank you for sharing such a story. Now I know why we don't tolerate such narrow minded, greedy ignoramuses. Thank Goddess we don't have any of those in Mu!"

"And what did you think, Schizandra?" asked the rabbit.

"Well," she said quietly, still growing used to her voice. It sounded lower and more resonant than she remembered. "I heard the story a little different."

"How so?" asked Nestor.

"Well, it seems to me that *everyone* was beautiful."

"Not Pascal!" said the queen. "You'd have to have some kind of father complex not to see *that*! He was bad."

"That's what *he* thought." Schizandra said. "He felt guilty, and so he acted worse. He lived down to his expectations. And Aradia wasn't too sure of herself either. All that judgment, doom and gloom." She paused. "But that *mirror*."

"Yes, the mirror!" thumped Nestor. "What about the mirror?"

"When Aradia looked into it, she saw ... *beauty within* ... "

No one said anything, so the girl continued, "She saw beauty, and it terrified her."

"Why would beauty terrify her?" asked Frauke. "When I look in the mirror, I always like to look pretty." She patted her hair and winked at Sephora.

"Of course," said Schizandra, "and you're lovely. I'm sure every time you look in a mirror, you rediscover that." She smiled fondly at the queen, "But in the story it's not a normal mirror."

"'Za gate!" Sephora chirped and reenacted her dramatic knock.

"That's right," the girl said, "*people call it a pearly gate, but when someone knocks, the gate becomes a mirror.* Don't they call heaven 'the pearly gates?'" she asked.

"Beats me," Frauke said, "we just have the Gates of Mu."

"And what are those?"

"Um," Frauke looked up and around, studiously avoiding eye contact. "I never really thought of it?"

"What if the Gates of Mu lead to the eternal dancing kingdom? Maybe they open when we believe they *can*!"

Frauke stuck out her chin for a moment, considering this, and then put her hand into her pocket. She removed a yellow pod. "Cacao anyone?" She cut a piece with her tiny sword, but everyone else passed. "I suppose we should get going now. When my heart feels big, it's so much easier to see the king."

Nestor hopped alongside Frauke and Schizandra, as the hummingbird fluttered around all three of them.

"We'll go as far as Cat's Alley with you," the rabbit said, "and then Sephora and I will take our leave."

The name nudged Schizandra into another distant memory. *Walking through mosaic streets of the biggest city in Atlantis. Teal and turquoise. Smelling the sea air and feeling sunshine on her face. Sensing she should watch her words as she approached an alley full of cats behind the restaurants.*

Knowing that those who craved more power employed their spies, sometimes in the form of telepathic strays.

Despite so many artists and healers from Mu working to save the island, some key people in Atlantis had said "absolutely not" to change.

"What's Cat's Alley?" Schizandra asked.

"'Za very scary place," Sephora twittered, "with cats 'n' fangs!"

"Oh, sweetness," the queen lightly poked the hummingbird's breast, "so timid! I'm certain the cats would never eat *my* bird." She turned to Schizandra. "Even Lemurians fear Cat's Alley, but I like it there. It's by our compost piles. Cats from everywhere come there to scavenge. Even cats from *Kay Pacha*."

Schizandra raised her eyebrows in a question.

"You know, where *you* come from," the queen said, pointing up. "*Sedona, Chicago, Egypt, the British Isles*: Kay Pacha!"

"How do they get down here?"

Frauke and Sephora paused to laugh, while Nestor thumped her foot.

"What's so funny?"

Frauke tried to insert words between her giggles. "They—bilocate— silly. Everyone knows—that." She and Nestor started moving again as Sephora sprinkled the air with warbled laughter.

"Not everyone from Kay Pacha, or whatever you call our world," Schizandra said, hurrying to catch up. "Cats are pets."

The three continued their shared amusement as they journeyed. "I don't see what's so funny. Cats can't bilocate." Schizandra crossed her arms. "That only happens on *Star Trek*, or like, those *Highlander* videos my babysitter let me watch before Daddy fired her. People feed cats, and cats take naps. Sometimes they chase birds… "

Sephora stopped laughing.

Wiping a gleeful tear from her eye, the queen said, "Oh, darling, now don't get upset with us. It's funny because *you* bilocated here, like the biggest cat of all! Where do you think all the kitties go when they fall asleep?"

"But their bodies stay," said Schizandra.

"And so did yours, silly!"

"But—"

A cat hissed as Sephora and Nestor took flight. The little bird fluttered high, but Nestor hopped into the air and disappeared.

"Nestor's more advanced," Frauke said, then opened her hands, palms forward: "Welcome to Cat's Alley." She turned to the dozen felines at her feet. "Hellllo, darlings!" The queen smiled as five cats rubbed against her cloak. One jumped on her head, licking her face with its rough tongue. "Stick close to me," she whispered to Schizandra. "They're not always this friendly, especially to strangers."

"When the Hanged Man steps down, nothing will ever look the same again," Tom said. "After a period of suspension, the old paradigms just fall away."

"What's all this got to do with Schizandra dancing?" Melissa asked.

"Ah," he said, "it comes back to that thirty card." Instead of returning to the Four of Wands, though, Tom turned over another card. A pregnant woman in full crown and regalia sat in front of a spinning wheel. Above her head, hung a red heart inscribed with the female sign. The bottom of the card read 3—*The Empress*—3.

The Empress card meant abundance and other feminine, creative things. Melissa got that, but Tom lost her as he explained, "Thirty is the zero expressing itself through the three." She did manage to catch something about the thirty's emphasis on *spiritual* communication. Tom pointed to his graph paper and a bunch of cards. From what she could glean, they all had something to do with threes.

A synapse connected, and Melissa understood: the numbers of those cards each added up to three! She nodded as Tom pointed back to his graph paper and the Hanged Man card.

"Three is also the twelve, the Hanged Man, which she has here as her Core Essence," Tom said.

Right, thought Melissa, *Schizandra's an extraordinary psychic healer.*

Tom continued, "The next three is the twenty-one, represented by the World."

He flipped over another card, showing a floral wreath with a woman dancing inside its oval. In a white toga, she moved across a starry indigo sky. The bottom scroll read *21—The World—21.*

"The energy of the Star Dancer!" Tom said. "And this brings us to the fourth three, the thirty, which happens to be represented by the Four of Wands."

Tom launched into an explanation of what he called "the dance of life." It was esoteric, but Melissa thought she understood. The World card showed someone dancing in the cosmos, reveling in all sorts of starry wisdom, maybe even leaving the body to do so. Melissa imagined a hyper version of Gabriel Roth's trance dance where the mind became all-knowing Bliss. Schizandra could learn to embody this cosmic dance. Instead of dropping into a coma or trance, she would access all that energy in her waking life. The process would free her and help her heal the world.

"She could find herself becoming a very talented dancer," Tom said. "That would be good for her, because all her intense Scorpio stuff is fifth house. Traditionally, five *was* the dancer—flexible, adaptable, expressive. In one of the very old Celtic decks, the fifth card was the nymph—a sprightly wood nymph—a young female dancing naked in the forest glade. The Medieval Church replaced it with this one."

Tom turned over a card with a stern looking man dressed as a bishop or the pope. Two boys sat praying at his feet. The scroll read *5—The Hierophant—5.*

Melissa laughed. "What was the *Medieval Church* doing in the Tarot?"

"Good question," he said. "If you knew anything about Church History, though, you wouldn't find it so surprising. 'Money is the root of all evil: *wanna buy an Indulgence?*'" Tom raised his eyebrows and grinned. "*Repression!*"

Melissa laughed. "I forgot about that. Maybe if they made more things wrong, then sales went up!"

Her face turned serious. "Guilt and shame aside, though, Tom, I've met some amazing believers. As a midwife, I've always disliked the expression, 'don't throw out the baby with the bathwater,' but at times like these, I agree."

<hr />

Hundreds of cats dug through food scraps. The caterwauling was intense. Meows, screeches, howls, hisses. Catcalls played like an audience before a late-night concert. Tails flicked and wriggled in anticipation as enemies postured and old friends rubbed whiskers. Frauke seemed to thrive amidst the noise. Tabbies, kittens, old and sly ones, orange cats, black cats, gray ones, striped and brown ones, toms digging through banana peels and Romaine stumps.

"I thought cats liked meat," Schizandra shouted, "but you eat only fruits and veggies—"

"And cacao!" said the queen with a mischievous smile. "One must never forget cacao." She shook her cloak, discarding peels onto the compost pile.

"But *why* are they so interested in your leftovers? Why bilocate for scraps? Cats don't eat chocolate."

"They do here, don't you darlings?" Frauke picked up a short-haired Persian. She stroked her and said, "Helllllo, Audrey. How was your trip to the Pleeeeee-a-deeeeees?" Audrey meowed and the queen replied, "Ohhhh, I seeeeee." Frauke scratched Audrey's neck as the dainty feline purred. "Loveleeeee."

Cats continued to surround and rub themselves against the queen. "Audrey, darling, why don't you tell Schizandra why you come here?" Audrey pressed her cheek against the queen's, scenting her with the glands behind her whiskers. "Ohhhhhh, sweetness!" laughed Frauke, "*Beeeeesides* meeeee!"

Schizandra felt a tug on her consciousness and heard a quiet meow inside her brain. "Weeeeee reeeeestore ourselves with morsels from the Land of Mu. And weeeeee love our queeeeen."

Frauke glowed.

"So your food gives them their nine lives?" asked the girl.

"In a matter of speaking."

Schizandra raised her eyebrows. "Don't you mean a *manner* of speaking?"

"No, in a *matter* of speaking," said Frauke. "Words become flesh here."

"*Words?*" The girl stooped down and stroked a tabby. "Are you a word made flesh?" she asked, rubbing the cat behind its ears.

"*Some* words become flesh. Not all words, but some."

"How—"

A huge, resonant sound destroyed Schizandra's train of thought. Barreling through Cat's Alley, soothing savage beasts and twitching tails, a primordial sound obliterated space: *Aaaaaaaaaaaaaaaaaaah-ooooooooooooooooooh-mmmmmmmmmmmm.*

Everything stopped. The cats closed their eyes and posed like hieroglyphs. Nothing moved—a still point within the chaos.

A a a a a a a a a a a a a a a a a a a a h - o o o o o o o o o o o o o o o o o o h - mmmmmmmmmmmmmm. The sound rose on the *ah*, projected through the *oh* and shuddered through Schizandra with the mmm. Another pause. Her brain felt like a raindrop before it hit the earth.

She waited.

A a a a a a a a a a a a a a a a a a a a h - o o o o o o o o o o o o o o o o o o h - mmmmmmmmmmmmmm.

And then she splashed.

Chapter Twenty-Three

TOM CHUCKLED AND SHOOK HIS head. "There's one thing I haven't mentioned here yet:
one significant part of her chart that's the only standalone, oddball thing. We call it the Esoteric Life Lesson Number: only for initiates!" Tom leaned so far forward that his chair creaked. "Unless they're really on their spiritual path, people don't have a clue about this. The vast majority of humans go to their graves without ever realizing it."

Melissa leaned in, too.

"Even so, there's nothing quite so strong as this number, which sits in a very powerful part of the chart. Schizandra has a sixty-three there."

Melissa's mind tried to move with Tom like Greg Louganis. She missed the second twist but dove into the importance of the sixty-three. She swam to shore and toweled off with his allusion to the Life Lesson Number. If Melissa remembered right, that was the thirty-seven, that King of Cups card about humans evolving through the heart.

Tom had already executed this topic from several angles. She held her breath for his next performance. So many mental dives! Good thing he taped these things. It might take her a few months to swim through this reading.

"Thirty-seven added to sixty-three is one hundred," he continued. "Her Life Lesson Number and her Esoteric Life Lesson Number form a complementary pair. They complete each other."

"And that's not common?"

"It's extremely *not* common," he said. "Out of a thousand people, nobody might have the complementary pairing. Out of three thousand people no one might have it. Schizandra has it."

He flipped over another card: on a dark night, a young girl wrapped in a starry blue blanket hid her face and wept. Behind her, nine horizontal swords formed parallel bars like a prison. A small white circle enclosed the number nine. Tom explained how this dreadful Nightmare card really meant *Awakening* from the Nightmare. "Of course," he reminded her, "if you need to awaken, that means first you're going to sleep."

"Like a coma?"

Tom slowly nodded his head. "The Nine of Swords deals with shifting paradigms."

The disembodied spirit vowed revenge. No one brushed *him* off as easily as the aunts had shoved aside his follower, the cat man. If the spirit could strengthen himself, he might just find a way to jump inside a body. He needed to lower the world's vibration enough to accommodate his energy. He thrived on feelings of fear and judgment.

During the French Revolution, he surged when *"Liberté, Egalité, Fraternité"* fell into bloodbath. As heads rolled, he cheered with frenzied crowds, but that wasn't enough to bring him into body. Across the Atlantic, the newness of America offset the Reign of Terror. That hope and idealism raised Earth's energy too high for him to incarnate.

He assessed January 2001. He felt division, which he enjoyed, but if he really wanted to return, he needed more. Terror seemed like a good idea. It had almost worked in France. An undefined enemy—someone or something that could attack at anytime: he liked the way people reacted to non-stop stress. If he could get them to turn against each other, then global fears might invite him into body.

Schizandra inspired a sense of unity and love. She wouldn't just talk about these things. Her very essence generated them. Even from a coma, she brought people together. They healed themselves in order to help her heal—without knowing why they felt so called to do so. This was just the beginning. If she woke up, her influence would spread, synchronizing lives around the planet. Joy would follow, and once that happened, he could never return again.

He had a window of opportunity between 2001 and 2012. He needed something that would grab the world's attention, something to neutralize Schizandra's influence. A stronger, scarier Reign of *Global* Terror.

From what Melissa could follow, Tom had taken the sixty-three and reduced it to a nine, which led him to a card showing a hermit with a lantern. Tom liked to call the Hermit "the Adept"—someone who had already moved through all the other levels of awareness and could morph from one world into the next. He explained how Schizandra was the Adept. As an old soul, the girl needed to bring both compassion *and* detachment to her service.

"For someone with a good heart, the compassion comes easy. Detachment's the tough one to learn. Ironically, in this lifetime she needs to relinquish all the things that grew her into such a dynamic human soul. She needs to let go of all those old ways of being. She needs to become truly open to whatever Spirit wants to bring through her."

Melissa released her breath through pursed lips and asked aloud, "She's only thirteen. Why would change be so hard?"

"Ever play that game where you stand in the doorway and just push, push, push out against the doorframe?"

Melissa nodded.

"What happens when you step out?"

The midwife smiled. "We used to love that game! Your arms just fly up of their own accord."

"Right," he said, "there's something called momentum. Schizandra has thousands of years of momentum built up that she needs to turn around right now, really, really fast."

Melissa felt stupid. Of course he meant reincarnation. *How else would a thirteen-year-old have so much experience?* He went on again about Saturn and Uranus and the unique batch of kids born right after August '87. This week in 2001 would force intense energy to the surface, especially for those kids.

As Tom put it: "Saturn's very realistic, down-to-earth. In an inconjunct with Uranus, it's hard to get those energies to harmonize and go smoothly. An inconjunct presents an awkward time. You've got this down-to-earth Saturn aspect being formed with Uranus, which wants to kick out the jambs and go crazy. The result? *Chaos.* Totally unpredictable. Right now, even for other kids her age, any kind of weird stuff can happen on every level."

Chapter Twenty-Four

"HARU, WHAT'S UP?" HE JUMPED as Angie tapped his shoulder. "It's just me, silly!" Angie giggled. "Why are you standing by yourself in the middle of the hallway? We'll be late for English. Come on, I'll walk with you."

Fourth Period Bell tolled as they took their seats. Brielle turned around and motioned to Angie, who nodded. Brielle scribbled something quickly on a piece of paper, which she folded into a triangle and passed three rows back to Haru. He began to hand it off to the girl behind him when he noticed his own name on the note. No one had *ever* written him a note before! He blushed.

"Haru!" barked Mrs. Kingsley, "Would you please read us last night's poem?"

Haru scrambled to find his homework. He tucked Brielle's note inside his pocket and pulled out several sheets of paper from yesterday. Reading the handout, he realized that he had not completed any work last night. He read aloud:

"*The Pearl by Anonymous*
In the bottom of the bottom of the sea
I found an opening. I dove into
That narrow grave and found a cave of
Bubbling light.

Within the cave an oyster shell, within
The shell a pearl. The pearl too big to take
Away, and yet too beautiful by far
To leave behind.

And so, I dove inside of it, myself
Then not-myself: ten trillion particles
Of smiling sand, beneath uneasy sea.

160

> *We wait here knowingly—a womblike gleam*
> *Beyond our pearl."*

"Thank you, Haru," said Mrs. Kingsley, "well-recited. Now, who can tell us what this poem means?" She surveyed the raised hands. *"Brielle?"*

"I think it's about the spirit world," answered the straight-A cheerleader.

"Very good." Mrs. Kingsley smiled at her pony-tailed student. "Anyone else have anything to say about this poem?"

Haru felt queasy. He reached inside his pocket. The black pearl necklace had coiled itself around the note.

No raised hands, so Mrs. Kingsley continued, "What do you suppose this anonymous poet means by, *Myself then not-myself*?" More blank stares. She called upon a student fiddling with his mechanical pencil. *"Charles?"*

"Um," the boy squirmed, clicking the lead in and out.

"Go ahead and reread the poem to yourself," Mrs. Kingsley said. She waited a moment then asked again, *"Myself then not-myself. Charles?"*

"Um," said the freckled boy, "maybe it means the poet thought she knew who she was and then something happens to make her, like, disintegrate?"

"Excellent!" Mrs. Kingsley said. "Interesting that you assume the poet's female. Who else wants to comment? What can someone tell me about pearls?"

Brielle's hand shot into the air. "The natural ones are rare, and they form because of an irritation."

Haru's stomach churned. He felt cold and clammy, sweating and shaking at the same time. As the class continued discussing pearls, he pondered the frog queen's words, *You'll need these later.* He didn't know how much more strangeness he could take. By the time he started paying attention again Mrs. Kingsley had moved on to another poem.

Angie began reading:

"On the Beach at Night, by Walt Whitman

> On the beach at night,
> Stands a child with her father,
> Watching the east, the autumn sky.

> Up through the darkness,
> While ravening clouds, the burial clouds, in black masses spreading ..."

Haru suddenly saw a vision of Shazzie, watching waves with a man who must have been her father. The boy could feel Lake Michigan's cool breeze blowing against her tears. He could feel her heart even as it broke.

Angie continued reading:

"... *And nigh at hand, only a very little above,*
Swim the delicate brothers the Pleiades.

From the beach the child holding the hand of her father,
Those burial clouds that lower victorious soon to devour all,
Watching, silently weeps.

Weep not, child,
Weep not, my darling,
With these kisses let me remove your tears ..."

Haru felt an overwhelming urge to hold the girl standing on the beach at sunset. *Oh, Shazzie!* His churning stomach had risen to his chest, and now it swelled with grief. He put his elbows on the desk, covering his eyes with his hands.

In an instant, he knew the girl had just learned of her father's terminal illness: *They sat together on two jagged rocks, watching roller-blades dodge baby strollers, bicycles skid on patches of sand—where picnic area and trail lost separate identities. Mostly, though, they watched the waves, rough and ocean-like in the sunlit gusts. And they watched each other, knowing this would be their last Chicago Fall together.*

Haru's arms ached to comfort her. Sobs escaped his throat, and he heard snickers behind and to his left. Someone poked him. "Hey, Haru Be-*Gay* likes poetry."

Haru wept silently as Angie read:

"... *The ravening clouds shall not long be victorious;*

'Jupiter shall emerge—be patient—watch again another night—
the Pleiades shall emerge, They are immortal—all those stars
both silvery and golden, shall shine out again,

The great stars and the little ones shall shine out again, they
endure ..."

Haru heard more giggles and laughter around him, but he couldn't halt the flow of feelings from his heart.

"That's enough, Ari," said Mrs. Kingsley. "What's so funny?"

"Be-*Gay's* crying like a girl." Four boys burst out laughing, unable to restrain themselves.

"Stop it!" Angie said.

Ari stuck out his tongue at her. "*Stop it!*" he mimicked.

Brielle got up from her seat and glared at Ari. "Cut it out, Ari."

"*What?*" asked the coolest guy in school.

"Haru's *my* friend now, so back off," said Ari's would-be girlfriend.

"Yeah," said Angie, "mine, too."

"That's enough, Ari. Brielle, please sit down," said Mrs. Kingsley. "Haru, why don't you go to the nurse? Here's a pass. Now, Angie, let's finish up here." She narrowed her lips.

Haru could still hear Angie's sweet voice as he made his way through the classroom door: "...*Longer than sun or any revolving satellite, / Or the radiant brothers, the Pleiades.*"

Despite his concern for Shazzie, part of him rejoiced. He had friends! As he walked to Nurse Baker's, he unfolded the note Brielle had passed to him at the beginning of class. He stopped walking and stared at the note, which read, "What does *this* mean?" Underneath Brielle's bubbly cursive was a rough picture of the symbol from his dream and vision.

Haru tried to grab a locker as he crashed to the floor. Heart pounding and soaked in sweat, he watched the ceiling churn above him. As it spun, he saw a California condor—his animal totem—flying through the vortex. After a few moments, he rolled over onto his stomach and crawled like a snake to the nurse's office.

Cracks in the tile floors reminded him of yesterday's black pearl and the frog's black egg. He felt the world begin to spin again. If he could just get to Nurse Baker's, she would call his dad to pick him up. *He should be back from that Chicago conference by now. Only one more hallway, Haru. You can do this.* For once, thinking of his Navajo father brought relief instead of fear.

Chapter Twenty-Five

AAAAAAAAAAAAAAAAAAAAAH-OOOOOOOOOOOOOOOOOOH-MMMM-MMMMMMMM

The sound continued to echo through Cat's Alley.

"What's that?" Schizandra asked as she recovered herself between the blasts.

"Shhh!" said Frauke, "That's the king."

A a a a a a a a a a a a a a a a a a a a h - o o o o o o o o o o o o o o o o o o h - mmmmmmmmmmmm

The cats sat in rapt meditation as the queen urged Schizandra forward. "C'mon, we're almost there."

"It sounds like a bell or a gong," said the girl, pulling herself from another period of silence. "Are you sure that's the king?"

A a a a a a a a a a a a a a a a a a a a h - o o o o o o o o o o o o o o o o o o h - mmmmmmmmmmmmm reverberated through the tunnels as they left Cat's Alley.

Frauke nodded, hurrying past a man standing on his head.

"Why's he upside down?"

"That's an inversion," said the queen, as she pulled her by the hand.

"A *what?*"

"An inversion. People stand on their heads to give their hearts a break. Turns everything upside down so the heart doesn't need to work so hard."

"Do you do that?" Schizandra tried to twist the top of her head below her chin.

"Don't need to yet, but you can bet I will if I ever see a wrinkle or start to sag." Frauke touched her face, lifted her chest and smiled. "No need to yet, though. I've got plenty of circulation."

"Melissa does yoga."

"And who's Melissa?"

"My grandmother. She'd probably like it here."

The queen moved them so quickly through the tunnels that Schizandra wondered why the queen didn't just teleport them to the king.

"No one knows I can do that yet," said Frauke, reading her thoughts.

"But why – keep it – a secret?" Both of them breathed hard now. Frauke's cloak trailed after her, fluttering through the air. Schizandra jogged to keep up.

"Because once people know you can do something, they expect it from you. Teleportation happens fast. Sometimes I like to take my time." As silent thought, Schizandra heard Frauke add, *"Especially when it involves the king."*

The mysterious sounds stopped just as the travelers approached an elaborate bead curtain. Painted on the beads, Schizandra recognized an image from Melissa's house. Gold flecks and a bronze background highlighted a colorful vision of a tall, dark-haired man passionately kissing the woman who knelt before him. The man wore a crown of vines, and the woman had bright circles and flowers in her hair. A gold blanket wrapped itself around them, as he kissed her. The couple embraced until Frauke spread apart the beads and yanked her through.

Schizandra squinted and blinked before she stared. In front of her sat a seven centimeter purple frog with a golden crown resting on his head. To his left loomed a proportionately giant brass bowl with a wooden stick wrapped in red, white, yellow and blue felt. The bowl itself was etched with funny crosses. It rested on an orange and green silk pillow, embroidered with a beta fish.

The king reclined on the pillow, beside the giant bowl. Unlike a normal frog, his head seemed too narrow for that flabby body. He looked like Jabba the Hut. *If Jabba the Hut were three inches long, pinheaded and purple.* His tiny eyes penetrated the new arrivals.

Schizandra suddenly felt a lot more compassion for the queen. "That's your husband?" she asked telepathically, attempting to hide her shock.

The queen nodded, blushed and reached for her cacao. Still there. Good Goddess, she could use some.

"Frauke, my dear, finally you arrive!" A booming, melodic voice belied the king's small size. "I said to my heart, be calm, and wait without yearning, but at last you come." He flashed a smile and seemed genuinely pleased to see her. "And this must be the long-awaited Schizandra, she whom the Ancients call 'the chosen one.'" He leapt into the air. "Welcome!"

The queen curtseyed and replied, "Yes, Timaeus, this is Schizandra, she who walks beyond the veil. I've done all that you required of me."

"The necklace?" he asked.

Frauke spread her fingers and eyes wide. "Gone!"

"Those pearls were very beautiful, yes? Difficult to give away?"

The queen looked down, fighting shame and irritation. Any moment he would start quoting Kabir or T.S. Eliot, or (worse) singing in that pompous Sanskrit he'd learned from his *guru* at the foot of the Himalayas. *Ha!* His name probably wasn't even Timaeus. Didn't all his disciples rename themselves things like Ganeshananda and Shakti-Patty? As if *that* qualified someone to be king!

The frog looked directly into Frauke's heart and said loud enough for all to hear, "'No man knows till the time comes, what depths are within him. To some men it never comes; let them rest and be thankful! To me, you brought it; on me, you forced it; and the bottom of this raging sea,'" he pounded a webbed foot upon his purple chest, "'has been heaved up ever since.'"

The queen rolled her eyes. "Yeats?" she asked.

"Dickens," smiled the king, " ... and *Timaeus*, my love."

Something stirred in Frauke's breast and she fought to control it. The way that *frog* stared at her. *Uggh!* It unnerved her. *Upstart.*

Four scantily clad women entered the room, lit candles and prostrated themselves in front of Timaeus. He nodded towards them then returned his attention to Frauke and Schizandra. "I understand you are still asleep."

"She is," Frauke said, pointing at Schizandra.

"'Kabir says: Only she wakes, whose heart is pierced by the Beloved's song.'"

Frauke's nostrils flared. *"Enough!"* She turned to Schizandra: "See how the Ancients reward my devotion? He's not a husband. He's a hopping anthology. *Kabir says.* I don't care what Kabir says. I was happy 'til they saddled me with this pretentious blob."

The king croaked loudly, "'Had we but world enough, and time, this coyness, Lady, were no crime,' but we will hit the Galactic Equator in slightly more than a decade. Every year gets shorter. The Ancients and I had sincerely hoped, nay, *still hope* that we can work and love together."

"I can't handle this," said the queen, popping an entire cacao pod in her mouth. Mid-bliss, she suddenly noticed the four scantily clad disciples staring at her. "Oh, go Downward Dog yourselves!"

Timaeus laughed. "Darling, you're angry. How sweet! You must learn to breathe through that frustration and turn it into—"

"Into what?" she asked. "*A fly?*"

"Perhaps you're right," he said stroking his narrow chin with a purple foot. "'I heard a fly buzz / When I died—'"

"I don't *believe* this!" shouted Frauke. "You want poetry? How's *this* for allusion?

"*I heard a Fly buzz—when I lived—*
Its wings weren't Magic but
Distraction, Maddening.
It flew in circles just beyond my Reach
And kept me spinning—
Eyes around an empty room.
I found a Swatter
But I could not bring myself to strike.
It's just a Fly, I said—
And let it buzz.

It landed on my food—
Regurgitating feces, old lettuce and other people's garbage—
Ancient, sickening meals
Spewed upon organic carrots.

I took my plate and threw it out,
But that Fly remained.
I heard it buzz around my head again—
It's just a Fly, I said—
And hit it."

The followers gasped as Frauke swept her cloak past them and stormed out of the room.

<hr>

"Well!" said Timaeus. "She's certainly lively, isn't she? I do love the color of her cheeks when they flush. I suppose we should get started, though. I understand you've got an even tighter deadline than we do."

"I *do*?" asked Schizandra.

"*You don't know?*" Timaeus looked stunned then muttered, "Oh, Frauke, Frauke, Frauke, if you weren't so beautiful..." The frog's eyes went dreamy for a moment and then he collected himself. "According to the prophecies, you have only three days to complete this journey. You've already used much of your third day, which means we have our work cut out for us. Did Frauke reveal anything else to you by way of preface?"

Not wanting to get the queen in trouble, Schizandra tried to think of something, but came up short. "Well, it wasn't her fault," she said. "I've had some health issues."

"Ah, so you *do* know! Yes, you're in a coma. We must awaken you as soon as possible."

"A coma! I just meant I had some stomach cramps."

"Haven't you noticed anything unusual?" he asked. "Shadows teasing memories down mosaic streets? Through gates you *might* have entered? *Into the pomegranate-garden?* Your footsteps echo, but can you say for sure where you are or who I am?"

"OK, now you're creeping me out," Schizandra said. It was one thing to have potential past life memories trickle in from nowhere, quite another to have a three-inch purple frog inquire about them! "*Where am I?*"

"In a portal through the turning world."

"The queen tells me I'm in Mu."

"But the kingdom is inside you."

"Because I'm in a coma?"

"Because you are," said the king.

"And who are you?"

"Who do you say that I am?"

"OK, how about this: where do you come from?" the girl asked. "I've never seen a purple frog before, and no offense, but you're kind of nasal."

"A fair observation," sniffed Timaeus. "In fact, no one has ever seen a purple frog before. You see, I haven't been discovered yet! In October 2003, over two-and-a-half years from now, Professors Franky Bossuyt and S.D. Biju will announce they've found me in the Western Ghats of southern India. I'm afraid descriptions of me will sound rather like Frauke's." He began to channel a future press release:

"'Scientists have named it *Nasikabatrachus sahyadrensis*. In Sanskrit and

Greek those words mean nose (nasika); frog (batrachus); and Sahyadri, the name for its mountain home. The fat frog with a narrow nose appeared in a "biodiversity hotspot" in the Idukki district of Kerala. What a blob! Swollen and purple with very tiny eyes, this freak of nature packs an evolutionary punch. And you won't *believe* how small its head is!'"

Schizandra reached for something kind to say. "Surely there's more to your story. Are you new?"

"Some people think so," sighed the king. "But I'm more ancient than the Ancients," he said.

"So how old *are* you?" she asked.

"About one hundred thirty million years."

"Wow!" the girl said. "You look even better for your age than Frauke!"

"Thank you, child, but I must disagree. No one looks better than the queen." Timaeus smiled at the bead curtain and blinked his tiny eyes. Schizandra wondered why Frauke resisted him so much. He was actually kind of cute.

She listened to the rest of his lineage. "Dr. Bossuyt's DNA tests will prove me unique enough to warrant my own family without any other members. My closest relatives are called *Sooglossidae*, and they live in the Seychelles about nineteen hundred miles away from where they'll find me."

The frog explained that his very existence would have some scientists extolling the power and influence of continental drift. They believed Madagascar, India and the Seychelles had once formed a single landmass. When the split occurred, his unusual species had grown up in India, while close relatives evolved in seemingly faraway lands. He was a "living fossil," proof of a very different map of ancient Earth. The frog implied that the scientists might have missed a few details but said that humankind could "only handle so much reality at one time."

Timaeus likened his heritage story to that of the lemurs, relatives of monkeys who only inhabited the island of Madagascar. When nineteenth century scientists found lemur fossils scattered from Pakistan to Malaysia, they had hypothesized a missing continental link. Plate tectonics eventually replaced that theory, but not before scientists had coined the term, "Lemuria" to account for a sunken island in the South Pacific.

Again, the frog suggested that present day scientists had erred in their interpretation. He didn't seem worried, though. Timaeus seemed to think that things would reveal themselves whenever enough people could absorb the message.

Some of these theories sounded like stories from her childhood, but she knew her dad had ultimately sided with the scientists. He'd stopped believing in Mu when her mother died. Schizandra sensed that part of him had still longed to believe in something. She marveled at how individual lives moved and joined together, and how one coming or going could alter *everything*.

"So how'd you wind up here with Frauke?" she asked.

"'When you vow a vow to God, do not delay in paying it. It is better that you should not vow than that you should vow and then not pay.'"

"So you vowed to marry the queen?" Schizandra asked.

"I vowed to find the Quintessence."

"What's that," she asked, "some kind of fruit?"

"A berry," Timaeus smiled wide, "a five-flavored berry."

"Schizandra's a five-flavored—" the girl's voice trailed off.

On the other side of the bead curtain, Frauke carefully peeled a cacao pod. After this, she only had one left. She popped it into her mouth without a sound. The queen worked hard to cloak her thoughts so that neither would catch her listening. Smoke from burning incense twirled around Schizandra and Timaeus, as candle flames flickered in the twilight. The frog's shadow loomed large on the cavern wall. His deep voice echoed as he revealed the history of Mu.

Frauke knew these stories, but knowing and living were two different things. Timaeus sounded so proud of their heritage. He explained how Mu marked the beginning of civilization, the original Garden Paradise, a verdant crawl space in the memories of many walking the Earth today.

When a flood destroyed the Motherland, some went to Atlantis, hoping to protect that island from a similar fate. Some escaped to a place called Og in the mountains of modern day Peru. Others settled in parts of Mexico and the North American Southwest. Some went underground, awaiting better times.

The Hopi tribe near the Grand Canyon believed their tribal ancestors emerged from three cave worlds deep within the Earth. They had ascended through the worlds with all the animals and brought light to a darkened planet. The Hopi still used *kivas*, subterranean caverns that worked as portals to the underworld.

Frauke had forgotten the sacred aspects of her home. She did not remember Mu in its original abundance. Living in tunnels for so long, she had nearly forgotten true reverence and light. She talked a decent talk, but in her heart, she only now began to sense the magnitude of her husband's revelations.

The Law of One, to which she occasionally paid homage, really did stretch through all of space and time. That was why the same symbols kept appearing and reappearing in different cultures across the world—reminders of an underlying unity.

Timaeus' stories revealed secret tunnels connecting Cusco, Peru to the Grand Canyon, and portals linking Earth's "power spots," including Sedona. Shared memories haunted all of humanity, replaying again and again until they rose to consciousness. Schizandra's visit to the underworld foretold a massive shift in collective awareness. What was once hidden would be made clear. Unlike previous prophecies that could take centuries or millennia to come to pass, this one would happen within the next twelve years.

The queen felt overwhelmed. So overwhelmed, in fact, that she swallowed her last cacao pod before realizing what she'd done.

Chapter Twenty-Six

MELISSA HUGGED TOM GOODBYE AND settled into the Jaguar. On the whole, she felt relieved. The reading with him had helped make sense of some mysteries around Schizandra, including her birth. She did feel disturbed by the possibility of "other entities taking over the body," but hopefully Tom was right that her granddaughter would wake up soon.

As Melissa passed the Red Planet Diner on her left and a packed Coffee Pot Restaurant on her right, her stomach growled. She glanced at the dash: 11:45. She should stop in to check on her sisters and Schizandra. If all seemed well, they could break for lunch, or she'd run to get some food.

She tried to recall any specific suggestions from Tom. Perhaps she just needed to hold the space for Schizandra to expand and heal. She didn't know about all that "Cosmic Portal/Starry Canopy" business, but who could fight that kind of destiny, if Destiny it was?

She continued west and pulled into Sedona Regional Medical. So much had shifted since yesterday afternoon. She noticed a green Jeep Cherokee in the lot and thought of Mark. Her chest and cheeks felt warm despite the January gray and she smiled as she crossed the Urgent Care threshold. How had the twins fared with their reflexology? No messages on her cell: Schizandra hadn't awakened yet. Oh, how she hoped their expertise would break through the barriers of consciousness.

As she approached Schizandra's room, she heard laughter. Rosemary and Lobelia all a-twitter!

"I tell you I've not laughed that hard in two decades!" coughed Lobelia.

"I don't *ever* recall sharing such mirth with a stranger," Rosemary giggled.

Melissa pushed open the door. The twins smiled, and Mark rose to greet her. "I hope you don't mind," he said, "I, uh, I came by to give you these." He held up a silver bag with the goddess Kwan Yin on it. Four items wrapped in lavender tissue paper and curly cue ribbons peeked out at her.

"Mark!" cried Melissa, as she closed the door. She eyed the twins and then returned his gaze. "This is certainly a surprise. I see you've met my sisters."

"Rosemary and Lobelia, yes."

"We've had a delightful time," said Lobelia. "He's quite a young man."

"So fit," Rosemary said, "both mentally and physically." She squeezed his bicep and giggled.

Melissa thought she might die right then and there, but Mark just smiled. "Ladies," he said, "the pleasure's mine. Who knew you could do such things with feet? Why, if I had known that in the Philippines, I'd have had a nicer tour."

"Now don't forget that pressure point," Lobelia said, grabbing his hand. "Press here," she pinched the fleshy part between his thumb and forefinger, "if you ever get one of those nauseating headaches again."

Melissa had never seen her sisters like this before.

"Lobelia, sweetheart," Rosemary said, "let's let Mark give Melissa her gifts." The twins winked at each other and returned to their seats.

Oh, my God, thought Melissa, *if there's any mercy left in heaven kill me now.*

But Mark seemed unfazed. The twins grinned at Melissa as he approached her with the packages. "Nice shawl," he said.

"Thank you," Melissa said. "I got your message last night. Sorry, I haven't had a chance to call you back. I thought you were in Phoenix?"

Mark shifted his weight as Rosemary's dimples reappeared. He motioned to two chairs next to Schizandra's bed. "Sit down?" he asked.

Melissa looked at her granddaughter. She hadn't noticed that American flag hanging above her before. "How is she?"

"She'll make it," Rosemary said.

"Once you give her a rebirthing," Lobelia added. The two spinsters positively glowed. "But for now, why don't you sit down and accept your gifts?"

"This man has driven all the way from Phoenix just to support you and Schizandra," said Rosemary. "Oh, my stars, it warms my heart."

Chapter Twenty-Seven

THE FROG DISMISSED HIS FOUR scantily clad disciples. "Cobra, Camel, Fish and Sphinx: keep opening the heart, ladies. In the immortal words of the rock star Madonna ... " Timaeus clapped his webbed front feet together and a thousand fireflies began to flash. They created a strobe effect that burst rainbows from obsidian walls. Dancing to his own falsetto voice, the frog ushered his followers away with a lively rendition of *Open Your Heart*.

The disciples danced to the ashram next door, where they could practice the prescribed *asanas*. Timaeus turned to a starry-eyed and bee bopping Schizandra. "Come, child, let us chat over something sweet."

He hopped to a niche that contained his private barista. A tall man wearing an indigo robe leaned on a carved wooden stick. His white beard grazed the ground. Schizandra wondered if he could make anything as tasty as Daddy's Mexican fried ice cream.

The old man surprised her with an impeccable British accent. "Your Majesty," he bowed to the frog. "Might I recommend a Dulcimer de Lethe for the girl?"

"Excellent choice, Malku." The king turned to Schizandra. "We have six flavored syrups: up, down, charm, strange, bottom, and top. Take your pick," he said, "up and down are sugar-free."

"Can I have two flavors?" she asked.

The Druid barista and His Majesty the frog broke into wide grins. "Brilliant!" said Malku, tapping his staff.

"Then I'll have a Strange Charm Dulcimer de Lethe. How about you?" she asked.

"I'll have a Light Expresso," said the frog, "in a cone."

Schizandra smiled. "Don't you mean *espresso*?"

Malku raised his eyebrows and prepared their drinks by aiming his staff at ingredients on the crystal shelves. Timaeus said, "I enjoy my Light in a cone with over the top *Expression*. As the good book says, 'Let your Light so shine.'"

Malku handed the girl a mug filled with something between a drink and a pudding. "Thank you," she said, "how will I know which is strange and which is charm?"

"May I, Your Majesty?" Timaeus nodded. "Strange is green," said the Druid, "and it tastes like candy cane. Charm is blue, and it tastes like a cross between cacao, açai, and blueberry, with a hint of cinnamon."

"What's ah-SIGH-ee?" she asked.

"A berry from the Amazon for my five-flavored berry from Tibet," the king said. He winked. Malku handed him an ice cream cone filled with shimmering Light, Expression nibs, and a silver straw. "Let's sit down," said Timaeus. "It's time you knew your Self."

"You've often begun to tell me what I am, but stopped," said the girl.

Timaeus nodded. "Spacetime is the set of all *possible* events in a universe: it represents the history of an entire universe—or an entire soul." He glanced at the clock behind Malku. All the numbers had fallen to the bottom and behind the hands, its face read, "whatever."

"Indeed," said the king, "there *must* be time for all the works and thoughts of humans that raise and drop their theories in your cup. Fortunately, that drink allows you to absorb only what you need. Poor Pythagoras believed we should all remember *all* our lifetimes, but I say," Timaeus yawned, "*how tiresome!* Take what resonates and leave the rest."

Schizandra stirred charm and strange into a blue-green swirl. She took a sip. "Wow! That's cocoa-minty-berry-spice!" She paused. "What do you mean 'take what resonates'?"

"Hummmmmmmmm," sang the frog, "listen, do you hear that? Hummmmmmmm. That's the sound of a healthy throat chakra. Hum it with me now. Hummmmmmmm."

Schizandra joined Timaeus and felt her voice begin to blend with his.

"Did you hear that?" he asked. "Hear how your voice wants to join with mine? Do you feel it inside of you?"

The girl nodded and Timaeus said, "We share a fundamental frequency. We *resonate*."

"But what's that got to do with remembering past lives?"

"The only reason to remember past lives is to release them. We *resonate* with joy and love and freedom," said the king, leaping into the air and flinging his front feet high. "Keep the gifts, but why burden our remembrance with a heaviness that's gone?"

Schizandra put down her drink. "Well, it doesn't matter anyway," she said, "I don't believe in past lives. My father was a professor, and he said—"

"Pythagoras was a professor," said Timaeus, "the *first* professor. He built the very first university in 536 B.C."

"*So?*"

"So," Timaeus laughed as he sipped his cone of Light Expresso, "just because your father said something doesn't make it so."

Schizandra took another gulp. "Daddy said *nothing's* true unless you see it with your eyes or hold it in your hand."

The frog looked at her. "Then when is nothing false?"

"I don't know," she said, wrinkling her brow. "Can I try some of your Light Expresso?"

"*Absolutely!* I wondered when you'd ask." He handed her his cone. "You can have it all."

As Schizandra filled herself with Light, she asked, "So what's the Quintessence?"

"You are," said Timaeus. "Schizandra contains all five flavors and unlocks the fifth element in all of us."

"Fifth element?" she asked.

"Earth, air, fire, water, and ether. *You've* been 'etherised.'" Timaeus croaked and slapped his purple knee. "*Etherised!* Good old Tom Eliot! Ether—or Spirit—connects everyone and everything. Human studies reveal that the schizandra berry not only improves vision; it actually enlarges the visual field. It also improves hearing, sometimes to clairaudient levels."

"What does *that* mean?"

"Clairaudient means you can hear things that most people can't: spirits, for instance." He winked. "Or subterranean frog kings." Timaeus croaked several times in his version of a loud guffaw.

Resistance began to close its fingers around her heart, but the king jumped in: "Schizandra also increases sensitivity in skin receptors. In fact, it alters the central nervous system allowing us to analyze data in entirely different ways. When humans change how we process information, we change our world."

"We?" she asked. "But *you're* not human!"

"The true revolutionary acts from feelings of love," said the king. "I wonder why a handsome young man would choose the body of a frog."

"You *chose* this form?" Schizandra eyed the three inch purple blob in front of her.

"I believe Sir Thomas Browne said it best." Timaeus cleared his throat and smiled. "Pardon me," he said, "I've got a frog in my throat." He chuckled. "Ah yes, Sir Thomas Browne: 'Thus is man that great and true *Amphibium*, whose nature is disposed to live not only like other creatures in diverse elements, but in divided and distinguished worlds.' The frog seemed an appropriate form for dimension hopping."

"So you wanted to become a frog?" she asked.

"It affords me certain advantages," said the king. "Most New Agers assume reptilians will orchestrate their evolution or destruction, but I tell you, it's the frogs!" The purple blob stood on his hind legs and took a bow. "'There's surely a piece of Divinity within us, something before the Elements.' Awaken our Divinity!" he said, "*Whyever not?*"

Schizandra scrunched her nose like Haru. "I don't know." She took another gulp of Light. "What's that uh-mig-duh thing you're thinking about?"

Chapter Twenty-Eight

HARU SAT ON A BLUE plastic chair outside Nurse Baker's office. She had called his father, and Professor Amaru Begay was on his way. The boy held Brielle's crumpled note in his sweaty left palm. He wanted to ask his dad about that symbol.

Professor Begay taught at Yavapai College in Prescott, about an hour over the mountains without snow. During winter, he often stayed at a hotel in town, rather than driving roundtrip from Sedona each day. Between that and all the academic conferences, Haru rarely saw his dad. And when he did, they barely spoke. Maybe that symbol would get them talking.

Professor Begay had left his hometown when friends accused him of 'iińzhįįd (translated, "evil-wishing magic"). This branch of *Witchery-Way* relied on the power of names, strands of hair or fingernails, and stolen personal items in order to curse or otherwise affect people. Whirlwinds and power animals like ravens or snakes could also curse. Some of the professor's former friends claimed he had moved to Sedona in order to harness the power of the vortexes. His father did have an interest in the occult, but Haru had only heard the rumors.

Haru's Japanese mother told him not to believe such things. Her grandparents had been imprisoned in California during World War II. Loyal U.S. citizens, they had lived in an internment camp until Japan surrendered in 1945. In 1988, Congress and Ronald Reagan had apologized on behalf of the nation. The legislation blamed "race prejudice, war hysteria, and a failure of political leadership." As a descendant, Haru's mother had collected a small settlement. "*A reparation.*" But her grandparents had never recovered from the shock of other people's fears.

Haru glanced at his watch: almost noon.

Melissa admired the goddess dancing with a lotus on her gift bag. "It's beautiful!" she said, "Is this by a local artist?"

Mark smiled and shrugged. "The folks at *Center for the New Age* say Kwan Yin's 'the bestower of children.' I thought with you being a midwife and all ... I don't know about the artist. I just liked the bag."

"I do, too," Melissa said. "Kwan Yin's also the goddess of mercy and a powerful healer. I think I'll place her right here by Schizandra." She removed the lavender tissue paper and gifts, then put the bag on a table near the hospital bed.

"*Om mani padme hum*," said Rosemary, "'hail to the jewel in the lotus!' I've always admired Kwan Yin, too." Lobelia nudged her sister to stay quiet.

"Are these all for me?" Melissa inspected the four wrapped items.

"Two for you and two for Schizandra," Mark said. "I hope they help."

Melissa's chest warmed and she felt her breath relax. "How thoughtful!" She untied the first curly cue bow around the tissue paper, removing a four-inch marbled green slab.

"That one's for you," he said. "Malachite: the stone of pregnant women."

Melissa's heart dropped slightly into her stomach. *What's wrong with you? He knows you're a midwife. Malachite's a lovely gift.* Mark watched her face and added, "Someone also told me it's 'a mirror to the soul.' Kind of like your eyes. Supposedly, it brings balance to all heart relationships. Anyway," he said, "it reminded me of you."

Melissa's heart smiled again. "Thank you!" She carefully opened the next package, which revealed a gray stone with a raised brown cross.

"Staurolite," said Mark. He reviewed a small typed card. "'Also known as fairy stone or fairy cross.' That one's for Schizandra. Staurolite works on the nervous system, especially in children, 'connecting and balancing the physical, astral, and extra-terrestrial planes.' It also helps with PMS if she ever gets anything like that."

"Menstrual cramps!" coughed Lobelia. "Schizandra's got those. Rosemary and I—" This time Rosemary nudged Lobelia to pipe down.

"Fairy cross," Melissa said, "how charming." She turned to her sisters and asked, "She's got cramps?"

"We believe so," Rosemary said, "but keep opening your gifts. I told you Mark was bright." She turned to him and said, "You're very intuitive: a natural healer."

The retired Army officer smiled impishly. "I just call it 'being in sync.' Here," he said, picking up the smaller of his two remaining gifts, "why don't you open this one next?"

Melissa untied the knot and unwrapped the purple stone. "Oh, I like this one!" she said. "It's got a nice feel to it." She ran her thumb over the smooth face. "Hmmm," she said, "I know it's not amethyst … "

"They call it sugilite," Mark said. "Apparently, it's one of the newest stones out there. According to this history," he glanced at his mini card before passing it to her, "a Japanese guy discovered it in 1944. 'It counteracts cosmic radiation. Some people hail it as the stone of the New Age.'"

"Is this for me?" Melissa asked.

Mark shook his head. "I bought it for Schizandra because it helps the nervous system. I think this one helps menstrual problems, too." He looked at the twins, who nodded their approval.

"These are lovely," Melissa said. "Thank you for thinking of us." She paused. "And for driving all the way up here. You've been very kind."

Mark watched Melissa place the fairy cross on Schizandra's forehead and the sugilite on the pillow, right above her head.

When Rosemary saw the staurolite, she exclaimed, "That's remarkably like the Chakana, isn't it? Melissa, what did that Tom fellow tell you about the Chakana? Anything beyond what we discussed last night?"

Lobelia stage whispered to Mark, "The Chakana's a cross from South America. We've been seeing it in the strangest places!"

Melissa looked down. "I forgot to ask him, but from the reading, I think Rosemary had things right last night: connecting the three worlds."

Mark shivered and looked around. "Anyone else just get goose bumps?" The twins giggled, and he handed Melissa her last present. "I hope you like this one. It's for you."

As she unwrapped the Lemurian, Mark touched something in his coat pocket. Melissa held her gift up to the light and watched the rainbows. "There's a city inside here! Look at this!" she turned the crystal to face Mark. In this light, he could see snowcapped mountains above snow covered roofs and trees. The bottom evoked ice caves.

He spun the crystal a few degrees and said, "Hey, a UFO!"

"Where?" shouted Lobelia.

"Here," he showed Melissa before they walked the crystal over to the twins. "An unidentified *floating* object!" Mark chuckled. Melissa and her sisters marveled at an inner saucer shape that flickered above the snowy town.

"I've never seen anything like this," Melissa said.

"It's a Lemurian Seed Crystal," Mark said. "They're new. Or," he consulted his card, "I guess I should say they're really, really old. More than twelve thousand years old, but they were only rediscovered last year. *Melissa?* Are you OK?"

The midwife had grabbed Rosemary's chair to steady herself. She focused on Schizandra and asked, "Did you just say *Lemurian?*"

"Yeah," said Mark, "they say it's an ancient civilization that went underground and off to some other star system." He grinned. "Natives call it the Motherland of Mu. Ever hear of it?"

Melissa squeezed the crystal and felt a jolt of energy towards Mark.

"All the Lemurian Seed Crystals are connected to each other." He showed the three sisters the one he had bought for himself. Black spots spun around Melissa's eyes. She barely heard Mark say, "I guess they're kind of like that Chakana thing, connecting the inner earth with the surface and the stars. *Melissa!*"

He caught her before she fainted and carefully walked her to a chair beside Schizandra's bed. Lobelia gave her a bottled water while Rosemary squeezed an acupressure point.

"Philip," said Melissa. She gulped the water and continued. "Schizandra's father, he taught archeology at Chicago University. When he met Ginger in 1986, he had come to Sedona on a research sabbatical. That summer, he believed he'd found the Gates of Mu."

She told Mark about the way Philip had shut her out after Ginger's death. Mark listened. The twins each touched one of her shoulders from behind, and Rosemary smoothed Melissa's hair with her free hand. They remained that way for several minutes until Lobelia shouted:

"Enough is enough! You have *got* to let this go. You're a midwife. For heaven's sake, Melissa, *rebirth that child!*"

Chapter Twenty-Nine

AH-MIG-DAH-LAH," TIMAEUS SAID. "YOU'RE VERY bright." Schizandra finished her Light cone, and the frog continued, "The amygdala's a tiny, almond shaped structure in the brain. It deals with our conditioned fear response—how we learn to keep ourselves from danger."

"What's wrong with that?" she asked.

"Well," the king said, "unlike the rest of the human brain, which developed all sorts of higher thinking and learning abilities, the amygdala has not evolved since the time of the dinosaurs! It makes humans easy prey for those who manipulate through fear."

Schizandra slurped the last of her Strange Charm Dulcimer de Lethe. "Yeah, but can't we just think our way around the fear? I mean, smart people *know* better, right?"

"Indeed, they do," Timaeus said, "but knowing in the mind won't override the old programming. Humans have far more neuro-pathways leading *out* of the amygdala than in."

"So?"

"So," the frog smiled, "that means the fear and anxiety go out to our cognitive and emotional centers, but the calming thoughts don't always make their way back in. Too often, the amygdala gets stuck in fight or flight."

The king tapped Schizandra with his purple feet, "Zzzz, zzzz, zzzz. It's like singing the body electric with electric shock therapy!"

"Hey, that tickles!" she said. She zapped him back.

"When we awaken, we feel a surge of power and awareness." Timaeus flexed his muscles. "But then the old programming kicks in and says, *'Hey, you can't do that!'*" He brought webbed feet to his skinny head and open mouth—a purple version of *The Scream*. "The amygdala associates sensation with reward or punishment. It fears the damnation society *says* will come, and so it halts the music." He looked at Schizandra and asked, "What happens when the music stops?"

"The serpent strikes." She snapped her hand at him as he jumped out of the way. They both laughed.

But Schizandra's face grew serious. "If our minds can't escape the fear, then how do we break the cycle? How do we awaken?"

Timaeus fluttered his tiny eyeballs at the bead curtain. "We awaken through the heart," he said. "In Sanskrit, the word for heart, *Hridaya*, is also the word for the Gateway to the Highest Reality. As an adaptogen, the Quintessence knows exactly how to lead us there."

"I do?"

Timaeus nodded. "The prophets say the mountains and the hills will burst into song before you. *The music will never stop again.*" He paused, then leaned in to whisper, "In scientific studies, rats with recalibrated amygdalas will snuggle up with cats. Sound familiar?" he asked. "*The lion shall lie down with the lamb.*"

"And the lady with the frog?"

Schizandra smiled as Timaeus leapt onto her hand. "One can hope," he said, "one can always hope."

※

As the girl looked at the frog, she realized something else about amphibians. They could breathe under water. Another ancient scene rose before her eyes—a past life memory infused with extra clarity. Instead of seeing things from her own perspective, events played across her mind like a documentary:

The last night of Atlantis. The eve of a triumph of human evolution. A night of secret celebration and ultimate potential.

Schizandra and a group of scientists and crystal healers had joined forces for the betterment of humankind. At that time, several humanoid species had risen to greatness, and some members of the older species had recognized the unique potential of homo sapiens DNA. Those who wanted to maintain their power in the Old Guard felt threatened by such promise.

Even with only two activated strands of DNA, humans had quickly risen and altered life on planet Earth. If they activated their ten additional strands, homo sapiens would become key players on a galactic stage. They would morph into homo luminens. The radiance from their hearts would allow Earth to enter a realm of "power to, not power over."

Most humans didn't know what they could do or be, but this small team of scientists and healers planned to help them out. Deep in the bowels of the Earth, in a room connected by tunnels from basements of the Temple Beautiful and the Ministry of Science, this group had built a magnificent machine. Schizandra herself had chosen the colors. Formed of aquamarine and clear quartz, the machine offered three chambers. At any one time, three human beings could enter and activate all twelve strands of DNA.

Visionaries had worked for centuries to perfect this DNA machine. Sound healers, engineers, and crystal guides; astrologers and sacred geometers. A few soldiers from the Atlantean Army had provided covert protection for something special, but they did not know what.

Everyone involved was taught discretion. Not a word near Cat's Alley. Not even a hint in pillow talk. In order to succeed, this project needed to escape detection by overwhelming forces of resistance. These twelve visionaries had come together quietly in the night, decade after decade, running test after test, until finally they had worked out all the kinks. They knew the machine would work.

But they did not know that a traitor had worked within their midst. Masquerading as one of their own, he had tried to sabotage the process from inception. Forces seemed against him, though. Every trick he played resulted in a superior machine. Each part he damaged meant creation of a better replacement part.

On this particular evening—the last night of Atlantis—there came a time when the DNA machine was done. A glorious moment in human history, about to reveal its true potential via grand announcement the following morning. The saboteur summoned the strongest and most powerful, though not the wisest, members of the Council. They, in turn, summoned all the forces from the sky and sea and sand.

Ascension or destruction? The question echoed across the planet. Earth cracked with the choice, and annihilation won. Earthquakes, fires and floods. Volcanoes erupted into growing waves, displacing water that formed higher and higher swells. A tsunami devoured the island, sinking the DNA machine and all Atlantis with it.

A torrent of sorrow ripped through Schizandra's heart as she grieved the shock of those events. The next day would have changed it all. If only they could have unveiled the potential, and revealed it to the willing few. If only the resistant ones had let the dreamers live.

As a still point within her stormy heart, Schizandra realized that time had recycled. Yes, Atlantis had sunk into the night, and no, she couldn't bring it back. But in this moment, she remembered the underlying promise of Atlantis, that sweet hope of returning to the Garden, of finding the way back to the Paradise of Mu.

She could see where Earth was headed then. And it looked familiar:

A world on the cusp of scientific discoveries that could alter life as people knew it, for good or ill. A world riddled with wars—at the same time individuals had begun to open their hearts in unprecedented ways. A world in which concern for the greater good had finally begun to surpass embedded racism. A world that had nearly maxed out its current energy sources at the same time government, financial and religious institutions had begun to crumble. A world of paradox: one that faced a great deal of darkness, which encouraged people to reach inside and let their light so shine.

Like today, DNA experiments occupied much scientific and spiritual attention in Atlantis. Science had begun to validate spiritual ideas, and people looked forward to new worlds of possibility. But a few details had escaped their notice, and those tiny blips turned out to be important. Vital. By the time they realized the damage, their window of opportunity had closed.

In a vision, Schizandra saw herself sinking with the others, but *this* time she felt herself embrace instead of running from her fear. She imagined breathing underwater. Inside her head, she heard a voice, beckoning her through the bottom of the sea. "Come here," it said, "you know the way where I am going." And suddenly, *she did.*

Chapter Thirty

PROFESSOR BEGAY DID NOT LOOK happy. Haru followed him outside to the blue Buick and climbed into the passenger's seat.

His father put his right arm on the seat to look behind him as he maneuvered out of a tight spot. "Buckle your seat belt." His expression didn't change. He looked forward again and left the school parking lot. "What's wrong with you?"

Haru's stomach began to churn again. He still held Brielle's crumpled note, but he had lost interest in talking with his dad about the symbol. "I don't feel well," he said.

"So I gathered. Do you need my help?"

"What do you mean?" Haru watched his dad out of the corner of his left eye, without turning his head. The car's motion was making him sick. He clutched the door grip and tried to swallow his heart. Beads of sweat slid across his forehead, dripping over eyebrows and mingling with salty tears that had begun to taunt his lips.

"Are you crying?"

The floodgates were creaking open. Tears, sweat and mucus threatened to merge with vomit. Haru rolled down his window, but the wind on his tears reminded him of the girl on the beach. "Dad, I need you to pull over."

"We're on a highway," said Professor Begay.

"If you don't stop now, I'm gonna puke all over your car." Haru was shaking and sobbing now. His right hand hovered near his mouth, prepared to catch the worst.

His dad signaled and made an illegal U-turn on 89A. The car lurched forward as he hit the gas.

"What are you doing?" Haru yelled.

"We're going to Urgent Care. Here," his father handed him a tissue. "Try to clean yourself up."

As Haru blew his nose, he dropped Brielle's note. The Chakana stared up at them, and Professor Begay saw it. He pulled into the parking lot of Sedona Regional Medical and asked, "Where did you get that symbol?"

Haru swallowed hard. His dad handed him an antibacterial hand wipe. "Use it. Do you still feel sick?"

His urge to vomit had passed—for the moment—but the world continued to spin. "Yeah," Haru said, "I'm really dizzy."

"Then let's get this over with. I haven't even unpacked yet, and I've got papers to grade." Professor Begay opened his door and glanced at Haru before stepping out. "Wait until I get by your side." He helped his son out of the car, and supported him as they approached the ER entrance.

When the doors flew open, Haru and the six-foot-two Navajo crossed the threshold.

"I'm so happy I could kiss you," Schizandra said, with a wider smile than she'd worn in months.

"If you kiss me," said Timaeus, in a louder voice than necessary, "I'll be yours forever."

The bead curtain clattered as Frauke suddenly ran through it.

"Why, of all the backstabbing, ungrateful things!" she shouted. "Schizandra of all people! About to kiss *my* frog." The queen's chest heaved, as she rushed towards the revolutionaries. "Get away from him!" Her purple cloak swirled behind her.

Timaeus hopped from Schizandra's hand back onto the pillow. "My love, you misunderst—"

Frauke's eyes locked onto the girl's. "Back off," she said.

Schizandra lifted her palms into the air. "It's just an expression. It wouldn't have been *that* kind of kiss. I swear."

"The way I see it, there's only one way to kiss a frog," the queen said. "You stay away from my husband, or I'll, I'll!" Her face went white with rage. She had no more cacao pods, but she did still have her knife.

Timaeus read her thoughts, "'When our actions do not, our fears *do* make us traitors.' Come, Frauke, you know she and I must finish our work together. The universe depends upon it."

"Don't take me for such a fool," Frauke said. "All this time, I thought you loved me, but you were seeking that *Quintessence*. A likely story. That's all I was for you."

"Oh, Frauke, Frauke, I am 'constant as the northern star, of whose true-fix'd—'"

"The north star of a moving galaxy," she snapped. The queen rolled her eyes then narrowed them, looking from Timaeus to Schizandra. "If I so much as *think* there's anything going on here besides evolution, then I'll start quoting Shakespeare, too:

"'Oh, happy dagger!'" Frauke brandished her cacao knife and ripped Schizandra's shirt with it.

"Ow, get away from me, you freak!" The girl covered her scratched navel. Frauke had drawn blood.

<hr />

Melissa put one hand over Schizandra's heart chakra and one over her own. She closed her eyes and breathed deeply. The girl's breath began to flow with her grandmother's. Tears rolled down Melissa's cheeks as she allowed herself to return to Schizandra's birth.

"I can't believe I never thought of this before!" she cried, looking at Rosemary and Lobelia. "The trauma, oh, how could she *not* remember it?" Schizandra's breath grew ragged.

"You're upsetting her," coughed Lobelia. "Careful, or Amelia will come back and threaten to call Dr. Swinburne. Just breathe, honey bee. You can do it for Schizandra *now*."

"I remember when we first heard," Rosemary said, "you sounded so brave, Melissa. So calm. I'm sorry we never visited you. We just thought—"

"It's OK," Melissa said, returning to her breath. She whispered to her granddaughter, "You were so beautiful! Such a tiny spark of wonder. We didn't mean to make you feel unwanted. We didn't mean to greet you with our grief. We should have welcomed you with joy. When I first held you, your tiny hand grabbed my finger and I am so, so sorry that I ever let you go."

Melissa sobbed and laid her face on the girl's flat stomach. Mark gently rubbed the midwife's back as she pleaded through her tears: "Focus on your breathing, child. We want you to join us. We *want* to welcome you. Schizandra Ginger Parker. We welcome you, and whatever you need to do or be, I love you. I love you as my own. And because you're you. We *want* you, Schizandra."

Melissa lifted her tear streaked face, and Rosemary gasped.

"What!" shouted Lobelia, looking at her twin. "Spill it, sister."

All the color had drained from Rosemary's face. "There's blood," she said, motioning to the bed. Mark, Lobelia and Melissa looked from Rosemary's face to Schizandra's sheet. A red-brown stain had formed in the shape of the Chakana.

The three sisters stared with gaping mouths. Mark looked around for a towel. He found one and handed it to Melissa. "Do you want me to leave while you clean her up?" he asked.

The midwife looked confused. "You did it," he said. "Things are flowing again." The women looked from the sheet to Mark and back at the Chakana. He smiled and said, "Looks like it's that time of the month. I'll go wait outside."

As Mark opened the door, he saw Amelia leading a raven haired boy and his Navajo father down the hall. The boy glanced into the room and shouted, "Shazzie!" before running to her bedside.

He gasped for air but pent-up words exploded. "Oh, Shazzie! Are you OK? I've missed you. Feinman's class just isn't the same without you, and I've been so worried. I'm sorry I cut open that frog. I don't even like biology anymore." He grabbed her hand. "There's so much I want to tell you. Can you hear me? Last night I had a dream, and today at school—" Haru stopped talking as he sensed the silence in the room. His hair stood on end. When he turned around, everyone was staring at his father in the doorway.

Chapter Thirty-One

"SOME CUPID KILLS WITH ARROWS, some with traps.'" The queen glared at Timaeus and the girl. "I'll be watching." Her cloak and nostrils flared as she rushed to the other side of the bead curtain.

Schizandra looked at the frog and asked, "Should I be worried?"

"'A little water makes a sea, a small puff of wind a Tempest.' 'We that are true lovers run into strange capers.'" He leaned closer to the girl and whispered, "Do you really think she's jealous?"

"Sure sounds like it," Schizandra said.

Timaeus leapt three feet into the air in sweet anticipation. He cloaked his thoughts from Frauke and whispered to the girl, "'Why then tonight let us assay our plot.'"

"Um, not to dash your hopes, but don't I need to wake up soon?" Schizandra contemplated her navel. "I thought we had a lot of work to do."

"Journeys end when lovers meet," said the king. "Come. Let us go to the Heart of Matter."

Schizandra grinned. "Hey, isn't it, *get to the heart of the matter?*"

The frog leapt up and spun three times in front of her eyes. "Come," he said, "the universe awaits!" He brought her to a sacred chamber hidden in plain view.

<hr>

The Navajo took one look at the Chakana-stained sheet and removed a small, olive-green carved puma from his briefcase. He handed it to Melissa.

"This is for the girl." He motioned his head towards Schizandra. "It's made of serpentine, a powerful healing stone, especially for the heart chakra."

Melissa set her jaw. She could feel him trying to connect, but this time she was ready.

"The Ancients used serpentine to protect the soul against sorcery and the dark arts," he said. "It's a stone of Scorpio that guards one's vital energy."

"Who are you to give my granddaughter anything?" Melissa asked. She breathed slowly to control her fear. "Why did you tell me she was cursed?"

"It's a gift," the Navajo said. "The stone will protect her on the journey. One risks everything in order to return." He glanced at the Chakana again. "But I did not say that she was cursed."

Her violet eyes glared up at the Navajo. "You saw me Tuesday morning at the gas station on 89A. You gave me seven cents and grabbed my shoulders. You said, 'The child is cursed. Sins of the father.' Then you," she inhaled quickly, "you turned into a raven and chased me to my car!" Rosemary and Lobelia stared at them in silence.

Haru remained by Shazzie's bed. "What did you do to her?" Tears spilled over his cheeks and onto the girl's limp fingers.

"On Tuesday, I was in Chicago," the Navajo said.

"Chicago!" Melissa said, "What were you doing in Chicago?"

"Attending a conference at the Egyptian Institute. I saw a most extraordinary find—from Sedona of all places." He looked again at the sleeping girl then closed his own eyes. "She *is* cursed," he said, "but not by me."

Mark gripped the Navajo's shoulder. He spoke through gritted teeth. "Look man, if you've got something to say then say it. Can't you see this woman's suffered enough? The girl needs to wake up this afternoon. If you know something, you better say it or so help me—"

"Mark!" Melissa grabbed his right arm as he swung it back. Her eyes and touch seemed to soothe him as she said, "It's OK. I'm OK." She looked at the Navajo. "What can you tell us?"

The Navajo smiled at Melissa and put out his hand. "My name is Amaru Begay, and this is my son, Haru. Apparently, he knows the girl."

"Melissa Vreeland," the midwife said. She glanced at the bed. "Schizandra's my granddaughter, and these are my two sisters, Rosemary and Lobelia." She turned towards the helicopter pilot. "This is my friend Mark." The two men shook hands, eyeing each other carefully.

"The relic I saw at the Egyptian Institute was discovered by a Dr. Philip J. Parker."

Melissa steadied herself against Mark. "That was Schizandra's father," she said.

Amaru nodded. "The relic was a seven-foot high, hinged pair of

Egyptian ankhs with mirrors in the circular loops above each cross." He tore a sheet of paper from a small pad in his briefcase and used the pen dangling from Schizandra's chart to sketch a replica:

"They're made of orachalum," said Amaru, "a gold-like metal of unknown composition from before the time of Plato. These gates led into the pomegranate garden of Atlantis, created in memory of the original Garden Paradise. The museum has erroneously labeled them 'The Gates of Mu.'"

"Welcome to my p-brane," Timaeus said, "the Heart of Matter."

Schizandra giggled. "You don't have a pea brain!" She looked around. A three-foot-tall blue caterpillar played a Peruvian flute as a giant black-and-silver butterfly flapped its wings to the melody.

"Not P-E-A-B-R-A-I-N!" Timaeus croaked an amused guffaw. "I'm talking about my *p-brane*. A higher dimensional object. Your idea of a membrane would be a two-brane. A point's a zero-brane."

"So what's a p-brane?" asked Schizandra.

"According to SuperstringTheory.com, a p-brane's 'a spacetime object that provides a solution to the Einstein equation in the low energy limit of Superstring Theory. A p-dimensional ob—'"

"In English," laughed Schizandra, "I'm only in seventh grade!"

Timaeus winked. "This p-brane's technically a D-brane—a special kind of p-brane where the ends of the strings are all vibrating *on* the brane. It's the cosmic Chopin!" The frog began to hop and spin to a quickly hummed mazurka. Her eyes tried to follow him, but he moved so fast he made Schizandra dizzy. Finally, he lifted his purple foot and finished with a bow.

Schizandra stared at the frog and raised her eyebrows. She still didn't see what that dance had to do with a p-brane. The frog leapt high and tried a different route: "Pythagoras said, 'Number rules the universe.' Music is number expressed through time; astronomy is number expressed through time *and space*. They work together."

Schizandra began to understand as the caterpillar piped his song.

Watching her eyes follow the giant wings, the frog said, "I present to you the Galactic Butterfly, pulsating at the center of our Milky Way."

"She's beautiful," said Schizandra, mesmerized by the rhythmic wings and flute.

Timaeus leaned close and whispered, "In 2002, researchers at Socorro, New Mexico will analyze low frequency radio wave images taken by the Very Large Array telescope. A Dr. Hyman will detect an intermittent signal that seems 'intelligently directed.'"

"What's that got to do with her?" she asked, still tracking the cosmic dance.

The frog continued, "Five highly energetic radio emissions of equal brightness will last ten minutes each and appear every seventy-seven minutes from September 30-October 1, 2002. Our very own Galactic Butterfly will send the signal."

<hr>

"*Erroneously?*" Melissa said. "You mean the mirrored ankhs that Philip found really weren't the Gates of Mu?"

"He believed they were," said Amaru, "but no, those aren't the Gates of Mu. You can't put that sort of thing in a museum."

"That's exactly what Philip said! The discovery thrilled him, but he worried about taking the ankhs away from Sedona."

"He did more than worry." Professor Begay shook his head and then looked at the sleeping girl. He walked behind his son.

Holding his left hand between Schizandra's brows, Amaru said, "When her mother died, her father went mad with grief."

Melissa's eyes welled up.

"Professor Parker started thinking those ankhs contained spells to punish anyone who dared remove them. In his research, he found a Navajo curse that could target pregnant women."

Melissa forgot to breathe as Amaru continued, "A practitioner of Witchery Way cuts open a horned toad, places the woman's personal effects within it, and repeats a chant. Then the woman dies."

Her heart raced. "Schizandra's mother died in childbirth! Are you saying Ginger was cursed, too?"

The twins stared at their exotic visitors, and Haru looked at his father with expectation.

"Only in Philip's mind," he said. "Philip *believed* he'd been cursed and that the curse then spread and morphed to include his wife and child. He believed it so much that the curse became his truth. *Sins of the father.* This is very important."

Amaru paused and walked over to Melissa. He placed his huge hands upon her shoulders and looked into her eyes like she remembered from before.

In a firm voice, the Navajo said, "*There was no such curse.*"

⚬——◆——⚬

Schizandra pondered iridescent wings. The dancing butterfly was larger than New York's Twin Towers, yet fluttered silently behind Peruvian song. "What kind of signal will she send?"

"A confirmation," Timaeus said. "Some call our Galactic Butterfly *Hunab Ku*. Ultimate Consciousness. That which organizes all matter from a 'whirling disk' into heavens and solar systems, bodies and souls. The Ancients say this Creation process still directs everything in our galaxy through bursts of 'Consciousness Energy' at the center of the Milky Way."

"You mean the Ancients were right?"

"More right than not." The purple frog smiled. "Our *galaxy's* a 'whirling disk.'"

Timaeus explained that Hunab Ku provided a portal to other galaxies. He showed Schizandra how to enter and return without seeming to go anywhere at all.

"It's like that movie *Contact*!" she said. "No one knows we're gone!"

Timaeus nodded. "On that fateful night in 2002, scientists will realize that there really *is* a black hole at the center of our galaxy. A black hole that both consumes and gives birth to stars. The Galactic Butterfly will redirect them to Ancient wisdom."

"But why's that so important?"

Schizandra found her mind both lulled and sharpened by the dancing butterfly. Each flutter perfumed the Heart of Matter with frankincense, cinnamon, and apricots. Listening to the flute, Schizandra relaxed into the frog's disclosures.

"Scientists already know that on December 21, 2012, the Earth, the Sun, the Pleiades star cluster and the center of our galaxy will align exactly as Mayan astrologers predicted over fifteen hundred years ago."

"Wow," Schizandra said, "Daddy always thought astrology was bunk!

What else did they say?"

His purple chest swelled with pride and excitement. "People misinterpret things! *El Fin de los Tiempos* doesn't mean 'The End of *All* Time.' The Ancients knew what humanity only now suspects: that linear time moves in circles. An *ouroborus*: the snake that swallows its own tail. On Winter Solstice 2012, the Mayan Long Calendar ends."

"But every end marks a new beginning?" Her heart began to flutter.

Timaeus jumped into the air, spinning twice. "A new beginning for humanity!" he said. "We have *so* much to prepare." His eyes twinkled in the light and shadow of the dancing butterfly.

Frauke started to wonder at the silence. On the other side of the bead curtain, she had heard nothing for a full five minutes. A mixture of suspicion, anger and anxiety gnawed her tiny waist. Why hadn't she saved at least one cacao pod for such a time? She tried to follow her breath, but the effort left her topsy-turvy. What were Schizandra and the king *doing* in there?

The queen decided to take a peek. As she poked her face through the painted beads, she could feel but no longer see Timaeus or the girl. A tear slid down her cheek and she began to fear the worst. A thousand emotions swirled inside her brain. And at their center pulsed the darkest one of all.

Regret.

Frauke's sorrow threatened her complete annihilation. She had run from him for years. Distracted herself with bitter fruit, silly antics and half-performed agreements. He had offered love. And she? Scorn. He had offered wisdom. And she? Ridicule. *Where can I go from your Spirit? Where can I flee from your presence?* She had asked these questions ten thousand times without expecting to find answers. Turned out she didn't need to go anywhere! One day, he just disappeared. Frauke's chest ached with the pressure of unspent love.

Her coquetry. The names. That total disregard for what he'd offered. Very slowly, a crack began to spread itself across her chest. Frauke sobbed. Her voice squeaked with the splitting stone of her heart, a vast chasm about to flood.

Chapter Thirty-Two

I DON'T GET IT," MARK SAID. "You're saying there's no such thing as a curse?"

Amaru shook his head. "Curses exist, but they rarely come from the places we suspect."

Everyone's eyes asked questions.

"Take Philip, for instance. He was in the process of receiving everything he'd ever wanted: beautiful wife, new child, recognition from his peers. Full tenure at a prestigious university."

"Sounds good to me," Mark said. The twins nodded.

"Perhaps too good," the professor said. "When things go too well, we often curse ourselves."

Melissa's face grew somber. She remembered Tom's refusal to show the Devil card. *As a species, we've forgotten how to recognize the Garden.* And that quote he shared from the Gospel of Thomas. What was it? Something like: *If you bring forth what's within you, then what you have will save you. If you don't bring it forth, then what you do not have within you will kill you.* Her skin tingled. "So how do we break the curse?" she asked.

Rosemary chimed in. "If memory serves me, there's liberation in that cross." She pointed to the Chakana.

"Oh, just purge the whole damned thing!" Lobelia coughed. "Curses, shmurses!"

Mark laughed. "I'm with her!" He nodded his head towards Lobelia.

Amaru looked at Mark and asked, "Anyone ever call you superstitious?" The Warrant Officer stopped laughing.

Professor Begay turned to Rosemary and said, "Yes, there's liberation through the cross."

"What *does* the Chakana have to do with this?" Melissa asked.

Haru held his breath.

"It's a bridge," Amaru said, "uniting the underworld with the surface and heavenly realms; the soul with the ego and Spirit; the past with the present and future. It's certainly not the only bridge," he added. "Consider the ankh, an Egyptian symbol of life, but also the *crux ansata* of the Coptic Church: that's another cross combined with a circle. And what about the Celtic Cross with that circle in its center? Or the Rosicrucians with their round white rose at the center of a cross of light? It's not the symbol itself, but the intention behind the symbol."

Amaru explained how symbols worked—that they vibrated with our own feelings, perspectives and desires. They held not just personal and but also *universal* meanings. Because of this, one need not believe in symbols in order for them to take effect. Archetypes acted on collective consciousness, even if few could understand their meaning.

He added to Rosemary's comments from the night before. She had known that the Inca embedded the Chakana into Machu Picchu, but Professor Begay knew more. He described—in detail—ancient prophecies regarding the alignment of Machu Picchu's stairs with the Sun, the Moon, and the Pleiades star cluster on December 21, 2012. Some of his talk sounded like bits of Tom's reading, but most of it was new to all of them.

They learned what would happen at 11:11 "Universal Time" on Winter Solstice 2012—something about the Sun lining up with the Galactic Equator. Later that day, light and shadows would move down the temple steps like a plumed serpent, announcing *The Return of Quetzalcoatl*.

No one, not even the professor, knew exactly what that meant. Some people thought the serpent symbolized awakening all twelve strands of human DNA, which coiled like the snakes on a caduceus. For centuries, Western religions had linked serpents with "the Devil," but *Quetzalcoatl* signaled a golden age of light. Humanity wouldn't just *return* to the Garden. Events up to and including 2012 would offer chances to grow *beyond* the Garden—ushering Earth into the next dimension.

Quetzalcoatl was an Aztec creator god. The Maya called him *Kukulkán*, and he appeared in the Hopi tradition as *Pahana*. The Latter Day Saints said tales of *Quetzalcoatl*'s return sounded so close to the Second Coming of Christ that the two prophesied events were one and the same.

The three sisters stared at the Navajo in silence. Haru's hair wiggled, and Mark got goose bumps.

When Amaru mentioned binary code and UK crop circles, the pilot's mind imploded. "Man," he said, "how do you know all this stuff?"

Professor Begay caught his son's eyes and smiled. "It's a gift."

"Good old, *Hridaya*, Gateway to the Highest Reality," said Timaeus. "'*The mandrakes give a smell and at our gates are all manner of pleasant fruits new and old which I've laid up for thee, O my beloved.*'"

Schizandra was about to ask the king if he had lost his mind when Frauke appeared. The queen rushed over and kissed the frog, but nothing happened. Timaeus looked pleased until he saw her crestfallen face. Crying had wreaked havoc on her eyes. They looked puffy and red, and her porcelain skin was blotchy. Her cherry lips had dried in the saline of her tears, leaving cracked white lines and flakes. Strands of ebony hair clung to her forehead and slashed their way across her cheeks. *She had never looked more beautiful.*

Frauke wept. Each sob tenderized her heart a little more until she felt completely raw. When no tears remained, she dry heaved and hiccupped on the floor. The Galactic Butterfly's wings went unnoticed. Even Schizandra's hugs and soft words could not console her friend. But slowly, Frauke began to hear the flute. She followed its melody until she could open her eyes again. When she did, the purple frog sat in front of her. His gaze looked sad as it caressed her cheek.

"'In the evening of life, we will be judged on love alone,'" Timaeus said in his softest voice. He kissed Frauke, and she did not recoil. "'Tell your piteous heart there's no harm done.'"

At that moment, Timaeus revealed himself. No more amphibious disguise: before them radiated a handsome and unmistakably human king.

Schizandra could conjure only one word. She turned to the queen and whispered, "Wow."

"How *beauteous* mankind is!" Frauke's tears had turned to those of joy. Timaeus buried his face in her fragrant hair as they embraced.

Schizandra's heart fluttered faster for her friends. She tiptoed away to give them privacy.

"Stay," said the king through Frauke's lush black waves.

"Aren't I finished here?" Schizandra asked. "I get it: *journeys end when lovers meet.*"

"And sometimes the end brings more than a beginning." The king's face lit up even more. "Why don't you dance for us, Schizandra? And as a thank you, *please*, feel free to ask me anything."

"*Me?* Dance?" Her eyes quizzed a glowing king and queen. They nodded their approval.

Frauke blew her friend a kiss and said, "'When you do dance, I wish you a wave o' th' sea, that you might ever do nothing but that.'"

Schizandra giggled over her shoulder before she turned her head and twirled away. On a whim, she asked, "What can you tell me about the Gates of Mu?"

The king and queen looked cozy as they watched her spin. In his deep, resonant voice, Timaeus said, "'The lock of error shuts the gates.'"

Schizandra whirled by them and the king continued, "'Open them with the key of love.'"

She danced faster past the joyful pair. On her next round, Timaeus sang in harmony with the flute, "'The opening of the gates awakens the Beloved. Kabir says: Sweetness! Don't pass by such good fortune as this!'"

Frauke hugged her husband and planted a kiss upon his lips. That kiss became a smile.

Schizandra synchronized her turns with the butterfly's pulsing wings and the caterpillar's music. As the wings closed, she glimpsed a boy with raven hair. *Haru?* The wings reopened and the young man disappeared.

Schizandra whirled and twirled through the Heart of Matter. Each time she saw the dancing butterfly, her flashing vision of Haru grew stronger. She could see his face between the flutters. Haru stood behind the Galactic Butterfly and offered his right hand, beckoning her to reach for it. Schizandra's heart sang as she spun her way ever closer to Haru.

The wings flashed a searing white light and everything spun black and silent.

A moment later, she felt a hand in hers. When she opened her eyes, Schizandra found herself surrounded by turning faces and excited voices, only two of which she recognized.

Haru squeezed Shazzie's hand, and he knew her room stopped spinning. He sensed she wanted to lift her arms to hug him, but nothing happened; she couldn't move. She seemed trapped inside herself, screaming for release. She looked at him from far away and tried to speak, but he knew she couldn't.

Her eyes pleaded with him until he remembered Queen Froggy's gift. *You'll need these later.* The adults were still talking about crop circles, binary code and the Mayan Calendar. The old ladies and that guy seemed quite worked up about it, and his father kept them plied with stories. Haru never knew his dad enjoyed talking to people. He had always seemed so reserved.

No one else noticed that Shazzie had opened her eyes again. Haru felt time slow down in order to help him help his friend. He knew what he had to do. He also knew that he needed to act fast. Soon, Shazzie's grandmother would get in the way, and he would have to explain himself.

He pulled out the black pearl necklace before anyone could stop him.

Haru heard his friend—even without words—and he replied. Not out loud, of course. They didn't have time for *that.* He could tell Shazzie received his message, though, because she lifted her chin. Invisible in real time, this tiny motion looked obvious to him. It was enough to slide one end of the necklace behind and through. If he could just finish before her grandmother swooped in. Haru's heart and hands trembled as he clasped the pearls around her neck. *Got it!* He backed away before anyone noticed what he'd done. Time returned to normal.

When the black pearls touched her throat, Shazzie inhaled fast.

"I'm Schizandra."

"Oh my God, she's awake!" Her grandmother's eyes overflowed with tears, and everyone huddled around the bed. Haru let his fingers touch her hand again.

<hr />

"I'm Schizandra."

Melissa smiled and kissed her forehead. "Yes, of course you are." She kissed her granddaughter again. "Welcome home." The midwife had witnessed another miracle. Silently, she thanked Tom Brown for believing in this moment.

"I'm Schizandra." The patient lifted herself to sitting.

Melissa noticed that her granddaughter's voice sounded much more resonant than it had three days ago. She glanced at the American flag above Schizandra. *A Starry Canopy?* She caught her breath as she remembered Tom's prediction: *this mission will get done through this body.... Don't kill* the body. *We will take over the body.* Melissa shuddered.

She shook her head to clear it. The important thing was that Schizandra had awakened. The midwife glanced at the bloodstained sheet and kissed her granddaughter again.

"I'm Schizandra."

———◆———

Sitting now, she stretched her spine up towards the flag. "I'm Schizandra, come back to change it all, and I *can* change it all, but do I dare?" She paused. *"Do I—? Do I dare—?"*

"Do you dare what, child?" Lobelia said. "Go on now, spit it out!"

Rosemary and Lobelia each held a foot. Mark stared at Melissa, and Amaru glanced from the Chakana to the being behind it. Schizandra knew them all already, knew their names and knew their secrets. She was happy that Haru now held her hand. She wrapped her fingers around each of his and smiled.

As she sat beneath the stars and stripes, her soul embraced the Lemurian Seed Crystals, the serpentine puma, the black pearls and other stones. The fairy cross had fallen next to her, and the Galactic Butterfly pulsed inside her heart. She could feel Timaeus and Frauke, Nestor, Melissa, and Haru. She knew how the pilot felt about her grandmother and that the Navajo had always meant well. The other women were her two great-aunts, proud to have finally played their part. She loved them all. In the background, she could hear Sephora sing, *"'Za gate!"*

Schizandra closed her eyes and inhaled deeply. She paused. Exhaling, she reopened them. In the space between breaths, Schizandra said to no one and to everyone:

"Do I dare prepare the galaxy?"

Haru responded first. "You can count on *me* to help!" Professor Begay tousled his son's wild hair and smiled approval.

Lobelia asked, "What do you think, Rosemary? Should we stand guard? Leave Madison for Sedona?" She actually *remembered* the earlier imposter. No one was going to mess with her grandniece, not if *she* could shoo him away.

"The two of us retiring to the desert!" exclaimed her twin, "Oh my stars, I never thought I'd see the day, but yes. *Absolutely, yes!*"

Melissa felt unnerved. Things were moving way too fast. She saw a flash of Rosemary and Tom Brown together and wondered why the twins had offered to "stand guard." Sensing her discomfort, Mark walked over to her side. For once he felt bad keeping secrets from a woman, but he couldn't tell her now.

Schizandra silently agreed. *No, not yet.*

Instead, he whispered in Melissa's ear: " I suspect we're about to witness lots of things we thought we'd never see."

The midwife mused aloud, "The time has always been too soon."

"But that doesn't mean the time won't come," he said.

Schizandra smiled at Rosemary's dimples and felt joy bubbling in her chest. Glancing at the clock, she squeezed Haru's hand. She knew it! 1:11 on 1/11/01.

Oh, yes, Schizandra knew the date, and now she knew the time. She could feel things sliding into place: people, animals, events. In that instant, she realized Frauke had conceived a child. And someone from *Peru* needed her attention. Schizandra saw the stain on her sheet and recognized the Chakana, portal between worlds. She smiled at Mark then turned to her grandmother: "He's right, you know. *The days are coming when the time is now.*"

The End

STAY TUNED FOR

SCHIZANDRA AND THE PERUVIAN JAGUAR

HTTP://SCHIZANDRASERIES.COM

Acknowledgements

The last few lines of dialogue echo a line from page 220 of Daniel Pinchbeck's *2012: The Return of Quetzalcoatl* (New York: Jeremy P. Tarcher/Penguin, 2006). I highly recommend this book for anyone who wants to delve more deeply into the science, myth, prophecy and shared experiences pointing toward 2012 and the Mayan Calendar. Although I had written much of *Schizandra and the Gates of Mu* before discovering Pinchbeck's book, I found his work eerily in line with the inspired *Schizandra* series.

I'd especially like to thank Tim Glenn (www.soulpurposereadings.com) for providing so many accurate details regarding astrology, numerology and tarot. Your insights gave me the courage and direction to go where I felt led.

Huge gratitude to Visionary Artist Tania Marie (www.taniamarie.com) for your rendition of the Chakana and double ankhs; for your amazing spirit; and for introducing me to the original Nestor.

Special thanks to Traci Moore (www.tracimoore.wordpress.com) for your editorial expertise and insights. Your light touch has had far reaching effects!

Thanks to Cathi Stephenson for cover design and to Gwen Gades for interior formatting.

Additional thanks to Giacinta Vosika, Cassie Margraf, Erin Pavlina, Mike Gillick, and Karen Lang for ongoing feedback and enthusiasm from early to later drafts.

Thanks to Dr. George N. Dever for hiring me after my brain injury. This saga began in your office when I first learned of the schizandra berry. You explained the nature of adaptogens and helped me choose Melissa's name.

For helicopter details and accuracy, I owe many thanks to Sharon Robie and the mechanics and pilots at Guardian Air, along with helicopter flight instructor, Clint Davis. Thanks also to Sedona and Flagstaff Medical Centers for explaining why and how a patient would require air evacuation from SMC to FMC.

Special thanks to Anita Dalton at *Center for the New Age* for hiring me and facilitating my research during our short stay in 2004, and thanks to Shirley Andrews for writing *Lemuria and Atlantis*, an invaluable resource on prehistory. Thanks and blessings to Seann Xenga for your abundance of crystal knowledge and for gifting me my second Lemurian Seed Crystal. And thanks to Patrick Moore for details about running routes in Phoenix.

Blissings to Shazzie and David Wolfe for writing *Naked Chocolate* and introducing the world to raw cacao. Shazzie, Schizandra had your nickname long before you and I "met," but I'm so glad we did! Your love and support have sprinkled themselves throughout this offering.

Hats off to Uncle Ken for helping me understand neurological terms and implications. Any inaccuracies are mine, not his.

Thank you to Dr. Patricia Schwartz for creating "The Official String Theory Website": http://superstringtheory.com/index.html, and to the creators of http://www.aztlan.net, where I first learned about the 2002 discoveries at Socorro, New Mexico. I first learned about the translation of the Sanskrit word, *Hridaya*, from Sally Kempton's *Awakened Heart Meditation* CD. Dorinda's breathing evokes Alan Finger's *Ishta Diksha*.

Full-bellied thanks to *Café Raw Bliss, D'Lish, Café Gratitude, Seed, Cousins Incredible Vitality*, and Cecilia Benjumea for fueling me with amazing raw food treats that kept the vibe high and the creativity flowing.

Hugs, love and thanks to all the clients, colleagues, friends and family members whose stories and lives remind me how diverse and wonderful twenty-first century life on Earth can be.

Sweet thanks to Wendy Vigdor-Hess for believing in Schizandra way back when she was just a glimmer of a short story. In that same conversation, you told me I could "go vegan" and you first introduced me to numerology. You've had more influence than you know!

The highest praise, love and thanks go to my husband, Stephen Bruno. You believed I could do this before I did, and you have always supported my writing, beyond what anyone could rightfully request. Thank you for listening to countless oral readings and for allowing me to speak of my characters as real entities. You indulge my need for writing time and you force me to relax when I'm too scene-obsessed to take a break. Thank you for the back cover photo and for talking about your p-brain all those years! You've inspired me in ways that even I don't understand. For your love, loyalty and faith, I offer my eternal gratitude.

OTHER BOOKS
By
LAURA BRUNO

If I Only Had a Brain Injury

A TBI Survivor and Life Coach's Guide to Chronic Fatigue, Concussion, Lyme Disease, Migraine or Other "Medical Mystery"

Laura Bruno, M.A.

AFTER COMPLETING A MASTER'S DEGREE in English at the University of Chicago, Laura Bruno spent two years in the corporate world. Just before her return to graduate school, she suffered a brain injury and could no longer read without debilitating migraine headaches. Years of misdiagnoses forced her to find alternative means of getting well. Now a writer and Intuitive Life Coach, Laura enjoys a full practice. From a woman once considered "permanently disabled," *If I Only Had a Brain Injury* is itself testament to the incredible resilience of human brain and spirit.

Unlike other books on healing from so-called "Medical Mysteries," *If I Only Had a Brain Injury* encourages readers to chart their own inspirational journeys. The book's structure follows *The Wizard of Oz* storyline (Dorothy's journey begins with a concussion), guiding readers to a "yellow brick road through recovery." A collection of personal examples, alternative treatments and spiritual growth exercises, this book also offers wisdom from thirteen contributors, including Robin Cohn (Vice President of New York State Brain Injury Association), Dr. William Padula (Neuro-Optometric Rehabilitation Association), Dana Reeve, and Kay Strom.

WWW.IFIONLYHADABRAININJURY.COM

Check out Laura's blog at

HTTP://LAURABRUNO.WORDPRESS.COM

A POPULAR E-BOOK WITH 192 PAGES of Information and support for the raw food diet—especially nutritional, mental, emotional and spiritual aspects that tend to slow people down, discourage them or otherwise make life difficult. It also covers dental issues, kitchen equipment, eating disorders, and living with non-raw partners. You'll learn how to make your own informed decisions, so that you can design and create a diet and lifestyle that work for you. Includes over 45 recipes by some of today's top raw chefs and the Lazy Raw Foodist herself, Laura Bruno. www.lazyrawfoodist.com.

Stay tuned for *Schizandra and the Peruvian Jaguar,* with a target release date of early 2010. For more information on the Schizandra Series, please see:

HTTP://SCHIZANDRASERIES.COM

3774397

Made in the USA